Sea of Thieves™

Athena's Fortune

Athena's Fortune

By Chris Allcock

San Rafael, California

PO Box 3088
San Rafael, CA 94912
www.insighteditions.com

Find us on Facebook: www.facebook.com/InsightEditions
Follow us on Twitter: @insighteditions

Library of Congress Cataloging-in-Publication Data available.

ISBN: 978-1-68383-487-8

Publisher: Raoul Goff
Associate Publisher: Vanessa Lopez
Creative Director: Chrissy Kwasnik
Designer: Evelyn Furuta
Senior Editor: Amanda Ng
Editorial Assistant: Maya Alpert
Senior Production Editor: Rachel Anderson
Senior Production Manager: Greg Steffen

Cover illustration by Ricardo Robles

Special thanks to Adam Park, Peter Hentze, Mike Chapman, Bret Allen, and the Sea of Thieves team.

Insight Editions, in association with Roots of Peace, will plant two trees for each tree used in the manufacturing of this book. Roots of Peace is an internationally renowned humanitarian organization dedicated to eradicating land mines worldwide and converting war-torn lands into productive farms and wildlife habitats. Roots of Peace will plant two million fruit and nut trees in Afghanistan and provide farmers there with the skills and support necessary for sustainable land use.

Manufactured in China by Insight Editions

10 9 8 7 6 5

RAMSEY

Long ago . . .

Ramsey's boots were filled with icy water and the howling winds drove sheets of stinging spray across his face as he struggled to keep his grip on the helm. He was fairly certain that the next wave was either going to capsize them or completely splinter their ship to matchwood.

This, he thought with satisfaction, *is what being a pirate is all about.*

Wrenching at the ship's wheel with an effort that made his aching arms scream in protest, Ramsey leaned forward to bellow an order to his crew below. He might as well have been whispering, for the storm snatched at his commands and carried them away. No matter. Each of the crew was an experienced sailor, and the last few days sailing through what felt like literal hell had taught them to anticipate each other's actions. For now, they would work without words.

Ramsey squinted through the darkness and the rain to make out Rathbone and Mercia moving in tandem. They had lashed ropes to the railings and tied them securely around their waists as they wrestled with the sails, desperately seeking the ever-shifting balance that would keep the ship darting between the waves without the sails being torn to shreds. Behind them, a flash of lightning illuminated Shan as he staggered up to the prow. He held a battered bucket in his hands and began emptying its contents overboard, bailing away rainwater that had trickled down into the lower decks.

Those three pirates, along with Ramsey, represented the entire complement of the *Magpie's Wing*, the tiny ship he'd commissioned especially for this voyage. His friends and rivals had scoffed at the idea of setting sail with such a tiny crew, least of all into the Devil's Shroud, but that was precisely why they'd failed where Ramsey had succeeded.

The Devil's Shroud. Every pirate grew to know its name, even if they preyed upon waters a hundred miles or more from that cursed region. Ramsey had never been a superstitious man, but you didn't have to believe in undersea gods or arcane rituals to experience the fog's effects for yourself and learn swiftly that it was a very real threat indeed. The Shroud ebbed and flowed across a vast region of the sea, writhing like a living thing. Unwary ships could easily be drawn into its fringes, even if they'd sailed that route without incident for years.

Any vessel that did slip its course and find itself in those strange, ethereal clouds would soon realize it, for its crew would begin to taste an odd tang upon the air—not quite sour and not quite rotten, but cloying on the tongue and in the back of the throat. It was like trying to take a deep gulp of black treacle, Ramsey mused, but a treacle that soon began to burn cold like a hand held too long in ice. Masks and scarves across the face would do nothing to help, and before long, once-able seamen would be coughing and spluttering, choking on the very air around them. Often, they'd be so overcome that they wouldn't realize their ship was dying too.

Whatever fell curse the region inflicted upon people foolish enough to enter it would also work its will upon wood and metal. Beams would begin to split and twist, buckling and warping the planks that made up the ship's hull. The nails that held them in place would start to rust away to a fine red powder. The beleaguered crew would be fighting a losing battle against an onslaught of leaks and breaches as murky water poured in below decks, new ruptures appearing faster than the old ones could be bunged or repaired.

Yes, any seafarer with a promising career and a decent life expectancy soon learned not to sneer at the existence, or the threat, of the Devil's Shroud, though the challenge just made each ambitious pirate all the more determined to see what was on the other side.

Ramsey had hardly been the first to dream of the uncharted waters encircled by those malevolent mists, imagining an oasis at the center like the eye of a storm that would contain . . . well, anything. Everyone had their own notions of what might lie beyond the veil, and the topic was a favorite talking point during fireside conversation or whenever drink had been shared liberally.

Fabulous riches usually featured heavily in people's imaginations, although long-lost civilizations (hoarding said fabulous riches) and exotic beasts (who could be captured and sold for fabulous riches) were also common. A few naysayers would dismiss the idea of there being anything behind the Shroud at all, but they would be quickly jeered out of the conversation. It was far more fun to believe.

Still, Ramsey had always been sure that until the day mankind learned to fly like the birds, dreaming would be the only way anyone would peek beyond the Shroud. There had been so much to see and do in the wider world, so many places to plunder and battles to be fought, that he'd been content to leave the mystery unsolved. Unsolved and largely unheeded for many years—until, one day, he crossed paths with Mercia.

"You're blocking my light," the pirate said curtly.

Ramsey shifted apologetically as the pirate Mercia glanced up in irritation. The library in which they'd met barely seemed able to accommodate a tall and imposing pirate like Ramsey. He felt distinctly out of place in the serious and musty building, with his unkempt hair tied back using scraps of cloth and a bristly beard that made him seem older than his years. His seafarer's garb—breeches, a rough linen shirt, and a bulky greatcoat topped with a wide-brimmed hat—only served to make him more incongruous among the crowded shelves.

Now well into his third decade, Ramsey had accumulated quite a bit of heft from the fine dining that success could offer. Thanks to the rigors of a life at sea, it was still mostly muscle, and he aimed to keep it that way for as long as possible. Squeezing himself onto the bench opposite Mercia, though, he found himself wishing he were a smaller man. His elbow brushed against a stack of books, nearly scattering them, and he apologetically clamped a suntanned hand down upon the pile.

"And now you're spoiling my work," Mercia sighed. "It's Captain Ramsey, isn't it? You've got quite the reputation around here."

"All of it deserved, I assure you." Ramsey grinned. Mercia did not. "You're an exceptional pirate yourself, I hear," he continued, beguilingly. "One with a lot of books and some curious ideas."

"Curiosity is correct," Mercia replied, considering Ramsey for a moment as if debating how much time to spend indulging him. "And I don't just mean poking my nose into other people's treasure. We've all seen things out there that we couldn't explain. Well, some of us want answers, and we have ways of finding them out."

Ramsey frowned. "Alchemy?" he ventured.

"Natural philosophy," Mercia said, patiently. "It's a way of approaching what you don't understand. Solving mysteries, like . . ." One gloved hand waved vaguely. "Why does a compass point north? Who built the old temples you find sometimes, and why? What precisely *is* the Devil's Shroud? Some people say it's a form of magic, as if that were any explanation, but I have another idea."

Mercia began to speak at length of the mysterious fog and the means by which by one might chart its boundaries, and Ramsey sensed his own interest in the barrier rekindling. He felt some measure of shame at this, for the last few years had been very kind to him, bringing him a wife and two young children. The black diamond ring upon his swarthy finger was a symbol of the promise he had made his beloved to one day provide her with all that she deserved.

Mercia had paused, and Ramsey realized he was expected to contribute to the conversation. "Truth be told," he admitted, "things are getting a bit too familiar around here. The same old taverns, stories I can parrot word for word. Finding a way through the Shroud, now, that'd be an adventure to stick in the mind. Think you're man enough for the job?" He'd chosen these words deliberately, and Mercia's eyes flashed in provocation.

"We'll need charts," Mercia shot back, with no hesitation. "Calendars, too. There's a shop in town that has some I've had my eye on. Smaller craft to use as scouts. Oh, and a ship, of course. She'll have to be swift and nimble, but tough."

"I don't understand half of what you've told me tonight," Ramsey admitted with a toothy smile. "But rest assured, I know what makes a fine ship. You'll be aboard her when we sail?"

Mercia smiled back for the first time. "Just you try leaving without me."

They'd had the *Magpie's Wing* built in secret, a craft tiny enough to thread its way through those twisting routes where a ship might sail in safety. Together, Ramsey, Mercia, Shan, and Rathbone had stuffed the hold with floats and coracles to send out ahead and stout wooden planks to patch up any damage they might take on their journey.

They packed their provisions and made their final preparations, until eventually there were no more reasons to delay. All that remained was Ramsey's choice: to stay at home with his family or sail headlong into the unknown and be the first man alive to see beyond the Devil's Shroud. The call of the sea claimed him as it always did and, perhaps, as it always would.

The course they plotted was contorted, and the ship was forced to travel at a veritable snail's pace. Finally, after days of inching their way through the stifling fog, starved of both food and sleep, they emerged into chaos. The Shroud had released its grip on Ramsey and his crew, only to spit them into the heart of a massive storm. With no idea of where land might lie and no possibility of reversing course, they had no choice but to press on into the downpour.

Another bolt of lightning, this one much closer, snapped Ramsey out of his reverie. They'd been lucky so far, able to angle through the waves without broaching and taking only minor damage to the hull, but their good fortune would only last so long. The *Magpie's Wing* needed shelter soon.

Feeling a tug at his shoulder, Ramsey whipped around to find Shan at his side. Even though the man was clearly bellowing, Ramsey had to bring their heads practically together to hear what he was trying to say. *Lamb?*

"Land!" Shan shouted again.

Eyes widening, Ramsey gestured impatiently and followed Shan's outstretched finger. There was something there, all right: a dark and craggy silhouette that he could barely pick out against the backdrop of the raging monsoon.

The ship gave a protesting creak as its captain spun the wheel once more, angling the bow toward the distant rock face. Shan picked his way down to where Rathbone and Mercia, both sodden and exhausted, were still fighting to capture the wild wind within the sails.

Rathbone in particular seemed dead on his feet, despite being the brawniest of the three, and he gratefully relinquished his position to Shan. "Never thought I'd be glad to accept bailing duty!" he barked over the cacophony, but he had barely filled a bucket before he paused to stare, mortified, at the horizon. "Ramsey *has* seen those cliffs we're heading toward, hasn't he? The cliffs that no one in their right mind would take us anywhere near?"

Shan pretended not to hear him and continued to wrestle gamely with the billowing cloth overhead, but Mercia snapped, "I'm sure *Captain* Ramsey knows exactly what he's doing!" before giving the sail a particularly vicious tug.

While Mercia's relationship with Rathbone had been civil, by and large, he was proving a hard man to really get to know. He was clearly a consummate pirate despite possessing a clipped English accent more suited to an officer of the navy; his skin was bronzed by the sun, his shoulders were broad, and his head was shorn to reveal a scar or two. Out of all the crew, he was most fastidious about his appearance and had come aboard laden with fine cotton shirts and gleaming shoes. Rathbone made a point of shaving every day and took every opportunity to trim and tidy himself. Mercia wondered if Ramsey knew more about the man and resolved to ask—assuming any of them of them survived the night.

More rocks were visible now, and the ship seemed to be sailing between two rows of stone columns that that jutted out of the water in rows like huge teeth. Lifeless and sheer, they rose up on either side of the *Magpie's Wing*. Rathbone suspected he could almost reach out and touch the stone as the ship bobbed wildly on the waves.

"He's gone mad!" Rathbone yelled, though Mercia's only response was to fully furl the sails, leaving nothing but their momentum to carry them forward. The looming darkness was almost upon them now, closer, then closer still, and Rathbone braced himself to hear the prow snap against the cliffs and feel the deck lurch beneath his feet.

Suddenly, there was no more rain pounding down on them, and Rathbone found that he could hear things again as Ramsey's call for light cut through the air. It took the crew a few moments to obey, groping for the ship's lanterns in the dark with their frozen and fumbling fingers, but one by one the flickering flames sprang into being and cast pools of orange light across their surroundings. The feeble fire was like a summer sun compared to the darkness they'd sailed through and more than bright enough to reveal the truth of their whereabouts.

The *Magpie's Wing* had sailed through a crack in the cliff face and was now drifting through a large cave filled with seawater, moving lazily toward the far wall. They dropped anchor at once, bringing the ship to a full stop, and took in their surroundings as Ramsey moved to stand with them.

The walls of the cavern were slick from the spray of the sea and the dark sandy brown rock was peppered with smaller exits and pathways—save for the view to starboard, which offered an unobstructed view of a windswept shore and the turbulent ocean beyond it. The walls extended upward to form a series of high archways—a ceiling of sorts that provided protection from the storm. There were gaps overhead, through which vegetation hung down and the sluicing rain cascaded in a series of miniature waterfalls. The nearest was just a few feet away, and Shan carefully hooked a bucket onto a long pole and filled it to the brim with fresh water.

One by one, they filled their flasks and drank deeply in mute appreciation until Shan, ever cheerful, broke the silence. "Funny how you only ever realize you're hungry when you've stopped being thirsty," he mused. "Are we sure there's no food left?"

"Never mind your stomach," Mercia admonished. "Getting warm and dry is more important."

"Easy for you to say. It's not your stomach."

Ramsey drained the last of his flask and stretched. "We can burn the floats, if they'll take," he declared. "Let's start a fire; it won't do if we all get sick. Then we'll see what we have to celebrate with, eh? We're wet, but we'll dry out. We're hungry, but we'll find food. Today, we four have made it through the Devil's Shroud! If that doesn't call for a belly full of grog, then nothing ever will again!"

This last remark earned a cheer, albeit an exhausted one, which rang around the cavern for a moment as all four roused themselves and went to work. The *Magpie's Wing* was eased carefully nearer to land until she was close enough to a rocky outcropping that the gangplank could be extended.

A circle of rocks was fashioned far from the reach of the storm, although finding wood dry enough to do more than give off a thick, protesting smoke proved a challenge. Rathbone's persistent use of flint and stone eventually yielded a cautious flame and, finally, a hearty conflagration around which they were all very pleased to warm their hands.

Shan disappeared off the ship wordlessly, though Ramsey knew the man well enough by now not to bother questioning his absence or his motives. Sure enough, his balding head poked back through a crevice in the rocks later, shining anew with fresh rainwater. "I've found a pathway that leads up to the higher reaches," he said, approaching his crewmates. Against his body he hugged both the motionless form of a scrawny rooster as well as a few plump bananas. Shan offered the bananas to Mercia, whom he knew avoided meat with a disdain most pirates reserved for an honest day's work, then set about cleaning and preparing the bird for its final resting place—a stained cooking pot that hung above their sputtering fire.

Ramsey, who had busied himself filling several casks with yet more of the fresh rainwater, took the opportunity to study the man from afar and recall their first encounter.

Every ship needs a quartermaster with a brain that can juggle a thousand calculations every hour, tallying every spilled pint of greasy grog and each shot fired in anger, not to mention working out where the crew's next meal is coming from. Ramsey had had no clue who might fulfill such a role on his voyage into the Devil's Shroud, but Shan had come recommended by Rowenna, one of Ramsey's few close friends despite the fact that she always kept her feet firmly on dry land.

As the owner and proprietor of one of the largest and most dependably disreputable taverns on the coast, Rowenna was the de facto matriarch of the town where she and Ramsey had grown up. They had played together as children, she'd introduced Ramsey to his wife, and he in return had used his earnings to help purchase the pub back when she was its only barmaid. When he told her of his plan to breach the Devil's Shroud, Rowenna had promised to reserve his barstool for him—so long as he promised to come back in one piece.

Rowenna had also pointed Shan out across the crowded bar: a lithe and balding figure with a pronounced tan, a series of silver rings in one ear, and an intricate tattoo that ran down his arm. He was older than Ramsey, perhaps fifty or so, which was both unusual and impressive. Very few pirates lived long enough to think about retiring. What little hair he had left was already a snowy white.

Dressed in a plain white tunic and simple knee-length breeches, carelessly barefooted, Shan might almost have been mistaken for a novice deckhand were it not for the aura of calm that seemed to surround him. He presented a lone oasis of tranquility amid the hustle and bustle of raucous enjoyment while his fingers worked deftly and ceaselessly on *something*.

Intrigued, Ramsey moved closer and wordlessly took a seat opposite, keen not to disturb the man in the middle of whatever creative whimsy had overtaken him. He watched with interest as toothpicks, carved wood, and scraps of cloth napkin were gradually whittled and tied to complete a tiny model pirate ship.

Once the miniature vessel was finished to Shan's satisfaction, he painstakingly tied a loop of string around the replica masts and slid the little boat through the neck of a clear glass bottle. Only then did Shan give the string the lightest tug, hoisting the sails upright, and glance up at Ramsey for the first time. "You're thinking that it's good, but nothing extraordinary," he said conversationally, as if the two men had been chatting effortlessly all evening.

Ramsey merely grunted in response. Shan took a jug of water and, tilting the neck ever so slightly, filled the bottle and presented it for inspection.

The little curio floated just fine, bobbing from side to side as the bottle was poked and prodded by a succession of inquisitive pirates, but it was the final bit of showmanship that convinced Ramsey. Shan placed another ship in its own bottle alongside the newly fashioned galleon, this one flying the colors of the merchant navy. Next, he pointed out the *other* string dangling from his latest creation and invited Ramsey to grasp it between two of his calloused fingers and tug. Ramsey obliged.

With a series of sharp cracking sounds, the miniature pirate ship let loose a volley from its diminutive cannons, unleashing pellets with such force that they escaped their bottle and pinged their way across the tavern's table and struck the merchant navy ship. Much to Shan's glee, Ramsey let out an audible bark of laughter upon spotting that the stricken navy vessel was already listing, taken down by the barrage of lead shot and sinking slowly toward the bottom of its own fractured container. "Welcome aboard," he said wryly, before going on to introduce himself and explain the nature of the proposed voyage.

Shan didn't agreed to a fateful journey into the Shroud right away. Rather, he listened intently as Mercia's findings—at least, the ones Ramsey was willing to share in such a crowded venue—were laid out before him. He suggested a couple of modifications to the design of the *Magpie's Wing*, too, but finally he grasped Ramsey's own paw in a wiry hand, clinked tankards, and asked when they'd be leaving.

Since then, Shan meticulously rationed the grog and what food they'd been able to squeeze into the hold. He also insisted on diving under the ship while it was moving so that he could make improvements to her rudder control, and he kept spirits up with the help of a gorgeous concertina. It was his one personal possession other than the unremarkable clothes he'd been wearing when he boarded. Watching Shan now as he tended to the roasting fowl, Ramsey felt a surge of gratitude toward Rowenna for introducing them and hoped he'd have his chance to repay her.

Mercia gave a luxurious stretch, tossing the skin of her banana into the water with a loud splash that startled several fish out of their hiding places. Standing, she began to tug at the buckles of the greatcoat she'd been wearing since the start of the voyage, removing it and spreading its soggy bulk out by the fire to dry. Her boots came next, but it was when she removed her tricorn cap and reached up for the pins that kept her long hair in place that she noticed Rathbone staring at her from across the fire. His face was a battleground torn between the twin expressions of fury and shock.

"Problem?" Mercia asked, mildly, shaking out curled tresses to settle around her shoulders. Her piercing, sapphire eyes gleamed as she faced him down. Finally, the others could see her as Ramsey had come to know her—a fair young woman with pale skin now framed by waves of blonde hair, whose stern demeanor and slender figure had served her well when seeking a life at sea.

"All this time! You're—" Rathbone's normally cold voice was rising in pitch with every syllable.

"Drying out," she replied firmly, peeling heavy woolen socks away. "I've no desire to end up with trenched feet or a peg leg thanks to a pair of wet boots, and you'd be wise to do the same."

"I thought women weren't *allowed* on pirate ships!" Rathbone whined, looking to Shan and Ramsey for confirmation and support, and finding neither.

"Quite a lot of men do," Mercia said shortly, sliding a small dagger from her belt and using it to neatly slice a second banana. "In the same way quite a lot of women think male pirates are a bunch of superstitious, swaggering boors who don't pay nearly enough attention to what's past the end of their noses unless it tastes nice. But out here..." The dagger glinted in the firelight as Mercia made a sweeping, dramatic gesture. "It's a fresh start. Medicines, maybe, and monsters too. The old legends have to come from somewhere. And it'll be waiting for anyone who's brave enough and bold enough to step up and take their share. Superstitions be damned." The blade stabbed downward, skewering a segment of banana, and Mercia popped it in her mouth with a fierce expression that indicated she considered the matter closed.

Rathbone's mouth opened and closed a few times, causing him to resemble a gasping codfish, until he stood up swiftly and stomped away into the dim recesses of the cave, along the path that spiraled to the cliffs overhead. Only now did Ramsey approach the fire, privately glad that Mercia had ended the conversation with her words and not her fists. While he figured she had every right to knock Rathbone flat on his back for blindly parroting the foolishness of his forefathers, it was just the four of them out here. The fewer broken noses, the better.

Mercia was staring at her own reflection in the shining blade, but glanced up as Ramsey lowered his bulk to sit beside her. "Think he'll be a problem?"

"I doubt it," Ramsey replied, accepting a bowl of hot, greasy meat from Shan. "I've known Rathbone a long time, and he's cunning enough to know a good crewmate when he sees one. He just doesn't like being left out of the loop, that's all. Did you mean what you said about monsters?"

Mercia shrugged. "Maybe. Why?"

"That doesn't seem very Natural Philosophy of you, that's all."

She scoffed at that. "I'd be just as bad as Rathbone if I didn't leave an open mind. If we do find a sea monster, the second thing I'm going to do is learn everything I can about it."

"Second?" Ramsey stifled a belch. "What's the first?"

"Slash at it with my sword until it stops trying to eat me." Mercia fastidiously oiled her dagger before returning it to its sheath. "So now that we've finally made it through the Shroud, what's next?"

Ramsey sucked the last of the hot fat from his fingers while he considered this. "We can't stay out here forever," he admitted. "Sooner or later we'll need supplies that can't be foraged and a proper layover at an outpost. Ammunition, maybe, if this place really is as wild as we think. Until then, we see everything we can. Chart and note everything we can. *Take* everything we can, and bury what we can't. Then we return home to tell our tales, and become legends."

Mercia pulled a face, but deep down each of them felt the same flicker of pride. Recounting their adventures if and when they made it home would see them plied with drink for days, no doubt. One by one, they shared their wild imaginings of what the next few weeks might have in store, talking through the night until the storm had blown itself out. Shafts of unfettered moonlight lanced through the ceiling and glittered on the water down below their camp as they spoke.

"When you've all finished daydreaming," Rathbone called out, his voice distant and reedy from high overhead and filtering down into the cave through one of the gaps in the ceiling, "I think you're going to want to come and take a look outside."

Intrigued, the crew rose as one and followed Shan up the winding path he'd discovered earlier. They moved in single file as they ascended, pushing through damp leaves and leaving footprints in wet soil as they wound their way higher and higher. Rathbone, lantern in hand, was standing atop the island's highest peak, outlined against a speckled night sky that was dominated by a low and yellow moon.

"New stars," Rathbone said simply, and he was quite correct. Not one among them could spot familiar constellations or point toward Orion's Belt. Even the North Star, brightest of all those distant lights, seemed to have different neighbors. Their compasses, at least, pointed the way as well as ever, but the implication was at once thrilling and disturbing.

Wherever their journey had taken them, they could no longer rely on the constellations to guide the *Magpie's Wing* on its voyage. From now on, they'd be sailing under unknown skies.

LARINNA

Here and now

Not even the jab of an elbow, delivered to her ribs by way of some careless reveler lurching past, was enough to wake Larinna. She was simply too stupefied for the blow to rouse her, though she'd later wonder where she got the bruise. Rather, it was the cascade of foaming drink that spilled down the back of her neck and across her tattooed shoulders that yanked her out of a blissfully dreamless sleep and back to the waking world.

As her eyes snapped open, Larinna had just enough time to deliver a lingering, vindictive glare at the pirate who'd splashed her before the first waves of recollection and nausea hit her in tandem. Her cheek, she realized with dismay, was stuck to the surface of the pockmarked bench by whatever puddle she'd collapsed into face-first the night before. It smelled like grog. She really hoped it was.

Carefully separating her head from the coarse wood that had served as her pillow for the night, Larinna began to run down the familiar mental checklist she used after any particularly heavy bout of celebrating. It *had* been a celebration, she was sure of that much, even though the details swam at the edges of her memory like silvery, slippery minnows refusing to be hooked.

Arms and legs? All present and correct, which was good. Larinna didn't consider herself the slightest bit vain, but she was particularly fond of the ink on her right forearm, so losing that would be a shame. Her brown leather clothes were likewise intact, if unpleasantly soggy. Still, they'd dry. What about her purse?

That, she discovered almost immediately, was now little more than a sad tatter of cloth at her side, the lower seam slashed expertly and its contents doubtlessly drunk or gambled by now. While annoying, this was hardly unexpected given the disreputable company all around her: all of them pirates, men and women alike, a heady mix of different tongues filling the air as they took in beer for breakfast.

Curling her toes, Larinna felt around until she located the reassuring weight of her last gold piece, the one she kept in her left boot for emergencies. It could stay where it was for now, she decided, at least while there was still the chance of a free meal somewhere out there. Bracing herself to stand, she cast a disapproving look around the tavern. That was when she remembered the map.

It was stuck to the bench in front of her with a knife she'd borrowed from a passing pirate's belt the night before, though its importance was another detail that had been washed away by the events of the evening. Removing the dagger, she turned the parchment over in her fingertips, eager for any clue that might remind her why she'd been so intent on keeping it close at hand. It was then she realized there were words on the back, though drink had smudged the writing and she could only make out three words with any certainty:

Not helpful, Larinna decided. Infuriatingly vague as secret messages went, in fact, not to mention irrelevant as all she intended to seek right now was something to fill the grumbling hole in her belly. Crumpling up the map and pitching it expertly into the embers of the large fireplace behind her, she stood at last, stretching her arms above her head to excise the knots from her back as she yawned loudly.

A smaller woman lingering in the doorway wisely made way as she approached, for Larinna was an imposing figure, even when she didn't mean to be. Tall and wiry, with olive skin and chestnut hair set into a tight ponytail, Larinna moved with the continual tension of a coiled spring. She had long ago learned to make good use of her height and ferocity when dealing with those around her, and if that wasn't enough . . . well, the spring could be made to uncoil with a swiftness that few pirates forgot in a hurry.

Striding into the sunlight, Larinna basked in the salty air for a moment before her head moved in a slow arc, drinking in the unfamiliar surroundings. There was patchy grass the color of fresh limes beneath the soles of her boots, though it gave way to a spider web of dirt paths that ran between ramshackle buildings: the tavern, a few storage sheds, and what seemed to be small shops that Larinna decided she'd investigate later.

The largest pathway zigzagged down the hillside toward a network of wooden boards that extended out into the water on stout poles. These boardwalks comprised a busy dock that bustled with crews and traders, shipwrights and swabbies rubbing shoulders as they went about their business.

A clucking chicken pecked hopefully around her as she stood watching two burly pirates. They staggered down a sun-bleached staircase and off toward the dock, arm in arm, still singing. She shook her head, bemused. It was almost funny how closely this place resembled old tales about the Sea of . . .

That was why she'd been celebrating. She'd made it to the Sea of Thieves.

Realizing she was grinning like an idiot, Larinna took a deep breath and outwardly composed herself, though her heart was still pounding. Every pirate capable of weighing anchor had heard about the Sea of Thieves, but few were bold enough to consider the crossing, let alone actually attempt it. But she'd made it through, against all odds. Even better, her traveling companions had never suspected a thing.

She sniffed once, then twice. A tantalizing aroma had wrapped itself around her as she stood in thought, and now her nose temporarily took control of her legs so that it could lead her to the source. It was the unmistakable scent of bacon, and it was coming from the private quarters at the rear of the tavern, suggesting the bacon currently belonged to somebody. But that wouldn't be a problem for long.

Poking her head into the tiny kitchen, Larinna spotted the tavern's barkeeper: a whiskered, red-nosed mountain of a man. His name was lost in the haze of last night's carousing, but that didn't matter. What did matter was the contents of his frying pan, which was sizzling plump sausages and fatty rashers of pork. He whistled cheerily as he worked on the beguiling breakfast, and it was only as he turned to dispose of two large eggshells that he spotted Larinna's shadow cast across the floor and bade her hello by way of a hearty wink. "Well now, I'm glad to see you're awake. Your snoring was disturbing the spiders."

"I don't—" Larinna began, hotly, and then remembered the bacon. "Er, that is, I don't suppose food comes included at your very fine establishment?"

"Bed and breakfast, aye, for them's what remembers to pay for a bed," the barkeeper replied agreeably. Larinna opened her mouth to protest this inequitable treatment but her stomach got there first, emitting a protesting growl that echoed embarrassingly around the room and drew a hearty chuckle from the ruddy-cheeked man. "We've got some eggs that needs eating up today, though, and only empty rooms upstairs." He paused and looked Larinna up and down, curiosity twinkling in his eyes as he assessed her. "It's rare to find a new arrival who doesn't have a crew to call her own. You've got to be very brave or very lucky to make it here by yourself."

Larinna arched an eyebrow. Was this a negotiation? "That's a long and very interesting tale," she replied, cautiously, inviting herself fully into the kitchen to take a seat upon a slightly wobbly stool. "The sort that would amuse your customers for months, I'm sure. Unfortunately I'm so hungry I'll probably keel over halfway through telling it."

The barkeeper scratched his bristled cheek for a moment, then nodded. "Fair is fair. A good meal in exchange for a good story." He bustled through the cupboards momentarily until he located a second plate, chipped and rather faded, and while Larinna's eyes roved eagerly over the contents of the sizzling pan, she began to weave her tale for the barkeep.

Her first memory was the sting of a smacked bottom after she returned from the woods that wrapped around her hometown like a highwayman's cloak. The forest was a dark, tangled, stinging, bramble-filled labyrinth that her mother had repeatedly forbidden her to enter. Naturally, this made it the most enticing place in the world.

As she'd grown older, the thrills she felt from stepping into the unknown had only become stronger. If there was a beaten path, Larinna would stray from it. When she was presented with a map, she'd immediately head for the edge because there was nothing more boring than following someone else's footsteps. How would anything new get done if everyone was just walking in circles?

It was a life of fierce independence, and it had taught Larinna many things: how to wield a homemade bow firstly, then later a rusty sword that she spotted while diving for crabs one day. She learned how to fasten a splint, how to sleep in a tree, which mushrooms were safe to eat, and how to run very quickly away from wild boar tracks when she saw them.

She signed on as a deckhand because she'd finally exhausted every nook and cranny of the island she called home—not that it felt like much of a home anymore, with Mum in the ground and Dad in the tavern more often than not. She worked hard and listened even harder, and soon she knew as much as anyone about a life at sea. She could furl a sail, swing from a rope, and use a pistol when necessary.

She scrimped and saved to buy a tiny sloop of her own because while she understood the usefulness of a crew she quickly tired of sailing only where the captain's orders dictated they go. Traveling from port to port was fine while you were learning the basics, but there were no adventures to be had at those sorts of places save for an occasional giggling rendezvous. These were almost always followed by flight ahead of the morning sun. Fun enough, but never a reason to stay.

Despite her misdemeanors, Larinna had never given much thought to piracy, but she'd been branded one just the same. A brief exploration into some caves she presumed were unoccupied had brought her into the heart of a smuggling operation being conducted by the local governor, who wasted no time in bringing her likeness to the attention of the authorities.

At first she fought to clear her name, but then she remembered an old saying of her father's: It was better to be hung as a wolf than as a lamb. From that day onward, Larinna embraced the epithet of *pirate*. She would indulge herself in acts of larceny and vandalism from time to time, particularly if she spotted one of the governor's ships on the horizon. His goods always fetched a pretty penny.

This had all been fine for a while. But little by little, the world was getting smaller. It was more crowded, too. Once-untamed islands were becoming homesteads, safe havens were hard to come by, and many proud pirates had given up their galleons for a life on land. The navy was everywhere, pitiless in its pursuit of people who just wanted to peek and prod underneath what few stones remained unturned.

Larinna had been clambering across the rocky shoreline of a deserted cove when she'd spotted the bottle gleaming in the sunlight. To her amusement there was an actual message inside, and she spent the afternoon carefully extracting the cork. To simply smash her way inside had seemed wrong, somehow, though she couldn't fathom why. Thanks to the map that had been safely sealed away through the bottle's long journey, she read the term *Sea of Thieves* for the first time and grew determined to learn what it might mean.

They—and "they," Larinna told the barkeeper, meant the grizzled old salts she'd been drinking under the table in some game or other—said there was no law on those strange seas. They spoke of lost civilizations sprawled across the bottom of the sea, of ancient cave drawings pointing the way to hidden treasures that could transform a person, body and soul. Above all, they spoke of entire regions that barely had a name, let alone charts that pinned everything down and drained the life out of the world.

For Larinna, the Sea of Thieves represented a solution to her wanderlust—and yet, it might as well have been a million miles away. As she was a lone wolf more concerned with exploration than extortion, her name and face were relatively unknown, her talents unproven. She could be captain to nobody bar a crew of novices, the sort whose inexperience would see them sunk before they were two days out of harbor.

In desperation, she'd taken to roaming every port in search of an open position on a ship that might be heading for the Sea of Thieves, but despite the map in her hand, many captains called her a gullible fool for believing such a place might even exist, and all denied her passage.

Finally, having eavesdropped on a pair of pirates whose tongues had been loosened all too easily by the contents of their glasses, Larinna followed them back to their vessel and accosted its captain, a squat merchant dripping with rings and gemstones who'd used his considerable influence to secure a map that matched Larinna's own. He stoutly refused her a position on his crew, and while he grudgingly offered a position as a passenger, the price—even if she traded away her trusty sloop—was far beyond what she could afford.

Frustrated and unwanted, she stormed out of the captain's cabin and was almost to the gangplank when she spotted the stack of barrels being lowered, one by one, into the hold. It was the work of a moment to tip several hundred pickled onions into the water below, though she began to regret her choice of hiding place the minute she sealed the lid back over her head. The smell was almost overwhelming.

After ten minutes of waiting on the dock, crouched in a vinegar-soaked cask with her eyes and lungs stinging, she was about ready to give up. Suddenly, Larinna found herself slung over a brawny deckhand's shoulder and thrown down unceremoniously atop a cargo pile, left to bounce around in the pitch-black mustiness, at which point a bad smell became the least of her problems as she now had to keep herself hidden for the duration of the voyage. (The barkeeper laughed so heartily at this part that he began to choke on his bacon, and Larinna had to thump him on the back until he calmed down.)

Only when she felt the gentle bobbing of a port's waters give way to the rougher waves of the open sea did Larinna dare to explode from her barrel, gasping, into the comparative bliss of the ship's damp lower decks. She spent the next three days lurking out of sight behind a dwindling cargo pile, barely daring to sleep and holding her breath whenever the crew approached to take more rations upstairs, desperate not to make so much as a squeak. She dared to sneak morsels of food and drink only when the ship's crew was eating, so that their commotion covered hers.

On one particularly windy night, she came within seconds of being discovered, as a pair of ham-sized hands reached for the crate she was crouching inside. Luckily, the ship struck a sandbar with a particularly violent lurch that sent everyone stumbling and slid the box clean across the room, giving her a chance to scramble to safety in the confusion. Another evening, she was pinned, furious and immobile, beneath a pile of sacks and a stupefied sailor who'd unwittingly passed out on top of her hiding place.

The indignities continued to pile up, one after another, and Larinna had increasingly frequent daydreams about storming up above deck and simply seizing the vessel single-handedly. Finally, there was a raucous cheer from overhead and she guessed that the ship had made it through to the Sea of Thieves. To her surprise and delight, she felt the ship weigh anchor shortly after with an unmistakable clatter, then heard the crew disembarking, chattering excitedly about the next leg of their journey as they ambled off to drink themselves into oblivion.

Sore and exhausted, Larinna finally clambered into the sunlight. She washed her face and hair in a basin she spotted in the captain's cabin, finally shedding the smell of onions, and briefly considered making off with the galleon. It would have been the sweetest revenge to do so, but deep down she knew that she was in no condition to sail a ship alone, particularly not one this size. Besides, she was incredibly thirsty.

Leaving the vessel alone, she swaggered into the same tavern as her unwitting shipmates, smirked as the squat merchant did a double take that resolved itself into a suspicious glare, and ordered what would be the first of many drinks. She raised a glass, silently toasting her newfound freedom, and another, and another until the moon was high in the sky. By then the air was full of song, but Larinna did not hear it, for she was asleep before her head even struck the bench.

"A tale worth every last rasher, as I'm any judge of them," said the barkeeper warmly as Larinna finished her tale. "Truth be told, I've seen a few young whippersnappers like yourself turn up with a mysterious map in their hand, but you're the first I've ever heard of who made it as a stowaway. And no," he added, chuckling as Larinna opened her mouth to interrupt, "I've no idea who wrote the note, but I'd like to thank 'em one of these days. They keep sending me customers!"

Larinna left her mouth open long enough to give a satisfied burp, then placed both her palms on the table as if to stand. "And what do these customers of yours do once they've sobered up?" she challenged. "This is a nice place to drink, but I don't want to be marooned here."

Cheeks flushed with the heat of a large breakfast, the barkeeper lumbered to his feet and began to clear away the crockery. "Crewing up, mostly," he said after a moment's thought. "Least, that's what they likes to call it. Finding people to sail with. Paying a visit to the shipwright for a vessel if they've got the gold." He tipped soapy water over the plates and began to scrub. "And you? Where might you be headed next?"

"Oh, wherever the wind carries me," Larinna said airily. "Somewhere *fresh*." Truth be told the question made her slightly uncomfortable, for her thoughts kept drifting back to the gold she didn't have. It had been a hearty breakfast, but she was well aware that her purse still needed filling as badly as her stomach had.

Having bidden the barkeeper farewell, Larinna took a brisk walk around the island, though it yielded nothing of interest beyond the outpost, which was apparently named Sanctuary Outpost—nothing, at least, until she spotted some laden banana plants high overhead, their fruit already beginning to drop and burst on the rocks below.

Staring first at the splattered mess and then at all the detritus the sea had washed up on the shore, Larinna saw the beginnings of a scheme. If she was successful, she hoped, she'd make some coin and orchestrate an encounter with a crew willing to take her out on an adventure.

Having gathered as many intact bananas as she could find, she selected the battered remains of a small rowboat that seemed to suit her purposes and began to dig it out of the sand, freeing it from the seaweed and other rubbish that had half buried it over the years. Dragging its husk back across the beach to a carefully scouted location at the dock was no mean feat, and while the other stallholders looked on intently, they made no attempt to assist her.

By the time the rowboat was in place, upended to stand proudly on the sands, Larinna was rasping her tongue across dry lips, beads of sweat tumbling and getting in her eyes. Visions of grog swam through her mind, and she gazed longingly back up at the distant tavern—but she had a plan to complete. Next, she placed the bananas in what she hoped was an eye-catching arrangement, though she'd be the first to admit she had no eye for aesthetics, and settled back to choose her first target.

So it was that an elderly mariner who wanted nothing more than to limp his way up the hill for a grog or two found his path blocked by an imposing figure who thrust a piece of fruit under his nose and demanded, "Buy these bananas!" with the tone of one committing a highway robbery.

The mariner moved to protest, but Larinna scowled at him so fiercely that he soon found himself sat morosely outside the tavern feeling altogether fuller, more sober, and less wealthy than he would have liked. In the distance, he could see Larinna hoisting her wares on yet more unsuspecting arrivals.

While the coins felt welcome jingling in her pocket, Larinna was less interested in a career as a grocer than in using her prime vantage point to keep watch for suitable crews. Had she been back home, she might well have approached each docked vessel one by one and attempted to talk her way aboard. She was all too aware, however, that despite their crumpled clothing and blemished faces, these were pirates who sailed the Sea of Thieves on a daily basis and had experience she lacked. She had to be careful not to bite off more than she could chew, even if that was normally part of the fun.

Instead, Larinna elected to bide her time, gauging the personalities and the proficiency of the pirates that surrounded her and making coin wherever she could. Sure enough, her patience was finally rewarded.

She heard the two men before she saw them, their banter carrying down the hillside at a volume that meant she'd have been hard-pressed to ignore them. Larinna was quiet by nature, preferring to let her actions speak for her, and the vivaciousness and volume of their quarrel nearly made her think twice about approaching them.

"Ned, my friend, you know I speak only with the utmost respect and concern for your reputation. So I know that you will forgive me when I tell you, again, that this fool's errand will see us all drowned!

You think we'll get our fair share from the Gold Hoarders? Hah! I say to you, hah!" one man scoffed.

"S'gud voyage, Faizel," the other responded. "S'better than yours, anyway. Cargo runs always make the ship stink of pigs an' I'm the one who always has to slop out afterward. You're just scared."

"We all have our talents, you know? Mine happens to be picking the jobs that will keep us all in one very wealthy piece. Your talents, on the other hand, are most certainly as varied as they are numerous. One day we may even discover what they are."

The bickering duo stepped onto the boardwalk as they rounded the corner, providing Larinna with her first chance at a proper inspection. While they were obviously close friends, the two could hardly have been more mismatched.

The one who appeared to be winning the verbal fencing match, presumably Faizel, was short and shaped like an egg. He possessed a great belly protruding over his belt that shook when he laughed, which was often. Most of his face was obscured by a curly beard that ran up the entire length of his face and framed twinkling, mischievous eyes. He might have been five years older than Larinna or perhaps fifteen—the sort of man for whom gray hair and wrinkles will never have meaning—and he was dressed smartly in long trousers and an emerald shirt that struggled to contain him.

The other, who had to be Ned, was a lumbering, craggy cliff of a man whom Larinna immediately decided was not to be pressured into buying fruit against his will, for he stood two full heads taller than she. He looked young and his skin was fair, though he was already sweating in the heat of the day. He was, Larinna was forced to notice, completely hairless save for his eyebrows, which were so blond as to be almost invisible. He wore no shirt, possibly because no tailor had sufficient stamina to sew something in his size, or perhaps just so he could appear even more terrifying. The drawn blade in his right hand only added to his intimidating countenance, and Larinna took a deep breath before stepping out in front of them, making sure to keep out of swiping distance.

"Gentlemen," she said, trying desperately to remember how to be personable after a day in the hot sun. "You appear to be at an impasse, but I can offer you a simple solution."

Faizel's patter silenced immediately as Larinna addressed them, dark eyes gleaming as he slowly, nonchalantly laid one hand on the hilt of his sword. "I'd accuse you of eavesdropping, but I suppose we were hardly inconspicuous," he replied, mildly. "And it would be ungracious of me to ignore free advice, even if we should choose not to follow it."

"Good," Larinna said flatly. "Show me both of these voyages you're considering, and I'll decide which one we should sail on." She glanced at Ned, who seemed content to let Faizel handle proceedings, and arched an eyebrow expectantly.

A flicker of recognition passed across Faizel's face, as if he knew the game he was being invited to play. "But stranger, there is no impasse, you see, for we are a crew of three. When the time comes to choose our next voyage, our captain shall break any deadlock. Your services are simply not required, I am sorry to say."

They're shorthanded, Larinna thought to herself. *That could be a good thing, if I play my card right.* She adopted a supercilious air, and sniffed. "You choose to sail as a crew of merely three, and you tell me I'm not needed? You should be sat with the rest of my wares!"

It took only a second before Faizel got the joke, and grinned. "Ah, because we must be bananas, yes? Very good! I think I like you. But even so—"

There was a low rumble, and Ned said, thoughtfully, "We're not supposed to be three, though. Always hadda crew of four, only we had to leave Kyrie behind."

Larinna felt her lip curl, as she did not like the sound of *that*. "You left her behind? Why?"

"We couldn't get the shark up the ladder."

Larinna glared up at him, but Ned's face was impassive, and it was impossible to read any trace of insincerity in his expression. It was like trying to out-bluff a rock.

"Kyrie," Faizel mused. "Most regrettable, indeed, and I suppose now that you put me to it, we are somewhat underhanded. In more ways than one, hah!" He studied the bananas for a moment. "You're quite sure you're a good pirate? A strong pirate? You can handle yourself in a fight?"

"If you want me to prove it," Larinna offered, "I could throw you into the sea."

Ned twitched, but Faizel laid a placating hand on his arm, breaking into a warm laugh Larinna couldn't help but find endearing. "I think I must tell our captain all about you. If she agrees, we will be back for you and your bananas. In the meantime, you will need a weapon, and I am certain our friend Wilbur will have something within your means."

Faizel's proclamation was accompanied by a grand gesture toward one of the larger buildings farther up the hill, where a faded sign depicting two crossed pistols was just about visible. "Shall we say an hour, then?"

Larinna nodded her assent and watched them stroll away along the dock before turning back to her makeshift stall. Whoever this Wilbur was, she hoped he didn't mind taking payment in fruit.

It was then she noticed there was something sticking out of the rowboat's hull—something that she was sure hadn't been there before. It was a knife, the blade of which had been stabbed through the moldy planks halfway up to its hilt. When she moved to pull it out, irritably, she saw the note it was pinning in place.

Larinna's hand flew to her sword until she remembered she didn't have one, and a low growl of frustration escaped her throat as she forced herself not to tear off in search of the culprit. Whoever was following her was clearly angling to end their days as an oversized pincushion, but she wasn't about to let some cowardly prankster ruin her chances of joining a halfway competent crew.

Gathering up the last of her bananas, she squared her shoulders and began to travel the long and winding path back to the outpost. Behind her, several scraps of viciously shredded paper were picked up by the wind and began their long journey out to sea.

3

RAMSEY

The Magpie's Wing sailed low in the water, her innards glittering with the spoils of a month beyond the Shroud. She plowed across the ocean at a merry pace, with echoes of a concertina tune and raucous, atonal attempts at song dancing upon the waves. *What a month*, Ramsey thought, tapping his foot in time as Shan dredged up yet another shanty from the depths of his memory. *We've lived like lords.* He glanced down at his fingers, which were laden with three new gemstones set in fine silver rings, and chuckled contentedly.

As Ramsey had always suspected, the sea they'd been sailing was utterly devoid of human civilization—an unclaimed paradise without as much as a campfire on the horizon. Well... *currently* unclaimed, he corrected himself. Exploration of certain islands had revealed crude paintings and sigils dotted here and there, barely more complex than a child's scrawl and clearly ancient in their origins. Mercia had explained how similar relics had been found back home and were not always simple cave paintings of hunts and beasts, but ways of expressing complicated ideas and even stories.

A long-dead people, then, but not as primitive as their art—if art was what it was—might suggest. By venturing into the caves and ruins where the drawings were at the most numerous, the crew soon learned that, whoever the area's original inhabitants were, they shared a love of precious metal that rivaled that of any pirate.

More surprisingly, some among them had shaped the gold into fineries whose quality far exceeded most anything Ramsey had plundered back in his homeland. Bracelets, anklets, staffs, and scepters were further adorned with emeralds, rubies, and a few kinds of precious ore even Mercia couldn't identify right away. There were coins, too, although Ramsey was rather less interested in these until Shan had pointed out that they were, by and large, made from solid gold.

It all seemed too good to be true, though their voyage through these untamed waters was not without its share of risks. It was rare that they went ashore without laying eyes on some predator or other lurking in the undergrowth, and on one occasion, Rathbone attempted to tug a vine aside only to find it tugging back. Only splashes of scalding water from the campfire's cooking pot was enough to convince the snake to uncoil from the man's arm, fortunately before it had chosen to clamp its sizable fangs down and deliver a fatal dose of venom.

Other animals, not used to being wary of humans, made a nuisance of themselves by trampling campfires and generally getting underfoot. Shan returned to the ship one evening to find a pair of plump piglets helping themselves to a pile of fruit he'd spent all morning gathering. The beasts charged at him when he shouted, bowling him over as they disembarked, squealing and slopping all the way down the gangplank and off toward the jungle.

They spotted a few telltale fins in the water as they sailed, too, and so Ramsey sternly forbade anyone to venture into the sea alone, not even to bathe. Back home, he might have risked tussling with a shark if it meant retrieving the loot from some sunken wreck, but these were strange and fearless creatures that not even a pistol could deter. Better to keep their feet dry.

Still, they persevered despite these dangers, and a glittering cargo was a testament to their success. Even more spoils now lay buried in boxes and casks, left beneath some of the more distinctive paintings and carvings that they'd found along the way. Mercia stored cryptic notes in the ship's journal so that it could be easily found again in the future.

Next time, Ramsey mused. He couldn't say for sure when that would be, for the last few days had seen the *Magpie's Wing* pick her way back through the Devil's Shroud, and now they were on the last leg of their journey home.

Independent and experienced a crew they might be, but there were certain supplies that not even Shan could re-create out in the wild. Grog, for example, was in short supply, as was oil for the lanterns. Mercia's compass had shattered when she tumbled from a high ledge, and a spell of bad weather had scraped the ship's hull against jagged rocks that no one spotted. Fixing the leaks used up many of the sturdy wooden planks they needed for repairs, and so they'd all reluctantly agreed it was time to head back to familiar territory.

Standing at the helm with his face concealed by a collar to keep out the early morning chill, Ramsey permitted himself a yawn. He'd insisted someone take a turn in the crow's nest once they'd emerged from the Shroud, and he himself had stayed awake and wary throughout their voyage. The prospect of losing any of their haul to rival pirates, let alone any of the local mercenaries who might fancy picking up a bounty or two, made his hands clamp so tightly on the wheel that his knuckles went white.

That was why he'd insisted on the detour. Oh, they'd arrive in port with plenty to trade and brag about, but much of what hadn't been buried behind the Shroud had now been transferred to Ramsey's private cabin. He remained aboard, staring at the darkened windows of a distant house and furrowing his brow in thought. The others had swiftly and silently followed his directions and stowed the riches away, ready to be shared once the noise and excitement surrounding their return had died down. Ramsey considered this arrangement proof of how the crew had bonded; pirates who didn't trust one another would never have agreed for a shared treasure to linger in the lap of any one person for too long.

Mercia, who'd been lingering by the captain's cabin, grunted as Shan's concertina wheezed out the final few notes. "I suppose that's one good thing about heading home," she said dryly. "You'll be able to learn a couple of new tunes. Maybe ones you can actually play."

Shan snorted. "That's all you're looking forward to, eh? What about a nice hot meal or a tankard of grog that doesn't taste like something drowned in it?"

"Did you carnivores not enjoy the captain's snake stew?" Mercia asked sweetly, beginning to pin up her hair with obvious reluctance until every last strand was tucked away neatly under her hat. "Going home has its downsides, you know. For some of us, at least. All boys together," she added sullenly.

"Very rich boys," Ramsey said matter-of-factly, which earned him a scowl, though Mercia accepted his assistance slipping back into the oversized coat that she'd dug out of the ship's clothing chest earlier that day. "It's not like we could have stayed out there forever."

"You would if you could, though," Mercia replied softly, lowering her voice so that only Ramsey could hear her as she fumbled with stiff buttons. "I've known you long enough to tell when something's troubling you. You've seemed restless ever since we first decided to head home."

"Yes, well, I'm sure we'll all feel better once we've made it ashore," said Ramsey, without an ounce of conviction in the words. Mercia spoke the truth; it felt like he'd left a part of his soul beyond the Devil's Shroud, buried along with his treasures.

"Land ho," Rathbone cried, quite unnecessarily, for Ramsey's keen eyes had long since fixed upon their destination. He scrambled nimbly down the ladder that led to the crow's nest, dropping the final few feet with a thud. "Can someone explain what's so special about this place? It looks a little shabby for my tastes."

"It's not so bad," Shan retorted. "This is where Ramsey and I first met. The traders are canny enough to take your haul in trade without asking too many questions, the food's hardly ever still alive, and we'll be able to repair and replenish the ship."

Though he continued to stare impassively at the distant buildings, Ramsey's chest tightened slightly at Shan's words. While it had been his suggestion that they head to the port where Rowenna's tavern lay waiting, he couldn't help but feel uneasy at the thought of seeing her again after so long, and of the question he'd have to ask. The answer he might hear.

To their surprise, another ship sailed forth to meet them as they neared the port, white handkerchiefs waving in the air as the crew signaled its good intentions. Another followed in its wake soon after. The *Magpie's Wing* weighed anchor, flanked on either side by well-wishers, some of whom they recognized but many of whom were simply curious strangers. It seemed that news of Ramsey's journey into the Devil's Shroud had spread shortly after his departure, and now his return was the talk of the town.

From the moment they disembarked, they were surrounded by gawkers, admirers, and skeptics in equal measure, and the crowd only increased in size as more townsfolk roused themselves from their beds and came to see what all the fuss was about. The crew members were bombarded with questions wherever they turned, and before long, the dock was bustling with such ferocity that Ramsey knew he'd never be able to unload any of their riches, let alone carry them through town. Not without starting a riot. Enough, he decided, was most definitely enough.

Ramsey was a tall man, and even more imposing once he'd climbed atop a sturdy crate, but it wasn't until he fired a single shot from his pistol into the sky that he really got the crowd's attention. He held his other palm outstretched to face the crowd.

"My friends," he began. That was probably a fair description of most of the crowd, he decided. It was amazing how kindly disposed you could feel to someone brandishing a gun. "My friends, I know you have questions. Doubtless you have heard plenty of idle gossip since we last sailed out from this port. But we have been a month at sea, and are in need of both rest and repair. That is why tonight, I shall be taking supper at my usual drinking den! Those of you who know me are welcome to stop by my table and hear all about our journey!"

There was a great roar of approval at this, but it subsided quickly as Ramsey continued, a steel edge now present in his voice. "Those of you who know me, of course, can also guess what will happen to you if you continue to dog me throughout the day." There was some laughter at this, but in quite a few cases it was tinged with nervousness, and before long most of the onlookers had cleared away.

"Nice speech," Shan commented, sagging slightly under the weight of a stack stuffed with gold and trinkets. "Mercia's volunteered to stay and guard the ship for as long as there are valuables aboard."

Rathbone cocked his head. "And miss out on the drinking? It's not every day a pirate gets a hero's welcome."

"But no one's going to give her a heroine's welcome," Shan replied. "At least we don't have to celebrate in disguise."

Ramsey nodded at this, picking up a heavy trunk stuffed with valuables and moving briskly to the first of their engagements, for they had much to do before nightfall. There were still whispers and furtive glances as they made their way through town, but at least their path remained clear as they staggered down cobbled streets and through a rat run of dingy alleyways.

At Shan's behest, their first stop was an unassuming little business in the old part of town. "This is it!" Shan said, waving a hand at a poky little building smeared with faded paint and fronted by foggy windows of thick bubbled glass.

"This? It's as humble as a sweetshop and looks as popular as a plague," Ramsey said skeptically.

"Just go on," Shan said, gesturing them toward the door.

Once inside, Ramsey was astonished to find an immaculate little jewelers' shop run by a fussy, white-haired man whose spyglasses dangled from a chain around his neck. He huffed and puffed at the pirates' boisterous entrance and muddy footprints, but his high-and-mighty demeanor vanished the instant Ramsey flipped the lid of the chest he'd been carrying. By the time he'd examined a few of the stones by the light of a sputtering candle, the prim little owner was practically their new best friend.

The crew traded their spoils for every coin in the jeweler's safe—Ramsey magnanimously agreed to throw in the chest for free—and the three pirates each took a share of the money and went their separate ways, agreeing to meet at the tavern after sundown.

Shan's destination was the marketplace, and he stuck his hands in his pockets as he drifted from stall to stall, nodding amiably at a platoon of soldiers as they marched past with expressions set in stone. He would hang back from each merchant for a while, watching carefully to see which cuts of meat or bottles of wine were offered up to the elderly townsfolk or to unwitting errand boys and which were reserved for the stern-faced cooks and canny housemaids who demanded the best for their masters.

Only then would he swoop forward and lay claim to the finest-quality items, rattling off a list of orders so quickly that the bewildered stallholders never even had a chance to try and swindle him before Shan was halfway down the street. In his wake, he left behind strict instructions to deliver any goods to the *Magpie's Wing* by sunset and, on the counter, exact change.

Rathbone, by contrast, had no need to hunt for bargains. On Ramsey's say-so, he was to seek out the finest weapons and tools the town had to offer—a task that required an imperious air and no small amount of arrogant self-belief. It was a mantle that Rathbone was able to adopt with ease, especially here on land, for his youth had been spent amongst businessmen and bankers cut from a viciously ruthless cloth. Having received the finest education courtesy of his father's fortune, his was a mind of debts and digits, of knowing precisely how much a person might owe you—not to mention remembering where they lived.

A businessman he'd been raised, and a businessman Rathbone surely would have remained had his lust for wealth not blinded him to his peers' growing dissatisfaction with his work habits. He had begun to snatch deals out from under his rivals' noses, undercutting and cheating powerful people.

When the governor's men arrived at his door one fateful morning carrying a warrant for his arrest and some particularly tight shackles, Rathbone was already halfway across the rear lawn of his sizable estate and accelerating, nightshirt flapping in the breeze. Publicly disgraced, his assets seized, Rathbone soon found himself in the company of smugglers and mercenaries—the kind of criminals he'd previously employed for some of his more underhanded business ventures.

For men of a certain background, walking into a thieves' den and asking for work would have been tantamount to suicide, but Rathbone had two advantages that separated him from most of the area's elite: Firstly, he was a large man who had always taken pains to keep himself fit and active. The regular fencing and hunting practice of his youth likewise lent themselves to skill with a cutlass and pistol.

Secondly, his excellent memory meant that Rathbone knew the details not only of his own business, but of many others as well. He retained an intricate understanding of cargo-run schedules and trade routes, knowing where ships loaded with valuables had previously been lost—and where they might soon be lost again. He took no small amount of satisfaction in building his reputation as a pirate at the cost of his rivals' people and profits, waging campaigns that sank their ships, their cargo, and ultimately their livelihoods.

It was around this time that Rathbone and Ramsey had first been introduced, and while many would have considered them strange bedfellows, they each saw in one another qualities to admire—and ambitions to be wary of. When they worked in tandem, however, their unique combination of experience and intellect, instinct and intimidation, proved a formidable force indeed. Before long, they were sailing together as regular accomplices, and Rathbone had long presumed he'd take over Ramsey's ship and its captaincy, sooner or later, when the man finally turned sufficient attention to his family and "settled down." It was a turn of phrase that made him shudder.

As Rathbone made his way around town, curling his lip and sniffing disdainfully until exasperated shopkeepers surrendered their truly premium wares for his inspection, he found himself wondering what this new turn of events might mean for his long-term prospects. There was no point in enquiring about Ramsey's plans directly, that much was certain. While he was undoubtedly a boisterous and passionate individual, Ramsey kept his private life extremely private indeed, even during conversations with his crew.

Even so, Rathbone had gotten the distinct impression that choosing to make the journey through the Shroud had cost Ramsey a great deal of domestic happiness. Could the man really continue to choose a life at sea over home and hearth? And what would happen to Rathbone's prospects if he did?

Rathbone couldn't know it, but Ramsey had been asking himself those same questions all day, even as he'd argued over figureheads and sail trim with the shipwright and made sure the *Magpie's Wing* was fit for its next voyage. Mercia's charts were growing more detailed and precise with every crossing, and he had no doubt that the little vessel would be able to make it back and forth through the Shroud as often as necessary. The question was, would he be aboard her?

It was a train of thought that took him up the winding hill to the tavern a little sooner than he'd intended, early enough that the stout double doors were still tightly locked. His mind elsewhere, he wandered around through the rear entrance and into the silent bar without really paying much heed to his actions. He settled back into his favorite chair, which creaked, startling the woman who was sweeping the upper balcony.

"We're closed," she said crossly, her voice drifting down from above. "And if the sign and the locked door didn't convince you of that, perhaps my foot up your arse will give you the hint?"

"I'd hope, since we're such good friends, you'll at least polish your boot first," Ramsey replied, wryly. His voice caused a little gasp of recollection, and Rowenna took the stairs at speed, bunching up her thick leather apron so that she didn't trip. She threw her arms around Ramsey's bearlike frame as best she could, kissing his forehead fondly before pulling back to look at him. "You've lost weight," she remarked. "That makes two miracles, what you sailing into that damn fog and coming back to tell me all about it."

"There'll be plenty of time for that," Ramsey assured her. "You can expect a crowded house tonight, and plenty of merriment. You'll need some extra sawdust for the floor, I shouldn't wonder."

Rowenna grimaced. "And here I was, thinking you might have dug up a few good manners on that voyage of yours." She stared at him, for a moment, her stony-blue eyes boring into his, and they locked gazes for a long while before she sighed and patted the sleeve of his coat. "You haven't been home yet, have you?"

Ramsey felt his insides drain away, as if Rowenna had uncorked him with the same practiced ease with which she'd decant a bottle of rum. "I thought I should—" he began, uncharacteristically struggling to find the words. "That is to say, given the circumstances ..."

"She's away."

The answer hit home like two physical slaps in quick succession, the first filling him with a profound remorse, the second, some measure of relief. "She's away," he repeated dully. "Where?"

She shrugged. "Family or some such. The littl'uns too, I shouldn't wonder. Of course, she wasn't to know you'd be coming back." It wasn't delivered as an accusation, just a statement of fact, for Rowenna had made it clear long ago that she wasn't interested in marriage—be it hers or anyone else's. Ramsey had always admired that honesty about her, even when it was currently twisting words into him like a knife. He sat and stared blankly at the floor, not knowing how to put an end to the uncomfortable silence.

"Well," Rowenna said after a moment. "If you really have invited half the town to come and hang on your every word tonight, I'd best get the place in order. You still owe me that present, mind you." With that, she resumed her chores, giving Ramsey some time alone to put his thoughts in order. He sat, brooding, until Rowenna finally unlocked the doors and the first of the pirates spilled in, Shan among their number. By the time she turned around, Ramsey's facade was back in place, and he was once again the avuncular pirate she remembered.

True to Ramsey's word, the tavern soon was packed fit to burst, with townsfolk hanging over the balcony railings and crowding onto benches to hear all about passage through the Devil's Shroud and what lay beyond it. Shan had brought a small sack of the most eye-catching and exotic valuables, including a jeweled horn that he claimed to have tugged from the dusty grip of a long-dead priest—a strange way of explaining that he'd really just stubbed his toe on it in the dark.

They told the story about the piglets, and after a few drinks, Rathbone was even persuaded to talk about the snake, but as the candles burned low and the hours passed, Ramsey refused to be drawn on two subjects: how he'd made the crossing, and how others might do the same.

Strong drink and heavy fumes of pipe smoke, coupled with seeing such fortune waved under their noses only to be snatched away, turned many pirates' moods sour at this point. A particularly devious rat of a man—known around town as Stitcher Jim—climbed unsteadily to his feet, roughly pushed his way toward Ramsey's table with the crimson of his cheeks matched only by his bulbous nose.

"*Liar!*" He meant the shout as a bellow, but it emerged as a belch. "Yer a liar, Ramsey, that's what I say! If as much as you say lies behind that bloody fog, then what harm is there in letting us all take our share? I say you just got lucky, found some old wreck or something, and now you're feeding us this ... this ..." Stitcher Jim's eyes unfocused momentarily. "This! You ain't been nowhere special!" Several of the man's friends grumbled in agreement at this, striking their mugs loudly upon the table and obliviously spilling their beer.

"Every man has his secrets," Ramsey growled, "and I'll not have you prying into mine! Are you telling us all, here and now, that you've no way to make a living, honest or otherwise, without my help? Perhaps," he added with his face twisted in a sneer, "you'd like me to wipe your backside, too, whelp that you are!"

Had the tavern not been so overcrowded, the bottle that Jim's crony aimed for Ramsey's head might actually have struck its target. As it was, a luckless deckhand who'd decided that now was a good moment to stand in search of the privy took the full force of the blow. The deckhand leapt up in one smooth motion, knocking two more pirates into a tangle of flailing limbs and plunging the entire tavern into a drunken brawl.

It was a messy, aimless tussle of pent-up aggression and too much grog, and no one made it home that night without extremely soggy clothing and a few bruises. It marked the only time regulars could remember soldiers needing to set foot inside Rowenna's establishment to round up the most persistent rabble-rousers, though both Ramsey's crew and the man he'd insulted were long gone by then. It never paid to be rounded up by the town guards, as pirates carted off for a night in the cells rarely made it to trial.

So it was that Stitcher Jim and his friends fled the scene and staggered home to the most disreputable part of town, nursing their wounds and clutching at their sore heads. Only Jim was in a state to speak, and he was busy ranting, so distracted that he almost collided with the cloaked figure as it stepped smartly out of a doorway into their path. Jim cursed, stumbled, and would have fallen were it not for the figure, who caught his arm in an iron grip.

Squirming, Jim made to deliver a threat, but it died on his lips as he caught a peek under the cowl. "You!" he spat. "You're one of Ramsey's lot! I ought to cut your tongue clean out!"

"If you do that," Rathbone replied amiably, apparently oblivious to the other two men closing in behind him, "then I won't be able to tell you where you can find yourself a map. Assuming you're still interested in crossing the Devil's Shroud yourselves, that is. I can only offer a copy, but I assure you I have an excellent eye for detail."

Jim eyed the taller man, warily, and yanked his arm free. He made no move for his sword, however. Not yet, at least. "Why would you help the likes of us, eh? Why betray your captain?" he asked, warily.

"Because I think he's wrong to hoard the knowledge," Rathbone replied, curtly. "The more of us there are out there, the more we can accomplish. Everyone needs to know they've got friends to rely on." He leaned closer. "We could be *good* friends, Jim."

Jim looked uncertain, his eyes almost crossed, but he shook his head. "This is a trick! Revenge for tonight, that's what this is. You're trying to get me to sail straight into that damn fog and sink the lot of us!"

"If that's what you believe, then copy the map yourself and send someone else through first," Rathbone scoffed. "If I were you, I'd make copies anyway. You can sell them to pirates who are actually brave enough to make the trip."

Stitcher Jim narrowed his eyes, annoyed at the insult, but if Rathbone was deceiving them, he couldn't work out how or why. "And how much will you ask for this precious map, exactly?"

"Noth—" Rathbone paused, because some part of him still churned at the idea of giving something for free. "Whatever's left in your coin purse will do, but what I really want is your loyalty." He was so close now, their noses were practically touching. "I want to know that the next time we see each other, you'll do as I say."

Jim could have refused. Had he been clear-headed, he might have done so and left Rathbone in a heap for the guards to find. But something about the intensity of the man's gaze was hypnotic. He heard himself say yes, and felt his fingers handing over coin.

"Excellent." Rathbone pulled back sharply, brusquely shoving Jim's companions aside and stepping between them. "You'll find the parchment in a bottle," he called, striding toward the dock without so much as glancing back at the bewildered group. "It's in the water barrel outside that dismal tavern. I look forward to our next encounter, friends."

Stitcher Jim watched silently until Rathbone was well out of ear-shot. "Friends, huh. He's cracked, giving away a map like that," he said finally.

"Definitely," the others nodded.

"Probably just a bunch of nonsense anyway. Probably doesn't even lead anywhere."

"Course not."

"Although," Jim mused, "even if it was a fake, it'd still fetch a pretty penny."

"Could be so, could be," the others agreed. One by one, they reached the same conclusion and stood for a moment, considering their options.

And then, scrambling and shoving at one another in their bid to get there first, each of the pirates ran back toward the tavern as fast as their legs would carry them.

LARINNA

A weapon within my means, he says. Larinna stood outside Wilbur's Weapon Emporium with her hands on her hips and scowled up at what could only charitably be called a building. More accurately, it looked like someone had taken two enormous piles of driftwood, pushed them up against one another, and hung a sign on the resultant mess.

Still, even getting her hands on a sharpened stick would be preferable to setting out on the open water unarmed. The shop's door grated against the uneven planks of the bare wooden floor as she entered, and Larinna had to apply the sole of her boot and force it backward before there was enough space for her to squeeze inside the little hut. Much as she'd expected, the place was as much of a shambles inside as out, with piles of rusting firearms half-disassembled and then abandoned. A selection of notched cutlasses hung haphazardly from an old hat stand, and a barrel had been stuffed full of what appeared to be cannon fuses, all different lengths and tangled together in a knot that might take lifetimes to unravel.

Wilbur, or at least who she presumed to be Wilbur, was a rotund, middle-aged man with a balding pate and an enormous moustache that drooped far down past his chin. Similarly impressive tufts of hair protruded from his ears. The overall impression was that someone had stuffed a walrus into an apron and left it in charge of their junk room while they were out.

He was pacing back and forth behind the counter in full theatrical flow, gloved hands gesturing at the various dubious weapons that had somehow earned pride of place as display models. The target of Wilbur's patter was a young pirate with a shaved head and an impressive collection of piercings. Her glassy-eyed expression suggested that she'd been here for some time and might continue to be so, for the dealer's grandiose showmanship showed no signs of dying down. Larinna folded her arms impatiently and leaned against the doorframe to wait her turn—gingerly, in case her weight was enough to bring the entire place crashing down around their ears.

"On the other hand," Wilbur was saying, "there will come a time in every pirate's life when the odds are stacked against her and the situation is grim, a moment when she realizes that her beloved pistol—up until that point her constant companion and her most faithful friend—simply lacks the pure punch to deal with the ravening hordes she's pitted against! Granted, yes, you're quite correct to say that the humble pistol can accurately pluck the pips from an apple from fifty feet away when in skilled hands, but when your back's against the wall, it's sheer stopping power that you need, make no mistake about it!"

Wilbur reached up and took hold of a beaten and tarnished blunderbuss, placing it on the counter with as much reverence as one might show a family heirloom. "It was the stopping power that saved the life of the notorious brigand known to his friends and enemies alike as Clumsy George, yes, the very same, when he found himself outmanned and outgunned by a crew of vicious villains with murder in their hearts! Oh yes, old George would have found himself in quite the sore spot had he not had this beautiful piece of craftsmanship clutched behind his back—for, like any good blunderbuss should, this fine firearm has the kick of a mule on mayday when you're nice and close." Here he gave a cheeky wink, as if imparting some great trade secret.

"If it's such a wonderful weapon," Larinna challenged, "why did this Clumsy George get rid of it?" She stepped up to the counter as the last of her patience ebbed away.

Wilbur merely shrugged and responded, "He tripped and lost it overboard." Pushing the blunderbuss to one side for a moment, he leaned forward on the counter. "Am I to take it from your unfamiliar countenance and sunny disposition that you're a new arrival to our little pirate paradise?"

"You are," said Larinna curtly. "And I have an appointment to keep. Faizel sent me," she added, as an afterthought.

Wilbur beamed. "Did he, indeed! Well I must say you've found yourself in some delightfully dishonorable company, so that's a good start. Faizel's been a regular customer of mine since I was back at the old place, before I went upmarket." He patted a nearby beam affectionately, dislodging a couple of woodworms. "I'm sure you're just as eager as our mutual friend here to learn more about the wondrous weaponry you see all around you. Such as this rifle, for instance, which has a long and surprising history in the hands of Gr—"

"Just a sword," Larinna interrupted. "And I don't need to know its life story, or which way you're supposed to hold it, or that the previous owner was a little old lady who only used it once a week to kill sharks. I just need it to be sharp, and well oiled, and for the blade not to fall off in the middle of a fight. Clear?"

"Ah," said Wilbur, thoughtfully. "One of our *deluxe* models." He reached underneath the counter and heaved a dusty crate into what passed for the daylight inside the little shop, wiping it theatrically. "Now, these don't come cheaply, of course ..."

"I have five pieces in my purse," Larinna said, refusing to let the blustering swindler take control of the conversation. "By the time I walk out of here, they could be your five pieces." She wrenched the box around to face her, and rifled through its contents, ignoring flashes of golden hilts or finally detailed blades that she almost certainly wouldn't be able to afford.

Finally, buried near the bottom of the selection, she found what she was looking for—a simple steel blade with a gentle curve to it and a handle wrapped with cloth to provide a sturdy grip. She swished it once or twice through the air, checking its balance. There were a couple of notches in the blade, but it'd do.

Wilbur could contain himself no longer. "Ah!" he exclaimed. "Now that sword—"

"—is worth five pieces." Larinna allowed the coins to tumble from her palm one by one onto the counter with a series of satisfying *thunk* noises, tilting her palm so that the final coin went into a spiraling roll before clattering to a halt. Wilbur's eyes followed it all the way. "My time here is over."

The weapon dealer let out a theatrical sigh, but Larinna could tell by the look in his eyes that the deal was already done. "Five it is," he agreed, "and you make sure you come back and trade it in just as soon as you're ready for the next model up, you hear me?"

"If your sword doesn't snap and get me killed, I just might," said Larinna reasonably, sliding the blade carefully into her belt and making for the door without another word. It was nice to be out in the sunlight again—but not as nice, she had to admit, as feeling the weight of a weapon at her side once more. Now it was time to meet her new crew.

As Larinna left for the docks, she could still hear Wilbur's booming rhetoric carried on the breeze. "Sometimes, young lady, you meet one of those customers who you simply have to get rid of as quickly as you can, or they'll talk your ear off all day. Now, as to that blunderbuss . . ."

The sun was brushing against the distant horizon by the time Larinna made it to the dock, bathing the handful of ships there in the orange glow of twilight. Deckhands busied themselves about them like bees around a hive, patching and repairing, loading and unloading supplies, and making ready to set sail by the light of the moon. Darkness could be a pirate's best friend, if the night was kind.

Even in a crowd, Ned was easy to spot. Currently he was hefting one lumpy object in each hand—to begin with, Larinna assumed they were casks or sacks of some kind. It was only as she drew closer that she realized she was looking at two struggling figures, a man and a woman. Neither seemed dressed for a life at sea, clad as they were in heavy leather tunics topped with purple robes made from some expensive fabric. Some sort of uniform, perhaps? Intrigued, she sidled a little closer so that she could hear what was being said.

Naturally, Faizel was doing more of the talking, and were it not for the way Ned was manhandling the strangely garbed pair, Larinna might have assumed they were all lifelong friends. "I am in my heart a gentle soul," he was saying, sorrowfully, "with a profound sense of love and respect for all things, for we are all the same deep down, yes? If you prick us, do we not bleed, swear, and hit you? That is why it fills me with such sorrow to see my companion here upset in any way." At this, Ned tightened his grip, hefting the two cloaked figures even farther from the floor.

"Since we are so alike, I am sure you both can imagine my despair when Ned tells me that we have intruders aboard our vessel, our pride and joy! Trespassers! Interlopers! Saboteurs! Had we not happened upon you scuttling around below decks, who knows what terrible fate might have awaited us, hmm? Now I find myself at a loss as to what should be done with you. I could have you locked in the brig, I suppose, but it really is only designed for one person ..."

"Yeah," Ned cut in with a gravelly chuckle. "We'd have to squeeze *really* hard."

"We had a contract!" one of the figures managed to choke out.

"Ah, this is very true," Faizel agreed. "A contract upon which, I admit, we sadly could not deliver. Even as we speak, our good captain is away explaining all of this to your superiors, who I'm sure are also gentle souls." He paused, moving around to stand disconcertingly behind the two prisoners, and lowered his voice. "But I think perhaps we are not so trusted, yes? You suspect that maybe we did indeed acquire what you sent us to find, and assuming that we were planning to hold it for ransom or perhaps make use of it ourselves in some way, you crept aboard our fine vessel to take it for yourselves. Ah, my heart is heavy again. You would rob us of the very clothes off our backs!"

Faizel rocked back and forth for a moment on his heels, frowning, then his face split into a delighted grin. "Then we must deliver payment in kind, I think! Ned, if you would be so kind as to bring our guests aboard for a moment," Faizel said with a sweeping gesture.

Larinna watched curiously as the two flailing captives were hauled effortlessly aboard and taken into the captain's cabin. She wasn't entirely sure how much of what Faizel had said was true, but she was eager to see how the intruders were about to be dealt with. These were people she might well need to entrust her life to one day, after all. How ruthless would they prove to be?

Her curiosity was sated a moment later when those same two figures—momentarily unrecognizable, as they were now clad only in their undergarments—were ejected from the back of the ship and fell, bellowing, into the muddy waters of the docks. They surfaced a moment later, red-faced and spluttering, and a chorus of jeers and jokes from bystanders on the dock floated after them as they sprinted shamefacedly out of sight.

When she'd finished chuckling, Larinna left her hiding place and approached the ship, noting the figure of a short-haired woman holding two crossed pistols. It would be wiser not to mention that she'd borne witness to the dispute just now, she decided, and she prepared to board and knock upon the door of the captain's cabin as if she'd just arrived.

She'd barely made it to the base of the gangplank, however, before Faizel and Ned reemerged. They didn't wave or shout but merely waited solemnly by the railings in what she could only assume was an invitation to join them.

"I see you have found yourself a sword," Faizel said mildly as Larinna's booted feet struck the deck. "And now I think it must be time for formal introductions. I am Faizel, and this is my fellow crewman, Little Ned."

"Larinna," said Larinna, "My—" She paused. "*Little* Ned?"

"I'm the younger brother," Ned said, helpfully.

"And this is our ship, the *Unforgiven*," Faizel continued. "Or to be more precise, she is the ship of the illustrious Captain Adelheid, who unfortunately continues to be occupied with ship's business on the mainland. Perhaps we can offer you a tour while we wait for her return?"

Larinna briefly considered declining. What, did they think she'd never set foot aboard a ship before? She was admittedly curious to poke around, though, if only to make sure that the little vessel was seaworthy. Nodding curtly, she followed after the pair.

The topmost deck seemed shipshape enough, she decided after a cursory inspection. The ropes and rigging for the ship's seven sails—split across three masts and currently furled since the ship was docked—were taut and well tied, while the heavy capstan responsible for raising and lowering the ship's anchor turned well enough at her touch. There were eight stout cannons primed and ready, four to port and four to starboard. The *Unforgiven* may have been small compared to the ships back home, but she was no less able to defend herself.

Larinna didn't bother with the long climb up to the crow's nest that crowned the highest mast, but she did spend some time standing at the ship's wheel, getting a feel for the vessel beneath her as it bobbed lazily. To their credit, Faizel and Ned both seemed to understand this behavior and stood patiently by until she was ready to move on.

A look inside the captain's cabin wasn't offered, nor did Larinna request one. A certain element of privacy was expected even when sailing in cramped quarters, and she wasn't part of the crew. Not yet, anyway.

Besides, there was plenty to see elsewhere on the ship, most notably the map table, which was dominated by a large and complicated chart. Larinna attempted to drink in as much of this as she could without making it too obvious that this was her first time studying the geography of the Sea of Thieves. She was privately delighted to see that many island chains were depicted as little more than crude notes and sketches, aching to be explored.

There was a tiny kitchen area near the table with a few half-emptied pots and bottles on display, though Larinna noticed a thin layer of dust atop it all and suspected that hot meals aboard the ship would be few and far between. No matter, for she was no cook and could get by on ship's biscuits or dried fruit for as long as required. There were hammocks here, too, strung haphazardly between the beams that comprised the skeleton of the ship. To Larinna, who'd spent three nights as a stowaway and a fourth slumped over a table, they looked like the most comfortable things in the world.

The lowest deck seemed to be used mostly for storage and was therefore the least interesting as far as Larinna was concerned. There was a poky little brig down here too, just as Faizel had said, though it was scarcely more than an iron cage with a very sturdy lock on its door. A few stains on the floor around the bars suggested that animals had been its only occupants of late, and that they had been particularly nervous ones.

All in all, she had to admit, it was a perfectly serviceable ship, if hardly the finest at the port. Ned seemed like the sort of man she could get along with just fine, and she could see herself tolerating Faizel's eccentricities on a voyage or two. The lingering question, of course, was whether or not she approved of this Adelheid woman. And, she grudgingly supposed, whether Adelheid approved of her.

She returned to the top deck to find Ned standing peaceably at the railing watching the docks. "That's the captain," he remarked, pointing one stubby finger out toward the distant buildings, and for a moment Larinna assumed he was referring to a middle-aged woman hauling a sack of potatoes toward a tiny sloop. As she stared in disbelief, a more distant movement caught her eye.

A figure, barely more than a silhouette in the dying light, was pelting over the rooftops, using beams and balconies as temporary footholds with an almost balletic grace. Her path was erratic, but she was certainly making her way toward the *Unforgiven*. As the woman drew closer, Larinna could see yet more figures, clearly pirates, judging by their outfits, and even more clearly desperate to catch up to their quarry. They were skittering through the streets and shouting to one another in confusion, though none possessed the dexterity to leap across the rooftops and follow her directly.

They did possess pistols, though, and Larinna could see flashes as the pursuers took potshots at their target, sending bystanders skittering for cover. Alarmed, she turned to Faizel, who now flanked her at the railings. "Should we help her?"

"And spoil all her fun?" Faizel grinned. "Our captain likes to show off from time to time."

Larinna could spot the showmanship to Adelheid's actions, now that she was looking for it. She slashed the ropes of a heavy canopy as she passed so that it collapsed onto two of the disoriented assailants, leaving them struggling under its weight. A third found a bucket slammed forcefully over her head as she rounded a corner, and then received a dizzying smack with the flat of a blade.

That left three, and Adelheid was on the ground now, sprinting full pelt along the dock toward the *Unforgiven*. She made it up the gangplank in three huge bounds, pushed past Larinna without so much as a second glance, and grasped one of the starboard cannons with both of her gloved hands. She wrenched it around so that its barrel was now aimed squarely at the dock—on which the pursuing trio, who had until that moment been racing toward the *Unforgiven*, were now frozen like something small and furry in the grip of a cobra's stare.

"Um," one began, but if there was more to that sentence, Larinna never got to hear it. The cannon in Adelheid's grip let out a vengeful roar that mirrored her own snarl of triumph, sending a speeding, soaring lump of iron right into the heart of the petrified pirate gang. The cannonball tore effortlessly through the gnarled planks of the jetty, reducing them to a shower of shards and splinters and flinging everyone atop them this way and that. By the time the smoke and dust had settled, the trio had beaten a hasty retreat, scrambling back up the sand and out of sight in case there was more gunfire to come.

"Bunch of idiots," Adelheid commented, rubbing her hands together. "Tried to stage an ambush on my way back, all because they're still sore about what happened at Barnacle Cay. Who's this?" She was addressing Faizel, so Larinna fought down the urge to step forward and introduce herself.

"This is Larinna, a woman with excellent taste in both bananas and traveling companions," Faizel informed her. "She would like to join our crew."

"Just 'Larinna,' is it?" Adelheid turned to look at her properly for the first time, and the two women began to study one another. Dark-skinned and dark-haired with eyes that flashed when she spoke, the ship's captain cut a striking figure—though it was, if you looked carefully, mostly due to her outfit.

The flared jacket, a wide-brimmed hat trimmed with an oversized feather, baggy pantaloons tucked into well-heeled boots—Larinna had seen plenty of pirate outfits in her time, but this was a costume being worn by a woman barely older, and significantly shorter, than Larinna herself. *A woman who just blew up a jetty out of spite*, Larinna reminded herself.

"Well," said Adelheid at last. "I, as I'm sure you know by now, am Adelheid, but I have never heard of you. Why might that be? Reputation is extremely important around here, you know."

"You certainly seem to have acquired one," Larinna remarked, glancing down at the shattered remains of the boardwalk. "I wonder if that always works in your favor."

Adelheid glared at her for a moment, and then nudged Faizel angrily in the ribs. "What did you tell her?"

Faizel looked genuinely hurt, as much by the remark as by the elbow. "Not a thing," he protested. "I think it is fairly obvious to anyone that our stay at this outpost has been not altogether tranquil. And without Kyrie at our side, we are running rapidly out of friends."

"You're right," Larinna cut in. "You don't know me. I understand that I'm a nobody out here. That's the point of this place, isn't it, a fresh start? Somewhere you're free to make what you want of yourself?" She folded her arms. "I'm not some swabbie. I know how to sail a ship, wield a sword, and raise a glass. I can look after myself and I can look out for others, but I don't expect you to take that on trust. What I do expect is a chance to prove myself."

Adelheid twirled a lock of her hair around her finger, musing on Larinna's words. "You made it this far, so you must be a halfway decent pirate, or a very lucky one," she declared. Larinna felt her fingers twitch and resisted the urge to make a fist. Already she was wondering how much more of the *Unforgiven*'s precocious captain she'd be able to stomach.

"And as you say, her face is not known around here," Faizel added. "Which may prove to be of some use to us tonight, yes?"

Adelheid smiled at that. "Why not? We'll be no worse off whatever happens. You see, Larinna, we recently were forced to back out of a contract with a particular group of people here in town. I don't like to lose, and I certainly don't like having to explain myself to a bunch of jumped-up, half-witted, snuff-smoking—" Adelheid cut herself off and closed her eyes for a moment before continuing in a far calmer tone: "Which is to say, we find ourselves interested in a new opportunity they have to offer. Unfortunately, we appear to be somewhat blacklisted for the present. Can't even show our faces without them making a fuss. But yours is a face that no one's seen before, either."

"So you want me to go in your place and get this contract?" Larinna looked deeply unconvinced by this. "This sounds too much like *employment* for my liking." Her lip curled in distaste as she spat out the word. "Who exactly are they, and why are you willing to do their dirty work?"

"Oh my dear Larinna, you really must be new around here!" Adelheid chuckled. "Let's retire to my cabin, and I'll tell you all about the Order of Souls."

RAMSEY

The day was bright but blustery, with a strong westerly wind that both billowed the sails and turned the sea wild and unpredictable, tossing anyone that sailed upon it back and forth. That bit of capriciousness was why the first volley of cannonballs collided with the water just shy of the prow, rather than striking the *Magpie's Wing* herself.

Rathbone, who was at the helm, let out a loud curse and spun the wheel as hard as he could, swinging the bulk of the ship out of the way. A second barrage of deadly iron splashed down to starboard, sending up great waves of spray that drenched everyone and everything on deck. Mercia and Shan were already fumbling with cannonballs of their own, preparing to retaliate, only for Ramsey to burst from the captain's cabin like a wild thing and shout them down. "If we try to fire back, they'll scupper us!" he bellowed.

Rathbone, who had the best view of the enemy vessel, had to agree. Their attacker was of a similar size, with a dark beechwood hull and crimson sails, already in position to launch as many broadsides as it cared to. To return fire, the *Magpie's Wing* would have to expose the vulnerable sides of the ship, presenting a bigger target. Their best option now, Rathbone suspected, was to flee.

Ramsey, however, had other ideas. Having instructed Shan and Mercia to tilt the sails, he lumbered up the stairs and bade Rathbone to surrender the wheel. "Have your swords at the ready," he growled. "We'll show these wretches what it means to start a fight with the likes of us!" Under his command, the prow of the ship turned in the water and began to speed directly for their enemy.

He's going to ram them, Rathbone thought, and dread twisted his guts as he drew his sword. Their assailants had obviously reached the same conclusion, because yet more cannon fire rained down around them. These shots landed even more haphazardly than before, doing little more than rattling the ship's windows, and it was clear that Ramsey's bold scheme had the crew of the other ship in a panic. One final shot arced high overhead before their guns fell silent. They were either out of ammunition, Rathbone suspected, or unwilling to waste any more of it with missed shots.

Rathbone risked a look through his spyglass and could see the opposing crew scrambling around in confusion as the *Magpie's Wing* bore down upon them mercilessly. Would their prow be weighty enough to skewer the other vessel, he wondered, leaving them locked like stags tussling with their antlers? Or would the two vessels simply broach, tipping to the point at which a torrent of seawater would flood into the ships and send both crews to join whatever fell creatures lurked at the bottom of the sea?

Suddenly, Ramsey was moving past him. To his horror, Rathbone realized that the furious captain had simply abandoned his position at the wheel, trusting their speed and Mercia's skill to keep them aimed toward their target. He'd moved to the capstan, placing both his hands upon it, and it was only then that Rathbone gained a full understanding of what was going through the man's head. Biting his lip, he took over at the helm, ready to go along with what was either a very brave or a very foolish thing to do.

The enemy ship was closer now, so close that Rathbone no longer needed a spyglass to see the terrified expressions on the other crew's faces. Less than fifty feet now separated then. Now, less than thirty. Now...

At the last possible moment, Ramsey heaved on the capstan with all his might, sending the anchor and its long, heavy chain down into the depths. Rathbone wondered briefly if they might be in such deep water that there'd be nothing for the huge weight to catch onto, but then he heard the familiar thud of metal on rock. It was now or never.

The *Magpie's Wing* groaned in protest, and Rathbone spun the wheel with all his might as they began to pivot. The anchor's chain was at full extension now, and its pull was transforming the ship's forward motion into a large, sweeping arc. Within a few seconds, they'd changed from bearing down upon the other vessel to matching her course, side by side and just a few feet apart.

That was when Ramsey leapt.

Rathbone found it astonishing that a man of his stature could throw himself forward with such agility, but there was a cold fury behind the move that sent Ramsey soaring across the gap between the two vessels. The pirate closest to the railing found himself taking Ramsey's boot to his chest, knocked helplessly to the ground as the crew of the *Magpie's Wing* began to board.

Mercia was next, taking a high dive from the rigging and rolling as she hit the enemy's deck and came up fighting. She pulled a slender blade free from its sheath and began to menace a young deckhand who'd been manning the cannons, but he clearly had no stomach for a fair fight and threw his weapon down almost at once. Mercia considered the quivering figure as he dropped to his knees before her, then coldcocked him so he couldn't cause any more trouble.

Rathbone hesitated, not so confident in his own acrobatic ability but prideful enough to try. His clumsy leap saw him falling just short of the other ship's deck, though his flailing hands were able to catch the rungs of the ladder that ran up her hull. Clambering aboard with his face flushed pink, he spared no time in taking out his embarrassment on the nearest pirate. The luckless man, who'd only just picked himself up from Ramsey's first assault, found himself on the receiving end of a flurry of blows that left him dazed and crumpled in the corner.

The enemy captain, however, had far more fight in her. Having leapt nimbly from the upper deck, she dropped down on Ramsey, staggering him and bringing her sword around in a blow that he was barely able to deflect with his own blade. "You should have run while you had the chance, old man!" she hissed, her eyes flashing as their swords danced.

"Now where's the sport in that?" Ramsey shot back, edging closer and closer to the railing as each of the captain's blows forced him backward. Little by little, he was losing ground.

Mercia was in no position to help him, for she was being terrorized by the final member of the ship's crew: a brawny woman with a scarred face and a split lip who'd managed to knock Mercia's sword away. She was shrugging off all the kicks and punches that Mercia landed, and her grasping fingers were reaching for the smaller pirate's neck, twitching mere inches from Mercia's windpipe when the first gunshot rang out.

Judging from the way the larger woman gasped in pain and clutched at her leg, Mercia guessed that Shan—standing calmly aboard the *Magpie's Wing* with a smoking pistol in his hand—had only been aiming to wound. *Fine by me*, she thought, and hooked her leg around that same limb, sending her opponent toppling sideways with a yelp and a stream of curses. Jumping down after her, Mercia followed this up with a vicious kick that sent the sprawled figure tumbling down the stairs and out of sight below decks. There was a loud crash, the sound of breaking glass, and silence.

Drawing his own sword, Rathbone approached Ramsey and the enemy captain while Mercia crept toward them on the opposite side. Their battle was so intense, however, that he didn't dare strike lest he accidentally cleave down the wrong captain. Besides, the hulking man seemed to be enjoying himself tremendously.

"You're surrounded, Captain!" Ramsey roared, pushing forward with a renewed surge of strength. Now it was his opponent losing ground, her feet dancing inch by inch across the deck until her back was against the railings. "Surrender, and I'll show you mercy."

She spat. "Mercy? From the great Captain Ramsey, the brave pioneer who breached the Devil's Shroud? Pathetic! Real pirates never show mercy. If you're prepared to let me go then you'd better learn to sleep with one eye open, because the next time I see you, I'm going to slit—"

Ramsey swept a long, lazy arc with his blade. As the other captain moved her sword instinctively to parry it his fist lashed out with a swift blow that caught her squarely on the chin, lifted her effortlessly into the air and carried her backward over the railing. There was a splash, and a scream cut short.

"Real pirates," Ramsey observed, "would have seen that coming."

With its captain lost and the rest of its crew defeated, the ship was a simple matter to secure. After some brief debate, the crew of the *Magpie's Wing* hauled Mercia's former adversary into the brig below decks, tied the youth who'd surrendered to a beam in the captain's cabin, and secured the final crewman in the map room. Separated as they were, it would be all the harder for them to conjure up a means of escape.

"We're leaving them to starve, then?" Shan commented, keeping his voice carefully neutral as he and the crew began to ransack the ship's supplies.

Ramsey shook his head. "We deserve a drink, so when we reach an outpost we'll spread word about a fine vessel out here for the taking. Someone'll pay us handsomely for her location, and then it'll be up to her crew to talk themselves out of trouble."

"Assuming some other ship doesn't stumble upon them first," Rathbone interjected. "There are more and more of these cocky little greenhorns sailing around every day."

Scowling, Mercia rounded on him. "And whose fault is that, I wonder? Who could possibly be responsible for every lubber with a dinghy to their name finding their way through the Devil's Shroud just as surely is if they had a map—*our* map?"

Rathbone's countenance darkened in return as he stepped up to her. "*This* again?" he snarled. "And yet again, I say, if you're going to accuse me of treachery without proof, you'd better be prepared to answer for it!"

"Just try it, you overbearing—"

"*Enough!*" Ramsey roared in a voice that shook the ship. "The hows and whys don't matter anymore. We're no longer alone out here, so let's take what we can and sail on before someone else decides to pick a fight." Chastened, Rathbone and Mercia moved to opposite ends of the enemy ship and joined Shan in the hunt for anything useful.

As he crossed the gangplank that was acting as a temporary bridge between the two vessels, a box of lead shot under each arm, Ramsey found himself musing on their journey to date. Almost a full year had passed since he'd stood in Rowenna's tavern and boasted about his journey, a night that had unintended consequences. The tales and trinkets Ramsey brought back had compelled others to follow in his footsteps, one way or another.

For better or worse, the region beyond the Shroud was no longer a secret. The pirates back home had even given it an informal name, and though Ramsey had snorted disdainfully the first time he heard someone refer to "the Sea of Thieves," the phrase had somehow seemed to stick.

He supposed he should be angry at the rest of the world for intruding into what he'd once considered his own private paradise. Certainly, Ramsey was furious the first time they spotted another ship, and he was ready to blow them out of the water for daring to approach him. But they waved a flag of truce and shared a meal. It turned out they merely wanted to offer thanks and a chance to dine with the famous captain who'd discovered the Sea of Thieves. He didn't know quite what to make of that.

Since then, there had been unexpected encounters wherever they'd journeyed. They no longer enjoyed the luxury of sailing without a lookout in the crow's nest as they had when they first arrived, secure in the knowledge that they were the most fearsome thing on the waves. Now, just like the old days, they had to constantly scour the horizon for distant sails lest they be caught unawares.

These constant distractions and the knowledge that a treasure left unclaimed today might be resting in someone else's hold tomorrow had served only to harden Ramsey's resolve. If these weren't to be his waters alone, then he'd damn well make sure that he was their undisputed master, and that every other pirate knew it. He'd been relentless in dealing with those who opposed him and wasted no time before detailing his exploits whenever they stopped off at an outpost.

Outposts! Now there was something Ramsey had never anticipated seeing out here, though he supposed it was inevitable. Previously unspoiled islands had developed first small campgrounds, then crude wooden shelters, and finally boardwalks and buildings. Even pirates needed to make camp from time to time, and others would come along later to build upon what went before, using their unique skills to improve the place whenever they stopped by.

There were at least two taverns in this region alone, both run by opportunistic pirates who knew about sugars, fermentation, and everything else that went into a good beer. These pirates had chosen to make their fortune by opening their doors to others, so that they might drink and relax without having to make the long journey home. He had even heard tell of a blacksmith coming to the region in the company of a crew who wanted to keep their weapons sharp and were willing to pay for the privilege. Before long, Ramsey mused, there'd be shipwrights and shopkeepers aplenty, all eager to hawk their wares to passing travelers and spare them the danger of the long journey home.

All told, the increasing likelihood of bumping into other ships while out on adventures, coupled with his own rising notoriety, had led Ramsey to insist that they find themselves a suitable hideout.

They needed a place where they could rest, relax, and repair; something that simply wasn't possible amid the hustle and bustle of an outpost, even if the folks around wanted to do nothing more than share a drink or hear stories. Mercia, true to form, had been keeping a careful log of everywhere that they'd visited and had suggested a number of suitable locations.

The first potential hideaway they'd visited was been an innocuous island near the heart of the region, where a soft crescent of golden beaches framed a huge rocky cave with a fine sandy floor. It seemed like an ideal safe harbor, and so they moored the *Magpie's Wing* and made camp inside. Their revelry lasted only until high tide, at which point seawater began to pour relentlessly into the cave from all directions, forcing the crew to abandon their cooking pot halfway through a meal and paddle hastily back to the ship. Shan continued to insist he'd seen a shark snacking on their dinner as they sailed away.

The second site, an imposing crisscross of rocky peaks surrounding a central lagoon, would have allowed them to hide the ship entirely. Shan even suggested mounting cannons on the high cliffs overlooking the bay's single entrance, allowing them to repel intruders. As they approached the island, however, tendrils of mist began to form around them and a familiar sourness filled the air. They had to execute a swift about-face to avoid sailing any closer, and by morning, the ebb and flow of the Devil's Shroud had swallowed the island up as if it had never existed.

Finally, Rathbone reminded them of the high, arched cavern where they'd spent their first night in the Sea of Thieves. The entrance was almost invisible unless you knew where to look, he argued, and they knew from prior experience that there were no ghastly surprises awaiting them when night fell or the storms swept in. He called it a Thieves' Haven, and the others agreed.

Shan in particular seemed to relish the opportunity to set themselves up a permanent home away from home and, by the time they set sail, had already dreamed up an extensive list of changes and renovations he wanted to make to the place. Mercia warned him not to get his hopes up based on their recent run of luck, joking that the whole island was probably an active volcano or the maw of some slumbering leviathan, but not even she could put a dent in his unrelenting optimism.

It turned out to be well-founded cheer, too, for the cavern was just as they'd left it all those months ago with its hidden entrance and all. Even the remains of their first campfire were still largely undisturbed, though Shan expressed a desire to build a more permanent dining area of sorts, tucked out of the way where the smoke and the firelight wouldn't make their hideaway obvious to passing vessels.

Mercia had bought into the idea of creature comforts, too, though she had some very different ideas as to what needed constructing first. Bedrooms, she insisted, or at the very least some sort of partitioned spaces, were needed for some modicum of privacy. Rathbone, perhaps looking for a way to ease tensions between them, helped her wedge a series of bamboo poles across the openings of cavities in the cave walls and hang sheets of thick canvas from them like curtains.

When they found treasures, they had begun to set the smaller items aside, offering them in trade for those little luxuries that were slowly but surely making their way to the Sea of Thieves. Sheepskin rugs for warmth, boxes of candles, and sturdy chests and boxes to hold their belongings all came together to convert Thieves' Haven from a gloomy cavern into a place of respite for the crew of the *Magpie's Wing*.

Only Ramsey had declined a bedroom of his own, pointing out that the captain's cabin was more luxurious by half than a rocky nook stuffed with gewgaws. Privately, the notion of spending too many nights apart from his ship felt deeply unsettling to him.

It was back to Thieves' Haven that the *Wing* sailed now, its deck strewn with everything the crew had been able to loot from the ship that had attacked them. "Well they may have been pretty pathetic pirates, but they certainly had some nice belongings," Rathbone commented, sorting through a collection of silks and fabrics. "We should consider raiding other vessels more often."

Shan pulled a face. "Waste of resources, if you ask me. You have to spend half of what you earn repairing the ship."

"Not if you take them by surprise," Rathbone persisted. "A sneak attack on a moonless night with all the lanterns turned off and they wouldn't even have a chance to retaliate."

Mercia made a disgusted sound. "We're surrounded by everything nature has to offer and you want to spend your time squabbling with other pirates? What a waste."

"Everything nature has to offer?" Rathbone parroted, unable to resist reigniting their earlier argument. "Like what, coconuts and pig droppings?"

Mercia shot him a withering look. "Even you must have noticed it by now. This place works... differently. Just little things, like how much faster injuries seem to heal out here." They all knew what she meant, of course. Shan had slipped on some rocks and fallen almost twenty feet on their last excursion. He had gained a few bumps and scratches to show for it, but by the time they got back to the ship he was back to his old self. A hearty meal, even something as simple as a banana, seemed enough to lift anyone's spirits.

It was, Mercia reflected privately, as if something about the region made everyone that much more resilient and filled them with a vitality that was missing back home. You got drunk more quickly, but hangovers passed faster too. Everyone seemed a bit stronger, a bit faster, could hold their breath a bit longer. The world itself seemed to be getting livelier, too, with more storms and unexpected bursts of wind. Almost as if the place was reacting to them. Almost as if it was a little bit . . . Mercia grimaced, refusing to let herself think the word *magical*, because that was a slippery slope back to the bad old days of superstition and stupidity.

They sailed back to the hideout in silence, each of them lost in their own thoughts, and Rathbone took his turn in the crow's nest. As they approached, though, he gave a sudden cry of alarm and slid down the ladder at speed. "There's smoke," he said in response to

Ramsey's questioning look. "Can't tell if it's coming from outside or in."

"Could have been a lightning strike?" Mercia said, doubtfully, for there had been no storms on the horizon. Ramsey said nothing, though his expression grew more ponderous by the moment.

They maneuvered the *Magpie's Wing* in through the gap in the rocks rather more cautiously than usual and with their cannons primed, half expecting to find another ship lying in wait within the shadows of the cave. There was no ambush to be found, however, and they extended the gangplank just as they always did, stepping one at a time onto the rocky ledge. Ramsey insisted on leading the way into the caves where they ate and slept, his sword drawn and his teeth bared, though gradually they split up to conduct a more effective search.

It was Rathbone's howl of anguish that sent the others dashing to his room, where the source of the fire had become clear. Greasy smoke was billowing from the smoldering remains of shattered boxes and crates onto which a lantern had toppled. They were the same boxes that had, until tonight, housed Rathbone's most prized treasures and the majority of his money. Together they doused the flames before rushing to their own belongings, leaving Rathbone to pick through what remained.

Each of their quarters had been plundered—every room methodically and ruthlessly ruined, its contents ransacked. Supplies for the ship had been looted, too, and what little had been left behind had been deliberately spoiled—burned, broken or simply tipped into the sea.

Someone, somehow, had found their hideout. Everything of value was gone.

LARINNA

There had always been those who sought to chain the waves.

First there were the navies: vast fleets of ships that sought to protect the sovereignty of the waters in which they sailed—joyless people in bright uniforms who flew their flag proudly as they went forth and conquered, driving their banners deep into other people's soil and warring with anyone who fought back.

For all of that, Larinna merely disliked the navy, as she could understand—if not sympathize with—the kind of people who felt most comfortable when following orders given from on high. The kind of people who would march to a beat, stand at attention, and polish their boots until they were precisely as polished as "boots should be." The kind of people who wouldn't kill out of fury or malice, but *would* kill because they were told to.

Growing up, Larinna had watched a few of the older children leaving their homes in the company of gleaming men with neat moustaches and shining medals on their chests. When they returned to visit their families, they always looked so smart and so prideful, but she could tell just by watching how they sat stiffly in the local pub and the way they flinched at unexpected sounds—even sudden laughter— that something had happened to them while they'd been away. Some flame inside them had been snuffed out, and now they didn't belong anywhere. They were just like chess pieces, she'd thought: soldiers in a box, jumbled up and waiting to be placed back on the battlefield where they could be useful.

On the other hand, Larinna *loathed* the Trading Companies. They were swaggering gangs of bullying merchants who were precisely as greedy and grasping as the most devious pirates but somehow acceptable to the stuffed shirts back on land. They tended to be run by wealthy, cunning, and unscrupulous people who were looking for ways to get even richer, and so had sailed out to the wilder parts of the world looking to ply their wares at ports and colonies far from home.

Larinna didn't have anything against someone trying to make a living by whatever means they chose, of course. Far from it. In her experience, however, the Trading Companies had no intention of sharing the seas where they wished to do business—not with each other, and certainly not with the pirates who sought to disrupt their trade and claim the spoils for themselves.

Years long past had seen lone company ships with their cargoes of fine silks and strange powders become easy targets for experienced pirates who'd grown up in the region and knew the waters far more intimately than their prey did. But the companies proved both rich and tenacious, and more ships came. Larger ships now sailed in convoys, laden with a veritable army of soldiers who dealt with any opposition as ruthlessly and efficiently as if they were sailing by royal command. Sometimes they were, for the larger companies began to hold sway back home and thus guarantee themselves the best protection king and country could provide.

Soon it was the locals who had reason to fear, whether they were pirates or not. Getting caught in the crossfire between two squabbling Trading Companies could *really* ruin your day, not to mention your livelihood if a fragile little ship was all you had. Larinna had heard tell of local traders being declared pirates and hauled away for questioning merely for being in the wrong place at the wrong time. Even if they managed to escape the jailer's cells eventually, they often found that their assets had been seized, and what had once been theirs now belonged, mysteriously, to the Companies.

Worse still, as far as Larinna was concerned, the proliferation of these big businesses made the world feel like a cage. The sea was more than just a series of territories and trade routes marked on a musty old map. You couldn't *own* it, even if you thought you could, and sooner or later it'd swallow up anyone who dared to try.

All this went some way to explaining why, in her first one-on-one conversation with Adelheid, Larinna damn near put her fist through the window.

Adelheid had led her into a sumptuous captain's cabin that was every bit as ostentatious as its owner, filled with pillows, gewgaws, and paintings of places Larinna didn't recognize. Once inside, she reclined in a velvet chair, placing her booted feet upon the desk with deliberate care before speaking.

"I'm sure you took a good look around the outpost today," she said airily. "You probably noticed a few tents and stalls that didn't seem to have anything for sale. Flourishing business ventures, you might say, with some more pathetic than others, of course." Larinna thought guiltily back to her rowboat for a moment, and then the truth of what Adelheid was saying dawned upon her.

"Businesses?" she hissed. "You're talking about more bloody Trading Companies! *That's* who you work for now?" Larinna smashed her fist against the surface of the desk with such ferocity that Adelheid's shoes momentarily left its surface, and the young captain looked genuinely alarmed.

"It's not like the old days," she snapped, defensively. "Not out here! Yes, some of them snuck into the Sea of Thieves looking to make an easy coin or two, greedy merchants who bribed or bartered their way here, sniffing for a profit. Do you know what they found?"

"Surprise me," Larinna said, sourly.

"Us." Adelheid smirked. "You can't tame this place. They sailed into our waters with their royal decrees and their fancy crests, and they might as well have painted targets on their backs. We pirates have got long memories, and we like to hold grudges. For once, *they* were outnumbered."

"I suppose I can see that," Larinna conceded. Although she'd been trapped, lurking below decks on her own journey to the Sea of Thieves, she knew enough about the Devil's Shroud to see how a huge vessel—loaded with soldiers, not to mention the kind of firepower needed to protect a company ship and its valuable cargo—would surely sink in any attempt at a crossing. "So they gave up?"

"Mostly," Adelheid agreed. "And for a long while. Until one day, some clever little clerk realized that if pirates were the problem, maybe they could be the solution. Some crews might be convinced into earning a little extra gold by handing over things we find and don't need, like animals or old artifacts. Stuff that might sell well out in the wider world."

The knot of tension in Larinna's stomach loosened slightly, and she began pacing slowly around the cabin as she considered Adelheid's words. "And you—Faizel, Ned, all of you. You work for these companies?"

"Occasionally, if it's to our advantage." Adelheid watched Larinna keenly as she moved back and forth, the captain seemingly eager not to provoke another outburst. "Most of the larger outposts have company representatives to trade with, and if you keep your end of the bargain you start to build a reputation. For better or worse," she added irritably, flicking an imaginary speck of dirt from her boot.

Larinna was silent for a long while as she reflected on what was being asked of her. Grudgingly, she had to admit that the relationship between pirates and profiteers sounded far more evenhanded than how things had been back home. More than that, she still needed a crew.

"I think I hate everything about this," she informed Adelheid, coolly. "Now tell me what you want me to do."

Sanctuary Outpost felt quite different bathed in moonlight, though Larinna wasn't surprised to see that many of the merchants and traders were still open for business. Even the shipwright was still at her stall by the dock, humming contentedly to herself as she worked on restoring a battered figurehead to some semblance of its former glory. Larinna had noted that almost everything on the Sea of Thieves had been repeatedly patched or repaired in some way; the people around her had a self-sufficiency she found quite admirable.

Except when they're begging for scraps from Trading Companies, she thought irritably, as the squat little building Adelheid had described came into view. It was lavishly decorated by the standards of the outpost, with strings of colored lanterns and a few hung banners cut from the same rich purple cloth that the cloaked figures had been wearing.

As they drew closer, Larinna realized that the Order had apparently colonized the underside of someone else's property, draping heavy fabric around its stilts to create a makeshift establishment of their own. There was a slightly bitter smell in the air that seemed to be getting stronger as she approached, and Larinna wondered if it had anything to do with the pale green smoke that was curling out from gaps between the drapes.

A scrawny young woman, barely more than a teenager, was sitting on a barrel near the entrance with her legs swinging, staring down at the ground in apparent contemplation as she gnawed thoughtfully on a strip of salt jerky. She glanced up sharply as Larinna approached, watching owlishly but saying nothing until her fingers were already reaching for the door handle. "We're closed!" she barked, suddenly, and flushed angrily as Larinna ignored her, pulling open a fold of fabric to bathe them both in a strange, pale light.

"It's hard to be closed when you don't have a door," Larinna remarked, stepping inside even as the girl hopped fretfully off her barrel and began to trail her, complaining peevishly.

The tent's interior was as gaudy as Larinna had expected, with chains of dark beads hanging in the entryway and a few crude stars painted on what passed for a ceiling. Yet more of the purple fabric hung in great folds from beams of the building overhead, muffling her footsteps as she moved deeper inside.

A sickly green fire, apparently the source of both the odd light and the strange smoke, crackled and sputtered fitfully in a large apparatus. It caused strange shadows to dance upon the ceiling, and also illuminated a large desk behind which a figure was hunched, an inkwell in one hand and a large black quill in the other.

Larinna was starting to feel that everything she'd seen so far was designed to foster a particular impression of mysticism and otherworldliness. The entire facade, she suspected, had been decorated to further the illusion that mysterious things were about to happen—a haunted house to get pirates suitably spooked so that they'd come away impressed. *They're still a Trading Company at heart*, she reminded herself. *And they need you more than you need them.*

"Don't linger, Aggie, you're letting fresh air in," murmured the man behind the desk to the young girl reproachfully, without glancing up from his work. His long, greasy hair fell messily down past his shoulders and across another purple outfit. Given the trappings of the place, Larinna was unsurprised to see him sifting through a box stuffed full of mysterious runes and diligently copying them down onto a scroll.

The man looked up from counting on his fingers as Larinna coughed, and shot a meaningful glare at the girl. Clearly she'd been posted as an advance guard tasked with turning away anyone who might interrupt him in the middle of some elaborate task, and clearly she had failed.

"I tol' her, Da'!" Aggie complained. "She worran listen!"

The man peered up at Larinna and she stared down at him, arms folded. "New in town, are we?" he asked, the tone of his voice indicating that he didn't particularly want to hear the answer. "My name is

Winston Phoebus, I represent the Order of Souls, and we are currently closed. Come back tomorrow." Like his daughter's, his speech was high and peevish, a voice born to complain and wheedle.

"I'll be long over the horizon when tomorrow comes," Larinna replied evenly. "But I could hardly pass through without coming to see this place for myself. Just to see if the rumors were true."

As she'd hoped, the man's expression was immediately awash with a mixture of indignation and curiosity. *He's a showman*, she realized. *Every showman wants applause.* "Rumors?" he snapped. "What rumors?" It was time to see if what little Adelheid had told her about the Order was true, or if she was about to make a fool of herself.

"Oh, more like hearsay, really. That your group possesses a great wisdom and a knowledge that sees far beyond the veil that clouds the sight of others. That through your tireless efforts, the secrets of the Sea of Thieves are laid bare for your eyes alone, and a thousand destinies revealed." She paused, wondering if she'd gone overboard, but Phoebus seemed genuinely pleased by the description, his whole demeanor having softened considerably.

"Oh, it's far more than hearsay, I can assure you!" There was an unmistakable smugness in his eyes as he reached into his desk and pulled out a number of neatly bound parchments, fanning them out with practiced ease. "Every one of these contracts may represent nothing more than a handsome sum of money to yourself, but they also provide our distinguished cartographers with invaluable information."

"I see," said Larinna, who didn't, but managed to look suitably impressed regardless. "The pursuit of enlightenment through the mystic arts is a responsibility that must weigh heavily upon your spirit." She glanced down at the box of runes, then around at the tent that passed for the Order's premises, before adding, "And your wallet."

Phoebus appeared to deflate a little. "Yes, well, from time to time we are *encouraged* to share our wisdom with others," he admitted. "For a price, of course. Not that we do it for the money, you understand, we prefer to focus on a more noble purpose, but everyone needs to eat. Unfortunately, our most recent contract fell through, which has left us rather in a bind." He paused. "You're quite sure you can't come back tomorrow?"

"It must be terribly frustrating, having to deal with small-minded scoundrels who can't appreciate that you're working toward a higher purpose," Larinna agreed, maintaining a sympathetic expression. "But as I said, tomorrow I shall be at sea, for I have a purpose of my own, though it's nothing so noble as yours." She patted the hilt of her sword, theatrically. "Before the day is done, my blade shall have claimed its final vengeance against that cur, Simeon, and his treachery shall be repaid!"

Adelheid had assured her that this Simeon, whomever he was, would mean something to the Order but had told her nothing else. Phoebus was staring at her with a curious expression. "Not 'Steel-Eye' Simcon, surely?" he pressed. Larinna, who had no idea, kept her expression inscrutable. To her surprise, invoking the name had lit a fire within the man, and he was frantically rifling through cupboards and cabinets, scattering parchments here and there until he emerged with a small box clasped triumphantly in his hands.

"I thought I recognized the name," he said triumphantly. "Steel-Eye Simeon, yes, we've had quite a few sightings of him recently!" For a moment he seemed to be about to offer the scroll, but hesitation overtook him. "It's not the sort of contract we'd normally give to a first-timer," he mused. "We prefer to offer lower-value work until people have proven they're capable."

Larinna had no idea what Simeon had to do with mapmaking, but she didn't have to work too hard at feigning offense. As far as the Order was concerned, this was her lifelong nemesis they were discussing. "I'll hunt down Simeon with or without your help," she growled. "And once I catch him, there'll be nothing left for your 'capable' pirates." She felt like she was bluffing on a hand of cards she hadn't seen, in a game where she didn't really understand the rules.

Fortunately, her gamble paid off, and Phoebus practically shoved the box into her hands. "It's all the information we have," he said beseechingly, "but we'll pay you handsomely when you return!" He insisted on taking Larinna's name into a leather-bound volume and pressing her thumb down onto an inky pad, badgering her to provide a print alongside her signature. As she signed, she spotted Adelheid's name farther up the page, though it had been viciously crossed out in bold strokes of purple ink. "Can't be forged," he explained.

Rubbing at her inky thumb absentmindedly, Larinna tucked the scroll into her belt and allowed herself to be shown out, still feeling like she was missing a piece of the puzzle. Finally she paused just outside the tent, her curiosity overwhelming her. "Remind me," she called. "What do I do with Simeon once I have him?"

"Do?" Phoebus had already returned to his runes but he looked up now, clearly puzzled by such an elementary and obvious question. "Why, bring us his head, of course."

Larinna returned to the *Unforgiven* with her thoughts in a whirl, more baffled now than before her mysterious errand and determined to get some answers at last. Striding into the captain's cabin and dropping the box onto the desk with a satisfying *thunk*, she placed both hands on either side of it and glared across at Adelheid, who was peeling an apple with a thin-bladed knife that she always kept on her belt. "What the hell did I just agree to?" she demanded. "Are we bounty hunters now?"

"In a manner of speaking," Adelheid said, clearly amused by Larinna's irritation. "They want what's in Simeon's head, and it's up to us to provide it. What did you think of the Order?"

"A bunch of tricksters pretending they're mystics and magicians," Larinna said coldly, forcing herself to adopt a less confrontational stance. "With some very strange business practices. When are you going to tell me what's really going on?"

"All in good time," the smaller woman replied, soothingly. "Think of this as your initiation, if that helps. I'm trusting you, and I want you to trust me in return." She reached into the box and removed a scroll from within, unfurling it and staring down at the faded lines and scrawled notes that covered it. Larinna thought she vaguely recognized one or two of the tiny landmarks from her brief time in the map room, but it was hard to say for sure.

"That far out, eh?" Adelheid mused, lingering over the parchment for a moment before suddenly springing to her feet. "This should be fun!" She left the cabin at a trot, and by the time Larinna followed her out she was already up at the helm, calling across to Ned as he began to unfurl the sails. Grumbling, Larinna took hold of the capstan alongside Faizel, who seemed as chatty as ever as they started weighing the anchor.

"I see that your visit to the Order of Souls was a success!" he called, over the clanking and creaking. "Their ways seem a little strange, yes, but they pay handsomely and I think they are harmless enough."

"Harmless?" Larinna shot back. "They tried to rob you!"

Faizel gave a little shrug. "Negotiations sometimes work a little differently out here. I guarantee that you will see many stranger things. But then, that is why you came to the Sea of Thieves, I think!" Much to her annoyance, Larinna found that she had no answer to that.

Once they'd cast off, the lanterns were lit, and the sails were billowing with a fair wind, the crew gathered around Adelheid in the map room. "It seems the last sighting of old Steel-Eye was at an abandoned fort near Cannon Cove," she told them. "Quite a nasty place, I hear, but we've got surprise and the night on our side."

"Yeah, I know the one you mean." Ned squinted down at the map and then pointed to a nondescript group of rocks, too small and insignificant even to have a name of their own. "S'got cannons all down the south side and onna top, though, so if they sees us . . ."

"I am *not* coming home empty-handed twice in a row," Adelheid declared, hotly. "We'll drop anchor here—" she jabbed her own finger at the map "—and swim the rest of the way if we have to."

"And if this bounty, this Simeon, is not at the fort after all?" Faizel asked, staring at the expanse of water under Adelheid's fingertip with a doleful expression.

"Then we'll get on those cannons ourselves and make some noise until he shows himself." Adelheid insisted. "The Order may be a bunch of irritable blowhards with delusions of grandeur, but they're not in the habit of sending people on wild goose chases. Simeon will be there."

With no more to say, they headed back above deck, and despite Faizel's suggestion that she get some rest in one of the hammocks below deck, Larinna volunteered to take a shift in the crow's nest. She felt restless and out of sorts, and when it came to it, she knew why. She'd come to the Sea of Thieves to be an explorer, not an executioner, and now her first voyage into the unknown was set to end with her sticking a man she'd never met, for reasons she didn't fully understand. Hardly an auspicious beginning.

She tried to distract herself by memorizing the more distinctive islands, memorizing their positions relative to one another and making mental notes of places she'd like to one day visit. Another ship appeared on the horizon at one point but veered away before Larinna could call out. Evidently they, too, had some dark business this night.

Finally, making use of the spyglass Ned had lent her, she spotted the fort on the horizon, and could tell at once that "nasty" was just the way to describe it. The core of the place was a large rock spire, devoid of vegetation, that rose upward in a twisting spiral with a flat, stumpy summit. The fortress spiraled up and around the spire in a complicated lattice of bridges and walkways, occasionally branching out to watchtowers and ledges on which she could spy the cannons Ned had mentioned.

Down below, huge wooden stakes jutted out from the base of the fort at various angles. Some were mere branches, others as thick as tree trunks, and any ship that dared to sail too close risked skewering themselves upon them—another reason to berth far, far away. Perhaps it was just her imagination, but even the clouds around the fort seemed ominous and foreboding. Once or twice, Larinna swore she could make out a death's-head billowing above them, though she was sure it was just her imagination.

Faizel and Ned were extinguishing the lanterns one by one as they drew closer, and Larinna climbed carefully down from the crow's nest to help furl the sails and slow the ship so it could be steered safely to its hiding place.

Then the crew clambered down the ship's ladder one by one and dropped lightly into the chilly water. It was cold enough to sting, and Larinna had to fight the urge to swim for the shallows at speed, for even that might be enough noise to give them away. Paddling quietly, they braved the freezing sea in silence until they reached the shallows, wending their way through the vicious stakes. Faizel in particular seemed uncharacteristically nervous, and even Ned seemed uneasy.

Only Adelheid was as cocksure as ever, drawing her sword once they reached the slimy rocks that served as both the foundation of the fort and the start of the pathway that led to its uppermost levels. Larinna had expected to see guards patrolling, if the fort was indeed occupied as Phoebus had claimed, and the knot in her stomach loosened slightly at the lack of movement. *Perhaps Simeon's not here after all.*

She remained as vigilant as ever, though, and as Faizel reached a sharp right turn and disappeared out of sight ahead of her, Larinna was sure she caught a blur of motion by his foot. She dropped into a crouch, wishing fervently that she could risk unhooding her lantern if only for a moment to get a proper look around. She poked out with the blade of her sword experimentally but found only old bones lying haphazardly in a pile of loose shale. *Probably a rat*, she decided, and turned to follow the crew upward, to the next tier of the moldering barricades.

She'd barely made it three steps farther when she heard it: the scrabbling behind her, getting louder and more persistent. For an instant, she feared a landslide—that the pathway might be crumbling away beneath them—but even as she turned to shout a warning, the truth sucked the breath from her lungs.

A skeletal arm was digging itself out from under a pile of rocks and rubble. As Larinna watched, frozen in horror, a bony cadaver began to emerge out of the ground where it had lain, half-buried, until the crew's passage had disturbed it.

It should have been impossible, the stuff of childhood nightmares, but within a few short seconds, the remains had erupted fully to stand just a few short steps away, and Larinna was staring at a skeleton a few inches taller than she, clad only in a few rags but clutching a sword of its own. She could see the moonlight streaming straight through its ribcage as it turned, slowly, as if taking in its surroundings.

The dead, dark eye sockets met her own mortified gaze. The lower jaw, yellowing and incomplete, fell slackly open to the accompaniment of a rattling hiss. It was not a happy sound; worse still, it was answered by other calls from farther up the trail. Dragging her gaze away from the shambling creature long enough to glance up the path, Larinna could see Faizel and Adelheid backing slowly toward her as two more of the creatures advanced on them. They weren't just under attack, she realized. They were surrounded.

RAMSEY

At first it seemed as though Ramsey's rage would last a lifetime—the fury burning white-hot in his belly and bubbling to the surface with every savage kick, every hack of his blade, every blow he inflicted upon the ruins of their supposed Thieves' Haven. He stomped back and forth until his footsteps had traced deep grooves in the sandy floor, ranting and threatening the unknown villains who had plundered their hideout.

Finally, when there was nothing left on land on which he could take out his anger, he stormed wordlessly past his crew and into his cabin on the *Magpie's Wing*. For the first time any of them could recall, they heard the door lock click, and then an eerie silence seemed to spread out until it permeated the entire cavern.

Rathbone leaned against the ship's railings with his head in his hands, staring moodily upward through two of the arches and watching the seagulls wheeling overhead. After being spooked by Ramsey's rampage echoing up from the caves below, they were now cautiously returning to their perches, their gray-white bullet heads peering reproachfully down through the gaps between the stone. Rathbone heard a scraping behind him and turned to see Shan dragging a large chest out of the hold. With everything that had happened, he'd forgotten the plunder they'd taken aboard.

"Where are you going with that?" he asked, gloomily, making no move to assist. "You don't really think he'll let us stay here now, do you?" This was accompanied by a tilt of the head toward the darkened windows of the cabin. "Not now that our little secret's out."

"Oh, things'll look better in the morning," Shan replied, cheerfully. "It's like my old dad used to say: When someone knocks you down, it's no good lying there feeling sorry for yourself. You've got to get back up and spit in their eye. He was a bit of a brawler, was my dad."

Rathbone permitted himself a thin smile. "Good in a tussle, was he?"

Shan paused. "Never saw him win a fight. Still had all his own teeth, though."

"Well, that's—"

"He used to keep them in a jar by his bed. For luck, he said."

Rathbone stared at Shan for a moment and wished for the thousandth time that he could tell whether or not the man was joking. Finally, he gave an exasperated sigh and moved to help with the cargo. Together, they carried the haul into the deepest recesses of the caves, a large, bowl-shaped room open to the sky but almost completely enclosed by a canopy of trees so that only slivers of sunlight made it through. The floor was covered in a thick carpet of leaves, twigs, and moss, and it was here that Shan dropped suddenly to his knees and began to root around on all fours.

Rathbone watched incredulously, deciding what insult he should hurl in Shan's direction, then spotted the glint of metal from underneath the leaves. Shan grasped a large iron ring in his hands and tugged as hard as he could, and the hidden trapdoor sprang open in a cloud of dust and mold. Beneath it was a square of inky blackness into which a rope ladder descended, and Shan dropped into it with an easy familiarity. Rathbone shook off his surprise and moved to join him, easing himself onto the ladder and clambering cautiously into the hidden chamber below.

The little room they were in was cramped and lit only by a lamp perched on a craggy ledge overhead, but Rathbone could just about make out the shapes of boxes and barrels in the gloom. A few cannonballs, a chest of gold or two. A pittance compared to everything they'd lost but the foundations of a new fortune nevertheless, all squirreled away by their consummate quartermaster. "Does Ramsey know about this?" he breathed, his voice sounding strange to his own ears as the echo bounced back and forth.

Shan shook his head. "Never got around to telling him. Besides, it's not really finished yet. I was hoping to turn this place into a proper workshop and get a few of my special projects ready first." He indicated a few scraps of paper and a handful of books, most of which seemed to be about tripwires, spring-loading mechanisms, intricate locking mechanisms, and—Rathbone squinted to get a clearer look—what appeared to be a crude drawing of a man sticking out of a cannon.

"You are a very strange person," said Rathbone slowly, "but I think I agree with you. Pirates don't just turn tail at the first sign of trouble. Let's get the *Wing* unloaded and take a proper look at what we've got left."

"Let's," Shan agreed. "And then you can show *me* where you've been hiding the good drink."

"Damn."

"Mercia."

Mercia, who'd been sitting cross-legged at the map table, staring dreamlike at her charts and notations without taking in a single word, jumped slightly at the sound of her name. Ramsey was framed in the stairwell, his huge figure outlined there in an unusually weary pose. "Am I disturbing you?" he asked.

Coming from the typically loud and boisterous Ramsey, the question seemed absurd. Mercia had to fight the urge to laugh. "Not at all, Captain. Please join me."

"Just Ramsey will do for now," he said, moving to straddle the opposing bench. "I haven't behaved much like a captain today."

Mercia tilted her head at that. "You got us out of an ambush without so much as a scratch and filled our hold while you were about it. That's the captain I'm used to. Besides, we both know how much we've still got buried out there. What was taken from us here was nothing more than spare change, if you think about it."

If Ramsey was cheered by the attempt at a compliment, he didn't show it. "It's not about how much was taken, not really," he said carefully. "I gave up everything to come here because I believed that the Sea of Thieves would be a better way of living—that we'd have freedom, that we'd make discoveries and find ways to live how we wanted to live without making the same old mistakes."

Ramsey paused, and took a deep swig from a mostly empty bottle Mercia hadn't even realized he was holding before continuing. "When I was very small, my father told me a story about a village—a magic village that only appeared in our world for one day every hundred years. Whenever it appeared, the people in that village wouldn't have aged a day. Just them and their village, contented, as the rest of the world happened by."

"And you hoped the Sea of Thieves could be like that village," Mercia said sympathetically.

Ramsey nodded. "Somewhere that the pirate life could always exist, even if the rest of the world fell under the rule of law and people forgot what it meant to be free. Now we finally have that place, and what are we doing? Wasting time and supplies on petty squabbles. Stealing from one another when there's still so much to see and do. Although . . ." He took another deep draft from his bottle and wiped his lips on the back of his sleeve, looking at Mercia slyly with just a hint of his old vigor returning. "There is one way this place is like that village. You've noticed it too, even if you won't admit as much."

Mercia groaned. "Please, Cap—Ramsey, not this again!" She threw up her hands in exasperation. "Yes, I'll admit I've heard some strange tales in recent months, and yes, we've all encountered things that are hard to explain. That doesn't mean we have to start believing in . . . in . . ."

"Magic?" Ramsey pressed, earning an exasperated sigh. "Well if it isn't magic, I can think of no one better suited to find out what it *is* than you, Mercia, with your books, your brains, and your Natural Philosophy. Remember the first night we arrived, and you told me about the importance about keeping an open mind? Here's what we're going to do," he continued firmly, even as an irritated Mercia opened her mouth to interject.

"At first light we're going to set sail and we're going to visit every last watering hole where a pirate might be found. I'll bluster and bellow and make out like we're looking for the wretches who ransacked our hideout, but what you'll be doing is seeking out more of those 'strange tales,' as you call them. You'll prod, poke, and ask questions just like you always do. If we're lucky, we'll start to see some patterns, some rhyme and reason to it all. Maybe even learn about somewhere we can see some of this 'magic' for ourselves."

"Are you talking about breaking up the crew?" Mercia challenged him. "The others signed up for excitement and adventure on the high seas. I'm not so sure they even believe there's anything mag—anything *unexplained* out there to find."

"We're stronger together," Ramsey said emphatically. "Besides, what pirate could say no to a tour of the local drinking dens? Who knows, they may overhear something useful."

"We'll tell them what we're planning, then?"

Ramsey scratched his beard for a moment, mulling this over. "Only that we're going hunting for the ones who robbed us," he said at last. "We've lost more than our fair share in recent weeks. The fewer people who know what we're searching for, the more likely we are to lay our hands on it."

It's no use, Mercia realized. *I'm not going to be able to talk him out of this. Not now that he's got the idea in his head*. Out loud, she said, "And if you do find some of this so-called magic you're so desperate to see for yourself, what are you going to do then?"

Ramsey smiled, grimly. "What any pirate would do, of course. I'm going to steal it."

Despite her reservations, the crew spent the next few days sailing from outpost to outpost, arriving just as the sun was setting and the taverns were at their liveliest. Having stopped at a few old haunts along the way and put their shovels to work, they'd reclaimed several stashes of gold and jewels—enough for Mercia to ply tight-tongued pirates with as much drink as was necessary to get them talking.

Almost everyone, as it turned out, had some fanciful tale to tell. One grizzled pirate, bare to the waist and coated with a fine spider web of tattoos, claimed to have discovered the phantom of some long-forgotten emperor within the crumbling rules of an overgrown palace. He had, he insisted to the pub at large, been appointed the old ghost's successor—and was, thusly, natural heir to the Sea of Thieves. His attempts to extract tributes from his subjects in the tavern had seen him firstly mocked, then batted aside, then finally pummeled and thrown into a nearby stream to sober up.

Others spoke of musical instruments that had begun to play themselves after a layover on a distant island, or a cup that could never be drained, but when pressed for specifics, it was remarkable how few of them could remember what had happened to these miraculous belongings.

Through it all, Ramsey threatened and swaggered, describing with gruesome detail what he'd do to the cowardly crew who had robbed him of his rightful hoard, while Shan and Rathbone lurked in the background, both bored and bemused at the nightly routine. Rathbone in particular seemed dissatisfied with the lack of treasure flowing their way and began excusing himself earlier and earlier each evening.

It was not until the fifth night that Mercia learned of anything that seemed even remotely plausible. She was squeezed into the corner of a bustling tavern, forced to share a table with an elderly pirate whose rheumy eyes had assessed Mercia with a keen intelligence as she took her seat. The woman was far and away the oldest person Mercia had seen upon the Sea of Thieves; her wizened face was partially obscured by stray wisps of iron-gray hair, and her chin jutted forward like the prow of a galleon.

The old woman said nothing by way of greeting, but sipped periodically from a bottle filled with a clear and sparkling liquid. Mercia couldn't remember seeing any pirate, young or old, come to a tavern craving anything other than grog in their bellies, and at last her inquisitiveness overrode her desire to monitor the crowd's conversations.

"That's an interesting choice of drink," she commented, continuing to scan the room offhandedly. "Is it alcohol?"

The old woman gave a low and melodious chuckle, her voice a stark contrast to her wizened appearance. "My my, love, no. I swore off the stuff years ago. This is my special spring water, found on our last voyage. I've taken quite the fancy to it, and it fizzes just the same!" She poured a small measure into an empty tankard for Mercia to try.

Mercia sipped. "Not bad," she said diplomatically, though in truth the taste put her in mind of the privy. "Not quite the magical elixir I was hoping for, though."

The old woman's eyes creased into a smile. "Magic comes in all shapes and sizes out here," she answered, coyly. "On that same voyage, we sailed right to the rim of the Devil's Shroud and found ourselves making camp on a tiny beach. 'Twas barely even an island, not worth a name, but there was a sinkhole at its center. Well, I'd barely been at the cooking pot five minutes when my daughter's calling to me. 'Mam, mam, look what's down here!'"

Mercia wasn't in the mood for an old woman's gossip, but something about the story seemed curiously plausible compared to the far-flung fantasies she was used to hearing in places like this. She found herself leaning forward, focusing intently on her companion for the first time. "And?" she pressed.

"When I was younger, my Charlie would take me dancing," the old woman said wistfully. "Even, one brave night, to a prince's reception at the palace. I'd never in my life seen such splendor! So when I tell you that the grand hall my girl showed me made that royal ballroom look like a pigpen, you'll know I don't mean it lightly."

She took another draft of her bubbling beverage before continuing. "A chamber fit for a king, hidden under the waves at the heart of some flooded caves and lit by an eerie fire we'd never seen the likes of. We didn't have to light our own path, you understand, the torches were already burning though there wasn't a spot of kindling to be seen."

An eternal flame, Mercia mused. A common legend, all the way back to the Promethean original, but it was an odd thing to boast about discovering nonetheless. You couldn't get rich from fire. She decided she'd listened long enough.

"And I suppose when you woke up the next day, there was no trace of this mysterious chamber?" she challenged, for this was where the stories she endured tended to collapse into rumor and excuses.

"Of course there was," said the old woman, so sharply that Mercia actually flushed. "I made a very detailed map, in fact. I was planning to pay the place another visit, see what else I could learn."

"You did?" Mercia struggled to keep the impatience from her voice, for she'd been led along like this too many times in recent days. "And you know where this map is right now?"

"Certainly I do," the woman replied, icily. "I'm not daft, you know."

"Sorry."

"It'll be in the wreck of our galleon, I should think." The old woman leaned back and began to fumble with a tobacco pouch. "We lost her in a firefight the next day. I've not been out to sea since. I'm too old to be salvaging scuttled ships, not at my time of life." She sighed, and then fixed Mercia with a crafty stare. "But if you've got a ship of your own, you could find the map for yourself."

Tenuous though the tale was, it was the closest thing to success Mercia had enjoyed all week, and she gladly bade the old woman tell her everything she could remember about the location of her abandoned vessel. Bidding her farewell, she forced her way to way to the bar where Ramsey was holding court and firmly gripped his arm even as he made to curse, once again, those who had plundered his hideout.

"It's time to leave," she said firmly. "There's a chance I've found something. A *slim* chance," she added at once, sensing his immediate change in mood and unwilling to raise his hopes too high.

Ramsey, though, was too full of residual merriment not to take the good news at face value. "I'll take it!" he roared, staggering through the throng behind Mercia and spilling several people's drinks as he did so. "It's about time fortune was on our side. What are we searching for, eh?"

"That," Mercia said diplomatically as she towed Ramsey through the tavern door and down toward the dock, "is very much a conversation for tomorrow."

Mercia had returned to the ship feeling curiously hopeful, looking forward to getting back out on the waves after days spent in smoky taverns. Ramsey, once his head had cleared, was more cautious. He gave a terse, curated explanation of their destination to Shan and Rathbone, saying simply that they'd learned of a shipwreck loaded with valuable treasures.

Privately, Mercia wondered if perhaps Ramsey's newfound interest in the supernatural was waning already, but she had no chance to put her question to him once they were out at sea. Their journey was a stormy one, and the driving rain pushed all other concerns out of their minds as they battled through to sunrise, until finally, Mercia found herself clinging to the side of the *Magpie's Wing*, staring down at the broken husk of a galleon upon the sea bed.

The sun was high and the water was clear; even from here she could make out the gaping wounds that had sunk the little ship. She'd have to swim through the largest of these to find the chest, assuming it still lay where they old woman had promised.

No time like the present, she thought, and plunged herself into the sea, kicking off from the hull of the *Magpie's Wing* and diving toward the waiting wreck. She passed Rathbone as she descended, as he was on his third trip to the surface both for air and to drop off the spoils from the captain's cabin. She waved cheerfully but he ignored her, focusing his gaze on the foamy waves overhead.

The ruined ship had come to rest almost upside down, its masts having been sheared away by cannon fire in the battle that sunk her. As she eased herself through a gap in the rotting planks, Mercia found herself in an environment that was both strangely familiar and entirely alien, thanks to everything being inverted.

Barrels and boxes that had been securely tied to the floor now hung ominously overhead, their looming bulk threatening to topple down upon her should any of the ropes and netting choose that moment to give way. Below her, a hatchway to where the stairs had once been led up—down, she reminded herself—to the middle deck.

Once her eyes had adjusted to the gloom, Mercia began to poke around, looking for anything that might resemble the outline of the chest the woman had described. She found it after a moment's exploration—small and unassuming, gilded with iron. Tugging it free was more of an effort than she expected, and Mercia was forced to tilt her head back and press her face up toward the inverted floor, finding a small pocket of trapped air she could use to replenish her breath.

Once she'd filled her lungs, she dropped back down, preparing to haul the little chest back to the surface, and that was when she saw the shark.

It was visible through the battered hull only for an instant, one deadly eye staring right at her as it passed by the hole she'd entered through. She waited, hardly daring to move, hoping that it had failed to sense her as anything more than a shape in the darkness.

No such luck. The beast had swum in a wide circle, and now she could see it approaching once again, eager to enjoy an unexpected meal. It looked old, with scars crisscrossing its body, and huge too—so huge, Mercia wondered if it would even fit through the gap in the hull or if it would simply become wedged, trapping her within the ship and snapping angrily as she drowned just out of its reach.

Deciding not to wait around to find out, Mercia grabbed the chest and used its weight to help her drop down through the hatchway, deeper into the ship. Overhead, she could hear the crashing of splintered wood as the beast collided with the wreck, trapping itself only briefly before it was able to force its way inside the battered hull.

Fighting a rising tide of panic, Mercia looked around for something she could use. Much in this room was familiar, too, though this ship's map table had toppled, managing to become wedged against the stairwell. It looked like oak—too heavy to move, too sturdy to shatter—and it was blocking the hatch that led to the ship's upper deck, cutting off her only means of escape. She began a frantic circuit of the room, hunting for a weapon or a way out, fearing that any moment the great gray face would poke through the hatchway and bear down on her.

Wriggling through the tangle of hammocks and ropes that separated this deck's front from its aft, Mercia's attention was caught by a tiny minnow as it zigzagged out between two crates. Startled by her approach, it and two others flitted past her nose and squeezed through another breach at the rear of the ship—one she hadn't noticed until now. It was barely a foot across, but it was a lifeline nonetheless.

Bracing her back against a beam, Mercia used the only thing she had at hand and began to repeatedly smash the silver chest against the hole. Her lungs ached more with every passing second as she used up her precious breath and at first it seemed as though her assault was having little effect, but finally one plank broke away. Another strike, and a second followed it.

Something touched her body as she pulled back to deliver another blow, and with a shudder of revulsion she realized it was the head of the shark. It was thrashing, blinded and flummoxed by a hammock that had become wrapped across its snout as it had approached her.

If not for the momentary protection of a flimsy piece of netting, Mercia might have lost an arm.

Desperate now, she struck again and again, widening the hole as much as she could before finally hauling herself and her prize through the breach. The arm of her shirt snagged on a nail as she made to flee the wreck, pinning her momentarily to the hull, and she tugged and wrenched with all her might until the sleeve tore up to the shoulder and released her.

Stubbornly refusing to abandon the heavy chest even as dark redness licked around the edges of her vision, Mercia kicked out with the last of her strength. She was grimly aware that she wasn't going to make it to the surface before she lost consciousness, at which point the weight of the box would drag her back down into the icy depths. She closed her eyes, furious at her own pride, and that was when she felt strong hands grip under her arms, helping speed her the last of the way back to where there was air, and sunlight, and life.

Once Mercia had been helped safely back aboard, vomiting what felt like a small lake's worth of seawater over the deck as she sucked in deep, blissful gulps of air, Ramsey turned his attention to the chest she'd salvaged. It was locked, as he'd expected, and so he took the helm and set a course to the nearest outpost.

As soon as they docked, Ramsey went ashore alone with the silver chest tucked under his arm, leaving the others to take their ease. He'd hoped for a blacksmith but had to make do with a lanky shipwright whose hammer and chisel made short work of the lock on the chest. Tipping gold into the craftsman's palm and thanking him for the favor, Ramsey returned to the ship and invited the crew into the captain's cabin.

Once unsealed, the chest turned out to be filled mostly with a selection of milky-white pearls, along with a handful of gems and gold coins. Rathbone scoffed, remarking that it had hardly been worth

Mercia risking life and limb for little more than a necklace, but she ignored him and groped around at the very bottom of the chest until she felt the rough texture of a parchment lurking beneath the jewels. Just as the old woman had promised, it contained detailed instructions for finding both the island and its hidden chamber beneath, and she pored over it eagerly.

The *Magpie's Wing* set sail at once on Ramsey's orders, and Shan was at the wheel when Rathbone, who should have been taking his turn in the crow's nest until they sighted land, approached him. "I suppose our illustrious captain and his new favorite are having yet another heart-to-heart below deck," he sneered, spitting over the side as if he'd a sour taste in his mouth.

"I suppose," Shan said evenly. He made no effort to continue the conversation, and Rathbone made as if to walk away in frustration, only to spin on his heel and continue.

"When I signed up it was to be a full part of this crew, and that includes getting a say on where we sail and why. What are we even looking for? If you ask me, Ramsey's been cracked ever since we left Thieves' Haven."

"I didn't ask," Shan said, then turned to meet Rathbone's gaze for the first time. "But I will say that we are low on supplies, and traveling here, there, and everywhere isn't helping matters. When we next make camp, that might be a good time to talk—"

"I've had enough talking to last a lifetime!" Rathbone exploded. "All Ramsey does is talk! There's gold out there, gold that's slipping through our fingers and into other people's purses every day we're out here sailing in circles."

"We'll *talk*," Shan said firmly, tugging at the wheel perhaps slightly harder than necessary so that the ship lurched.

"And if we don't like what we hear?" Rathbone persisted. But Shan had turned his gaze back to the sea, for their destination had come into view. Shan gave a piercing whistle that echoed through the whole ship, and a moment later Ramsey and Mercia had joined them above deck.

The old woman's description had been accurate indeed, for the island was little more than a series of sandy rings poking out of the water, concentric circles around a single fissure that cut deep into the sea bed. They weighed anchor and disembarked, the seawater barely reaching their knees as they approached the island's center, and it was here Ramsey explained that he and Mercia would be the ones to explore down below. Upon learning that he and Shan would remain behind once more, Rathbone looked thunderous.

Privately, Mercia wasn't looking forward to going diving again so soon, though she drew some comfort knowing that Ramsey would be alongside her. It looked strange to see him shorn of his usual hat, boots, and greatcoat, but he wasted no time in hauling himself into the pit and vanishing into the sparkling waters. Grimacing, Mercia did the same, and together, they dove down into the rocky labyrinth, carefully following the directions they'd memorized.

They made a left turn, and then a right, then a sharp left, passing through a narrow gap that Ramsey could barely squeeze his broad shoulders through. As they swam ever onward, Ramsey took the lead with a series of powerful breaststrokes. His excitement was mounting for the tunnel was growing lighter, not darker, and the way ahead was outlined by an unearthly blue light.

Where Ramsey felt anticipation, however, Mercia felt a growing sense of unease, for she could hear a strange keening sound that seemed to echo from the passages they hadn't explored. Every time she thought she knew which of the many tunnels must be the source of the eerie noise, it seemed to shift and twist away somehow. Still they swam, and now the floor of the tunnel was curving upward. Their heads broke water, and then they were paddling and eventually wading as they took the final soggy steps up the sloping passage. At last, they had reached their destination.

The hall in which they had arrived was both imposing and beautiful, making its location deep underneath the shoreline of some unknown island all the more intriguing. The floor beneath their bare feet was a lattice of mosaics—blues and greens and all the colors of the ocean represented by tiny stone trails that whirled and danced in complicated patterns. Fluted pillars carried the eye up to a high, vaulted ceiling, where carved frescos were fighting a losing battle against limestone stalactites that had formed in the years since the chamber was completed.

The center of the room was dominated by a large basin that appeared to connect back to the maze of flooded passages. The intricate patterns on the floor seemed to cluster and unite around the pool's perimeter, as if to signify its importance, but Ramsey paid it little heed. His attention had been captured by the ghostly blue flames that burned in braziers spread throughout the mammoth chamber.

Just as the elderly pirate had described, these flames persisted with no apparent source of fuel, seemingly able to endure the ravages of time regardless. They were magical, Ramsey knew, and he reached out as if making to cup one in his palm, only to discover that the burning lights were no mere illusion. He yanked his hand back and sucked at his fingers, swearing and grumbling.

Mercia ignored him, for she was once again searching for the source of that keening, echoing wail. Ramsey's cursing seemed to have triggered it once more, louder than before, and she began to patrol the hall's perimeter, twisting her head this way and that as she attempted to track down the source of the sound. She wasn't entirely certain Ramsey could hear it at all.

It was then that she spotted the earrings. Two simple pearl studs, far plainer than the golden hoops she usually preferred, placed without much care or heed in a small recess. Had she not been searching so determinedly for the wailing sound, she might never have noticed them. It seemed an odd thing to leave behind, and she plucked them curiously between damp fingertips and held them up, examining them by the light of the impossible flames.

She never knew what compelled her to delicately unhook her own earrings and slide the pearls into place. She could barely remember choosing to. But the moment she did, Mercia dropped to her knees, gasping as the keening wail began to shift and separate into a joyful chorus.

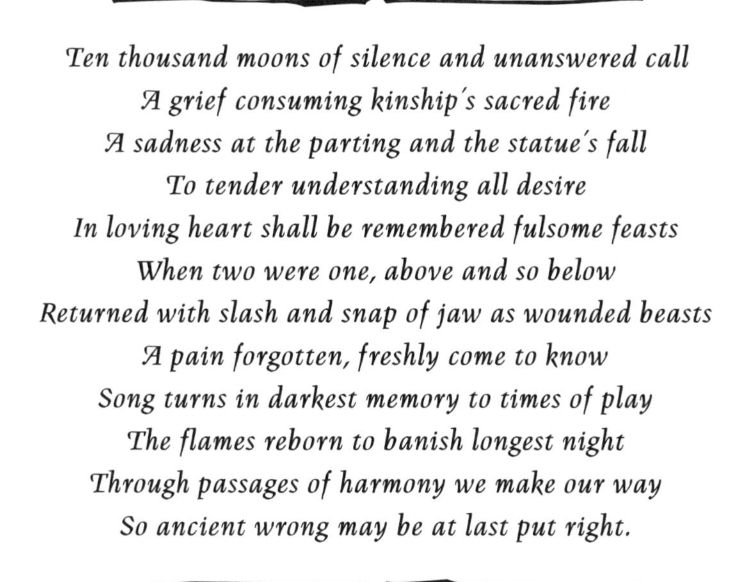

Ten thousand moons of silence and unanswered call
A grief consuming kinship's sacred fire
A sadness at the parting and the statue's fall
To tender understanding all desire
In loving heart shall be remembered fulsome feasts
When two were one, above and so below
Returned with slash and snap of jaw as wounded beasts
A pain forgotten, freshly come to know
Song turns in darkest memory to times of play
The flames reborn to banish longest night
Through passages of harmony we make our way
So ancient wrong may be at last put right.

"They're singing!" Mercia gasped in delight, bringing her hands to her head. Ramsey strode over in concern, crouching before her transfixed form. His eyes narrowed as he noticed the pearl earrings, which seemed to be sparkling with an inner light all their own. When he made to pull them free, however, she swatted his hands away irritably. "Not now," she snapped. "They're almost here. They need us!"

"Who does? Who is singing to you?" Ramsey persisted, resisting the urge to tug Mercia to her feet and drag her outside, away from whatever seemed to be intoxicating her.

A moment later, the central pool erupted in a shower of spray, and Ramsey got his answer.

It had taken Shan five hours, and an immense amount of self-control, to calm Rathbone down as he ranted and raved, stalking around the

ship and cursing Ramsey's name. Finally, Shan resorted to opening the final cask of grog and plying him into a stupor. Now Rathbone lay by their campfire on a golden sandbar in the shadow of the *Magpie's Wing*, snoring loudly as he slept in a fetal position.

Shan could feel himself starting to drift away out of boredom, his head growing heavier by the moment, and was therefore extremely gratified when a stream of bubbles announced Ramsey's return. He and Mercia staggered out of the pool, leaving a trail of muddy footprints across the sand, but neither made any attempt to come and dry out by the fire. Instead, they made straight for the *Magpie's Wing*.

"No treasure, then?" Shan inquired. "Seems a shame." He stifled a yawn and nudged Rathbone in the ribs, slightly harder than was necessary. There was a choking snort as the slumbering pirate snapped back to consciousness and glanced blearily around.

"Forget treasure," said Ramsey, firmly. "This isn't about treasure. This is about helping friends." And with that, leaving Shan and Rathbone to exchange bewildered glances, Ramsey hauled himself up the ship's ladder and out of sight.

8 LARINNA

The undead creature dragged itself closer and closer to Larinna as she stared at it, mesmerized by a kind of grotesque fascination. Only when it raised its ancient blade to perform a high sweep did her survival instincts kick in. She brought her own sword up reflexively to block the blow with a juddering clang that reverberated through her entire body, shaking away the last of the shock.

The creature raised its weapon again, and Larinna ducked underneath the attack, taking the opportunity to thrust forward with a sharp stabbing motion where the creature's heart should have been. Had it been alive, she'd have dealt a mortal blow—instead, the skeleton's ribs shattered under the impact but it kept advancing, seemingly impervious to any form of pain or fatigue caused by its advanced state of decay.

Got to focus, she thought desperately. *This is just like fighting any other opponent. You just have to find their weaknesses and exploit them.* She began to move around it in a slow circle, watching its movements carefully. The thing had no eyes, after all; perhaps it was tracking her based on noise or the vibrations she was making. To her dismay, the grinning skull turned smoothly to track her this way and that, and cadaverous feet shuffled around to face her, leaving dark scuffs in the dirt.

Worth a try, she thought, aggressively plunging forward to see if she could make the thing back off. It didn't, but each one of her blows made the creature slide backward, and that was enough for Larinna to adopt a new strategy. *It's just bones*, she thought. *It's strong, but not that heavy*. She feinted once, then twice, noticing that the skeleton's movements were clumsy and reactive; it wasn't adapting, but merely blocking any attack as best it could.

She began to land her blows higher and higher until their swords were sparking right in front of those empty eye sockets, and then Larinna leapt, landing a double-footed flying kick on the reaver's chest that left her sprawling on the rough ground. The full force of her impact was enough to knock the creature backward, its bony arms pinwheeling as it toppled over the edge of the path that wound around the fort and clattered onto the rocks below. Larinna resisted the urge to peer over the cliff, turning instead to sprint up the path and help the others. She needn't have worried, for they seemed far less troubled by the existence of the walking undead than she.

Now that she was able to watch more closely, the lurching creatures seemed to have personalities of their own. One was fumbling with a banana, apparently intent on having a midbattle snack until a stray shot splattered the fruit all over its rotten tunic. Two of its friends were embroiled in a tug-of-war over the same sword, snapping and snarling at one another as they heaved the weapon back and forth. *Were they once pirates themselves?* Larinna quashed the thought for now.

As she watched, Adelheid unloaded the contents of her blunderbuss into another of the skeletons at what amounted to point blank range, exploding it in a shower of bone fragments and smoke. What little was left crumbled to the ground, back to being lifeless bone once more.

Faizel, as Larinna could have predicted, seemed to be holding a one-sided conversation with his skeletal adversary, teasing and taunting it as he danced nimbly out of its reach. It was a distraction, but an effective one, for it gave Little Ned enough time to physically grab the creature from behind. His fingers curled around the exposed ribcage—Larinna suppressed a shudder at the thought of what that must feel like—and before the skeleton could work out what was happening, Ned had raised it bodily over his head and thrown it with all his might far out toward the ocean. "Get in the sea," he rumbled, dusting his hands.

That seemed to be the last of them, at least for now. Looking around with trepidation in case any more of the undead decided to burst out of the scenery and cause trouble, Larinna staggered over to the others and placed one hand against the rocky wall to steady herself. "What in the seven hells were *those*?" she hissed accusingly, glowering at her crewmates as if she held them responsible.

"Skeletons," Ned replied. "It's what's inside your arms and legs and things," he added helpfully.

"I know what skeletons are, Ned!" she snapped. "I also know that dead bodies don't just randomly decide to get up and go for a stroll."

"Not all of them, that's true." Adelheid was smirking, clearly amused at seeing the normally unflappable Larinna caught off-balance. "But you soon learn that on the Sea of Thieves, every rule can have its exceptions."

"And you didn't think it was wise to tell me there was a possibility we might bump into the dearly departed during our voyage *before* we set sail?" Larinna was feeling more focused now, channeling her uncertainty into the righteous fury of someone who has been left out and is now ensuring there's hell to pay.

Adelheid shrugged. "I assumed you knew," she replied blithely, before turning and continuing up the winding path that led to the summit of the ancient fort.

"I assumed you did not," Faizel interjected, falling into step alongside Larinna and grinning widely. "But I thought it would be funnier if you found out like this."

"Ow." Larinna replied, curtly. "My sides."

Faizel, at least, seemed happy to bring Larinna up to speed now that the crew had had their fun at her expense. "It is true that creatures like those are quite common in the wilder reaches of the world," he explained as they climbed. "It is fair to say that not every pile of bones is going to leap up and attack you, but it is better to be cautious rather than paranoid, yes? And surely you have heard tales of the undead?"

"Well, yes," Larinna admitted. "But only tales. Ghost stories you tell kids to make them shut up and go to sleep. Legends."

Faizel chuckled at that. "Hah! Out here, you will soon learn that many of the old legends are true. I did say you had strange things to look forward to."

"Well next time, warn me if those strange things are going to try and hack my limbs off," Larinna said sourly. "Really, though, skeletons? How does that work? Bodies need—" she floundered, teetering on the brink of her biological expertise, "blood, and a brain, and things. How can they even move around?"

Faizel shrugged. "I have never asked them." He caught her expression, and continued. "Some say that lost souls of long-dead pirates somehow find their way back to this world. Others suspect necromancy. Perhaps one day people will come with their contraptions and their microscopes and find out the truth and then the world will be just a little bit more ordinary, yes?" He chuckled, his eyes sparkling with mischief. "For now there is much we do not understand, and I like that very much indeed."

They continued to climb, the massive wooden stakes dropping away and the rough wooden bridges becoming narrower and more treacherous as they approached the summit of the rock spire around which the fort had been constructed. They were almost to the peak when a second wave of skeletons attacked, lurching forward out of shadowy alcoves with a loud hiss that was returned from on high.

There were many more of them this time, but now Larinna knew what to expect and was keen to make up for her earlier hesitation. She fought savagely, hacking and slashing at any bony body she could reach, seeing no need to exercise restraint as she might have done against a human opponent.

At one point, she gazed up and her eyes widened, for one of the skeletons had somehow managed to locate an old rifle, and its bony fingers were fumbling with the trigger. Larinna was able to hurtle across the distance between them and snatch the weapon away just in time, delivering four savage strikes with her blade that saw her foe collapsing into bone and dust. That seemed to be the fate of any undead whose body had been sufficiently damaged, she was realizing, as if whatever was reanimating the corpses could no longer hold them together.

She spotted Adelheid leaping nimbly from rock to rock, fighting a gaunt figure who, while certainly a skeleton like the others, seemed far more . . . *intelligent*, she supposed was the right word. He was larger, too, or at least seemed more imposing, for he donned a great brown cape and an old-fashioned tricorn hat.

It turned to deliver a blow that fell just short of cutting Adelheid down halfway through her jump, giving Larinna a glimpse of dull gray metal on its face. It was an eye patch, one that—back when the creature was still a living, breathing pirate—had been screwed directly into the skull. It also appeared to be the last remaining reaver, and Larinna moved to help combat it.

It was clear immediately that this final foe did not intend to go down without a fight. Reaching down and scraping bony fingers along the ground with a noise that set Larinna's teeth on edge, the creature snagged a second blade. It moved with surprising agility even with a weapon in each hand, slashing and stabbing as Adelheid's crew moved to surround it. Larinna wondered why Ned hadn't simply dispatched it with his blunderbuss, and began to fumble with the rifle she'd stolen, hoping to land a shot that would end the battle then and there.

"No!" Adelheid called urgently as she took aim, and Larinna paused, confused. The skeleton spun to face Larinna, now clearly convinced she was the greatest threat, and began to lurch in her direction.

Larinna stood her ground, rifle unwavering, though her finger itched to pull the trigger before those twin swords could get anywhere near her.

Adelheid seized her chance and leapt, bearing the skeleton to the floor from behind. Her sword cleaved away its fleshless right arm while her empty hand wrenched savagely at its left, pulling the limb free and tossing it aside to writhe obscenely on the floor. With all her might, Adelheid grabbed at the skull and tugged, keeping her fingers clear of the snapping jaws until the hairless head finally came loose with a sickening crack.

It was like watching a puppet with its strings cut; the severed limbs went limp immediately, tumbling apart. Only the skull clutched between Adelheid's dirt-caked hands remained intact, and even that was now as silent and lifeless as old bones should be.

"Here, Larinna," said Adelheid pleasantly, her voice echoing unnaturally loudly in the sudden silence as she held forth the skull. "Allow me the pleasure of introducing you to Steel-Eye Simeon."

Once they were back in the privacy of the captain's cabin, Adelheid hung her hat and coat on a pair of golden pegs above her bed and then turned her attention to the skull, placing it delicately inside the box the Order of Souls had provided and snapping it shut with a deliberate click. "I don't want it grinning at me all night," she admitted.

Larinna stood slumped against the wall, exhausted. She longed for a good night's sleep in anything approaching a proper bed, or even a pile of rags, but she guessed that retrieving the bounty was only half of the story. "So what happens now?"

"Now," said Adelheid, busying herself in the large, curved mirror that adorned one wall of her quarters, "you'll go back to the Order of Souls with our underfed friend and gain some understanding of the kind of business they're *really* in. They'll try to offer you gold as payment for the bounty and send you on your way."

She turned now, staring up at Larinna with an expression of utmost severity. "You are not to accept gold. Rather, there will be a parchment, and you are to insist upon *that* as your payment. They won't like that, but you have to insist. Do not walk away without the scroll. Not even a copy will suffice. Clear?"

Larinna had had enough. Enough of being patronized, enough of being tested. She'd gone through hell the last few days, and this upstart captain treating her like a child was about all she could take.

"On one condition," she said icily, drawing herself up to her full height. "When I return, I will be a member of your crew. Not a swabbie, not a novice, and *definitely* not the butt of your jokes or your snide remarks. You've seen me fight. You've seen me sail. I think we can work well together, but if you can't treat me like an equal than you might as well tell me and I'll jump overboard here and now. Only you'd better throw that box away if that's the case, because there's no way you're handing it back to the Order of Souls without my help."

To her surprise, Adelheid burst into a peal of laughter. "You're so cocky it's actually funny," she chuckled, slapping the table. "You have no idea how hard I want to hit you right now!"

"Not as badly as I want to choke you to pieces!" Larinna shot back, surprised to find amusement edging into her own voice. Adelheid's laugh was infectious, and Larinna felt her lips curling in a smile.

"I mean, I could just put your head through the window for speaking to me that way!" Adelheid guffawed. "It's so infuriating!"

"Try it, short-arse! I'll find you a box to stand on!" Both women howled with laughter at this, Larinna wiping tears of mirth away as the tension of the day evaporated and she found herself relaxing in Adelheid's presence for the first time. They traded laughter and insults in equal measure until the first rays of dawn, and when Faizel came to say that they'd sighted land, he found the two women surrounded by several empty bottles, collapsed side-by-side against the captain's desk, both still smiling.

The *Unforgiven* arrived at Sanctuary Outpost and Larinna made her way, rather unsteadily, toward the squat little building beneath which the Order of Souls did its business. There was no Aggie outside to greet her this time in the bright afternoon sun, so she invited herself inside, blanching slightly as she crossed the threshold. The smell was even worse than she remembered, and her stomach hadn't yet forgiven her for last night's reconciliation with Adelheid.

Rather than the hunched figure of Phoebus that she'd been expecting, however, occupying the room was a gaunt and willowy woman whose attire reminded Larinna of a fairy-tale genie, albeit a rather severe one. She seemed intent on studying the flame and did not turn around as Larinna approached.

"I'm looking for Winston Phoebus," Larinna declared without preamble. "I have something for him."

This appeared to rouse the woman from her trancelike state, and as she turned around, Larinna saw that her eyes were the color of midnight, surrounded by inky black streaks that cascaded down her high cheekbones and stained her face. Yesterday she would have found the sight quite startling, but her first full day in the Sea of Thieves had already taught her to expect the unexpected, and she remained steadfast and motionless as the slender figure seemed to glide across the room toward her.

"My brother is indisposed, I am afraid to say." It was a low and lilting voice with an indefinable accent, slightly thickened by the long-stemmed pipe that hung from the woman's mouth. Larinna had never taken to smoking and was no expert, but she was absolutely certain that what was smoldering in the pipe's bowl was something altogether stranger than tobacco. "I am Madame Occulia. Like him, I represent the Order of Souls. Unlike him, I possess some measure of magical talent." She took a deep draft of her pipe and exhaled a pale smoke ring toward the ceiling.

I'm struggling to see the family resemblance, Larinna thought to herself, but out loud she said, "I brought your brother a bounty, as we had discussed." She tapped the box for emphasis. Try as she might, she found Occulia's black-eyed stare quite disconcerting because it made it impossible to tell precisely where she was looking at any given moment.

The mystic's long fingers reached for the box without asking, but Larinna stepped smartly backward, tugging the skull out of the woman's reach. For an instant, she thought she saw a flash of annoyance on Occulia's face before she regained her composure and smiled serenely. "Is this your first time working with us, my dear? It is perfectly normal for one like my brother, who does not possess my gifts, to deal with the facts and figures while I remain attuned to a higher plane. You may of course deliver your prize to me instead. And then," she added with the air of one bestowing a tremendous gift, "perhaps you'd like to watch me at work?"

Larinna very much did, if only to finally gain a complete understanding of the madness she'd been embroiled in since first encountering Faizel and the others, and so surrendered the box without further complaint. She watched intently as Occulia removed Simeon's skull from its resting place with something approaching reverence, following when beckoned toward the rear of the tent.

There was a smaller table here, tucked behind a heavy velvet drape that provided some relief from the foul-smelling flames. It was stacked high with piles of parchment, all of which appeared to be curiously blank, and lit only by a circle of the dribbling green candles.

Simeon's skull already sat in the center of the circle, and Larinna squeezed herself into a small gap between the table and the wall so that she could watch Occulia intently. She wanted the best view of whatever sleight of hand this high-and-mighty woman intended to perform for her benefit.

Taking three great puffs on her pipe, Occulia tipped some of its contents into the skull's eye sockets so that they began to glow with an ethereal light of their own. Next, she bent toward the skull, and for a moment Larinna recoiled, believing that the strange woman intended to kiss it. Instead, Occulia merely whispered some sort of incantation into the hole where there was once a human ear before exhaling, blowing a ring of pipe smoke into the skull's open jaw.

The reaction was extraordinary, for the smoke began to curl around and writhe like a living thing, twisting through the skull in snakelike contortions before Occulia inhaled sharply, drawing the smoke into her mouth. Perhaps it was merely a trick of the light, but it looked for all the world like words and images were flowing across the woman's skin in the same dark ink that ringed her eyes.

Try as she might, Larinna could detect no mere conjuring trick at play. The mystic had grasped a tightly rolled parchment in her free hand, and the symbols appeared to be flowing along her outstretched arm and toward it. The skull's eyes were glowing white-hot now, the light becoming painful to look at directly, and yet more phrases spilled across the woman's skin toward the scroll. Suddenly, the skull flared so brightly that Larinna shielded her gaze instinctively.

Just as quickly, the glow was gone, Occulia's eyes were normal, and she was examining the parchment critically. Beside her, Simeon's skull was now little more than a pile of crumbling dust.

"Yes, yes," Occulia mused, still in that same lilting tone as her gaze roved up and down the scroll. "These are good memories. Very strong, very clear." Suddenly all business, she moved to the front of the tent once more and began to bind and seal the parchment with twine.

"Good ... memories?" Larinna repeated, skeptically, following in her wake. She was slightly discomforted to see that two of the Order's hooded lackeys had taken up position in the shadows, perhaps alerted by the sights and sounds of Occulia's ritual, or magic, or whatever it had been. "Memories of what?"

"Who can say?" Occulia examined the parchment critically, making sure it was just so. "Buried treasure, perhaps, or dark regrets."

"Well I suppose I'll find out—" Larinna began, reaching out for the coiled scroll, but now it was she who found her fingers closing around empty air, for it had been tugged out of her grasp.

Occulia's smile was still in place, but it had hardened slightly. "Did my brother not explain? Your recompense for the skull will be gold coins. We keep the parchment, for there are those who will pay us handsomely for such valuable information."

"You can consider me one of them," Larinna insisted. "Sell the scroll to me." She decided that now was not the moment to mention her empty purse.

"I'm afraid these particular memories have long been sought-after," Occulia said firmly, "and the Order has already agreed a sale of this document to another buyer. I'm sure you can understand that we would not wish to jeopardize future relationships with our clients by breaking our half of the bargain. Instead, please do enjoy your fee and the knowledge that, thanks to your courage, the Sea of Thieves is now a slightly safer place."

One of the robed figures thrust a bag of coins out toward her, and Larinna hesitated. She'd sworn to Adelheid that she'd come back with the parchment one way or another, and she was certain that Occulia herself would be a pushover if came to a fight. But in this cramped space, could she really take on three of the Order at once?

Looks like I'm about to find out, she thought, her expression hardening. "Well if these memories really are as valuable as you say, then I hardly think a purse of gold is fair payment. I say you're trying to cheat me. Since you can't very well give me back the skull, you can just surrender the parchment and I won't need to tell every passing pirate what a bunch of lying, two-bit swindlers you are." Larinna placed her hand on the hilt of her sword. "And if not, well, I'll just have to fight you. All of you, if I have to. If you're thinking that I won't make it out alive, you may be right, but I promise you that you won't either." She grinned defiantly. "What will they do with *your* skull, do you think?"

There was no longer any pretense of friendship on Occulia's face as she glowered over the desk. "You dare to meddle in our affairs, insult our ancient art, and threaten us! Then to declare that *we* are the disreputable ones? You, who are nothing but an odious pirate, come swaggering in here alone—"

"I agree, she could use a good bath," one of the robed figures interrupted. "But to say she is alone is, I think, quite incorrect, yes?"

Larinna stared in astonishment as Faizel pushed back the hood of the cloak he'd donned and stepped forward, abandoning his disguise and drawing a thin blade. Adelheid, who'd been concealed in the other robe, did the same. Occulia flinched as the scroll was tugged roughly from her hands, well aware she was surrounded.

"Now we will part ways," Faizel continued. "But to show you our good intentions, we will not be charging for our services today. Enjoy your evening, please!"

The three pirates backed toward the flap that served as the tent's exit with Faizel's blade still flashing menacingly in the firelight. Only when they were outside did they discard the Order's robes and sprint toward the ship.

"Ned's ready to cast off," Faizel explained breathlessly as they pounded through the busy streets, back toward the dock where the *Unforgiven* was waiting. "I think that perhaps we have worn out our welcome here at Sanctuary, at least for a while."

"Sure you want me aboard?" Larinna vaulted over a wandering cockerel who was too slow or too stupid to get out of her way. "I mean, *I* didn't exactly get the parchment."

"You were willing to die trying," Adelheid pointed out, shunting a startled stallholder out of her path. "That's the mixture of courage and crazy I'm looking for in a new crewmember. We can shake on it when nobody's trying to kill us."

Larinna laughed at that, then reached out to catch Faizel's arm, steadying him even as his feet struck a patch of loose gravel and he started to stumble. Shouting and bantering, they tore along the newly patched-up boardwalk, piled up the gangplank, and sailed back out to sea before anyone could stop them.

On the cliffs high above, an unseen figure watched them go.

RAMSEY

Mercia headed to the crow's nest immediately upon her return to the *Magpie's Wing*, for her head was spinning both with the night's revelations and with the dying refrain of the music she'd heard. She desperately wanted to clear her brain, to try and make sense of everything that had happened. She'd been staring blankly out at the horizon for less than an hour before the creaking of the ladder roused her from her thoughts.

She expected to see Rathbone, whose face seemed to be set in a permanent scowl these days, hauling himself up into the little wooden basket atop the mast. In fact, it was Shan who plopped down beside her, seemingly content to say nothing and just stare placidly at the horizon. Mercia would have indulged him, but the crow's nest was scarcely big enough for two. "Is my shift over already?" she asked, trying to keep the irritation out of her voice and only partly succeeding.

"I've always thought of myself as a bit of a tinkerer," Shan said conversationally, as if Mercia hadn't spoken. "Happy to let the ebbs and flows carry me through life. Never really needed a long-term plan as long as I've had something to keep me busy, content to go along with my crew. But it's just the four of us out here now, see. We need to be sure we're all dancing to the same tune or we won't survive, and right now it feels like you and the captain are dancing a waltz while the rest of us are standing around the maypole."

"That was some metaphor," Mercia said dryly.

"Well, let me put it another way. . . . What the hell is going on, Mercia? What did you find down in a soggy hole that's got us racing out to the middle of nowhere at full speed? The captain must know that Rathbone's angrier than a wasp in a wine bottle."

Mercia let out a deep sigh. "If I told you, you wouldn't believe me—and I *know* that sounds like an excuse, Shan, but I'm not sure *I* believe me. Ramsey thinks you need to see for yourselves, like we did. If we just told you, there's every chance you'd think us both cracked, and we're going to need all of us dancing, as you put it, together tonight."

Shan looked more pensive than she'd ever seen him. "Well, we've got a full hold and a fair wind," he said, finally. "It's trust we're running low on. Hopefully there's some to be found wherever it is we're heading."

"There is, I promise. Or do I have to swear an oath?"

"No oaths," said Shan. "But the next round is definitely yours." Mercia gave a nod and a small smile, and Shan swung nimbly back onto the ladder, dropping the last few feet to the deck. Rathbone, who was at the helm and grudgingly following Ramsey's directions, gave him an inquiring glance, but Shan merely shrugged and turned his attention to the sails. He could feel a cold glare boring into the back of his skull for the rest of their journey.

They sailed until their maps and charts could guide them no farther, and Ramsey came above deck to stand moodily at the front of the ship, one hand on his compass and the other resting on the railing as if urging the *Magpie's Wing* to move faster. When Mercia gave a curt whistle from on high, he began to move rapidly about the ship, extinguishing the lanterns one by one and half furling the sails to slow their approach.

It was easy to see why he wished to approach as covertly as they could, for three distinctive shapes were visible even at this distance—a trio of galleons at rest, moored in a line that bent to follow the curve of a sandy beach. Ramsey bade them weigh anchor, lurking out of sight behind a smaller atoll that disguised their profile. He led them down to the map room and unfurled a crude map he'd sketched so recently that the ink had barely had time to dry.

"I'll keep this short, for we've not much night left. This island's a hideout for a group who've laid claim to these waters," he explained. "As you've seen, we're outnumbered, but no one knows we're here yet. If we're shrewd, we can get the drop on them. Their camp is deep within a cave system at the heart of the jungle, and if you follow the river from *here* to here you'll spy it soon enough." He jabbed his thumb twice at the map.

"Now, there could be a dozen pirates here, perhaps more, but they'll likely not all be together. Some'll be asleep, some'll be on watch, and others . . . well, Shan and Rathbone, that's where you come in. Use the river, head downstream into the cave, and keep as quiet as mice. You'll get to see how many are still at the camp. If I'm right, you'll also come to understand why we've come all this way, but you're not to pick a fight you can't win, you hear me? Count heads and come home."

"You make us sound like a group of reckless thugs," Shan said dryly, tracing the outline of the river with his finger as if he was trying to commit every bend to memory. "And where will you be?"

Ramsey grinned in the moonlight. "Baiting traps."

To Rathbone's continued annoyance, Shan insisted on total silence as they crouched and crawled their way through a dense and tangled mass of vines and undergrowth. Once or twice they spotted drawings of the sort that always drew Mercia's attention on their travels: strange, runic depictions of what seemed to be swimmers praying to the sun—or was it a pig? Something else entirely? They had more pressing concerns, Rathbone decided, and put it from his mind.

They found the river easily enough, the babbling spring at its source guiding them by sound rather than sight. They traced its bank carefully as it wound its way through the disorienting labyrinth of trees and plants, though the thick jungle made it increasingly difficult to follow. Before long, they were forced to wade into the water, trying not to slip on sharp stones or lose their boots to the cloying mud.

Eventually, the river itself delved underground, plunging into a gap between two rocks and down into darkness. It was deeper here, and the two men were forced to swim a short way, carefully holding their lanterns high over their heads so that they could still see. Luckily, the subterranean tunnel through which they moved opened out shortly after, and they were able to clamber out onto a broad ledge that ran parallel to the river. The lamplight revealed yet more painted swimmers adorning the walls, suggesting that this passageway had once been used regularly, though to what end was anyone's guess.

They spent another hour crawling their way across slimy rocks, seeking out every safe handhold and foothold with painstaking care, for the river was flowing faster and more dangerously as they descended. They could hear the distant sound of a fiddle echoing in the distance and reluctantly snuffed out their lights. Both men inched forward in the inky blackness, guided now only by the music and the susurration of the ever-rushing water.

Finally, the path began to brighten with the flickering orange of a distant campfire, and they could hear the raucous laughter of people enjoying themselves. Here they paused, for moving any closer would risk stepping into view of a dozen unwelcoming pirates. Somehow, they needed to see without being seen.

As Rathbone chewed his lip in thought, his eyes came to rest on another of the faded cave paintings. Like the others, this one seemed to make little sense: two rows of stick figures, one above the other, with a zigzag of dots between the groupings and a boar's head in the center.

It seemed a strange place to have left such a doodle, and he stared at it for a moment before an idea struck him. What if it was more than just a piece of primitive art?

Reaching out to caress the wall around the drawing, Rathbone's questing fingers found the first foothold carved crudely into the rock. As he suspected, the image was instructional, guiding him toward a series of alcoves that would allow him to reach the hideout's upper level.

He began to haul himself higher and higher, moving each of his limbs in turn to find the next niche until he was eventually splayed out on a high ledge. He helped Shan climb up alongside him, and together, the two men wriggled forward on their bellies, peering down from the darkness.

The high shelf onto which they'd climbed acted almost as a gallery, surrounding and overlooking a large central cavern into which they could peek without being spotted. It was here that the pirates had made their home, and just as the drawing depicted, there was an enormous boar skull dominating the scene. It was huge, larger than any living beast Shan had seen, and it had been placed reverentially atop an ornate plinth carved out of the rock itself, with several smaller skulls and miscellaneous bones scattered around it.

The cackling revelers below paid it no heed, however. There were eight that Shan could see in total, though two were snoring loudly. Those who were still awake were focused on jeering and cavorting around a large wooden construction, and Rathbone eased himself out over thin air so that he could get a better look at it.

It's a cage, he thought in surprise. Stretching forward as far as he dared, he could just about make out two figures huddled within the stout bars. Prisoners, and mistreated ones, for those pirates who hadn't collapsed into a drunken stupor were poking at them with sticks and issuing mocking threats. For a moment, Rathbone feared that it might be Ramsey and Mercia—that they'd been captured and that the *Magpie's Wing* was now either seized or scuttled at the enemy's hands. *Ramsey would never sit that quietly*, he considered. *And he mentioned something about friends. Who could he have meant?* Well, if he couldn't see, he'd just have to listen.

"Oi, Douglas!" one of the pirates belched. "How comes I 'as to go on watch next, eh? 'S not like anyone even knows we're 'ere!" He blew his nose noisily on the hem of his coat and, upon discovering his bottle was empty, tossed it in a lazy arc into the river.

The largest man, whose ruddy face was framed by a lion's mane of bright red hair, growled. "You'll go because I said so, Gripper, an' because you don't want my blade in your belly! This is the biggest catch of our lives, and if I learn anyone's put our plunder at risk because they were too lazy or too stupid to stick to the plan, I'll personally feed 'em to the sharks one piece at a time, and I'll save the eyes till last so's they can watch!"

A bully, Rathbone thought. *But an effective one, if he's got three ships at his command. Once he's cut down, however....* It was tempting, here in the darkness, to simply draw his pistol and put a shot between those piggy little eyes, but it would also likely be the last thing Rathbone ever did.

Gripper, it seemed, was either too daft or too drunk to know when not to push his luck. "Yeah, well, that one won't eat what we gives anyway," he complained, delivering a savage kick to the cage. "If you ask me—"

Douglas moved so quickly that Rathbone never even saw the shot. He heard the bang, though, and felt it echo around the cavern with a deafening boom that silenced every pirate instantly. They, along with Rathbone and Shan high above, stared wordlessly at Gripper as he toppled forward. His limp form tumbled down the rocky slopes and into the river to bob away along with his bottle.

The scene was a frozen tableau, for no one dared to be the first to speak, at least until a rumpled-looking young pirate tore into the room. She was breathless, and looked to have sprinted for some distance. "Fire!" she yelled. "Ship afire!" That was enough to snap the assembled pirates from their horrified trance, and they began to clamor in confusion.

"Zounds!" Douglas bellowed. "Is it treachery? Or just another fool who wants to dance with the cat o' nine tails? Never mind!" he added, immediately answering his own question. Hauling the two sleeping pirates to their feet, he dragged them to the river and dunked their heads under for several seconds, assuring he had their full attention when he finally dropped them back on dry land. "Take Norris, Smiley, and Bo, and make sure every single ship is as it should be. And if you find the ones who've tried to scupper us, you're to leave 'em alive 'til I get there, you understand?"

"Smiley? But we can't *find*—" the pirate whimpered, then thought better of arguing. Wordlessly, she and her dripping comrades fled from Douglas's fury and out of the caves as fast as their unsteady legs could carry them.

"You two!" Douglas growled, rounding on two startled young men who were trying to linger at the back of the crowd. "Stay here and guard the prisoners! Everyone else, form search parties." He lumbered toward the cave's main entrance. "There's no one who knows this island better than us! Whoever's out there will be shark bait by morning!" Cursing and muttering, he and his crew filed out of the cave and out of sight.

That left just two bewildered pirates staring blankly at one another, so confused by the sudden turn of events that they were completely unprepared when Rathbone and Shan dropped from overhead and felled them like two sacks of potatoes. Once he was satisfied both men were out cold, Rathbone stepped out of the shadows and holstered his weapon. "Don't worry," he called out to the occupants of the cage. "We're friends. We're here to help."

"I'm not sure they'll understand you." Shan had already moved to the bars of the cage, which was half submerged in a deep pool, and gotten a clear look at its occupants. Now the older man looked as pale as a fresh sheet, the first time Rathbone could remember seeing him visibly shaken.

With some trepidation, Rathbone stepped and stared into the cage. From within its confines, their yellow eyes blazing in the firelight, two merfolk stared back.

Smiley the pirate was having the worst night of his life.

He'd been given first watch, which was bad enough. That meant that while he was out patrolling the rough pathways and passages that crisscrossed their island hideaway, the others were back at camp with the best of the evening meal and, more likely than not, a fresh cask of grog to accompany it. By the time Smiley got back, he was lucky to find a plate of cold leftovers to call his own.

Then there was the snake, which began coiling its way around his leg as he stopped for a quiet smoke out of the wind. Smiley hated snakes, and though he'd managed to slip out of his boot just in time, he hadn't dared approach the wretched creature to reclaim it. Now he was hobbling around the island with one stockinged foot feeling foolish.

To make matters worse, his arm seemed to be getting worse. He'd snuck another look at it earlier when no one was around. Four days had passed since he defied Douglas's orders and snaffled a golden idol for himself while exploring one of the island's many shrines. Now shadowy flecks of amber were visible in the veins of his hand and wrist, as if the little totem had been under some protective magic or other. His little finger was almost completely immobile now, but he didn't dare tell the others, in case they decided a solid gold arm was worth more than Smiley himself.

Finally, as Smiley trudged along his route feeling immensely sorry for himself, a man the size of a small bear had plummeted out of the treetops and landed on his head. Now Smiley was hanging upside down from a sturdy branch, bound and gagged. The terrifying figure and his accomplice made Smiley spill his guts about everything Douglas's gang had been up to, how many of them were on the island, and the plan for their two prisoners.

When Smiley mentioned the bit about taking the merfolk far from the Sea of Thieves to sell, the woman struck him with a blow that he felt sure ought to have taken his head clean off. Even so, he begged her to take him prisoner, lock him in the brig, or even make him walk the plank out at sea. Anything seemed better than being found by Douglas and made to explain himself.

He'd been left to swing regardless. High in the branches and too ashamed to even call for help, Smiley was forced to watch as one of their three ships was set ablaze, lamp oil burning brightly across her deck and flames bubbling the paint of the hull. Three of his shipmates raced aboard, buckets in hand to extinguish the blaze, only to be blasted into the ocean by cannon fire from their sister ship, which was now under control of the trespassers.

Douglas and his search party located Smiley shortly after, and he hung forlornly, confessing everything. He begged to be cut down, to be allowed to rejoin the fight and take revenge, but Douglas spat on the ground below him and declared that Smiley could be left there to rot, as far as he was concerned. An example to the others.

Now Smiley was swinging, trying to get enough momentum to hack his sword into the bindings that held his feet. His wild swipes were missing by mere inches as he rocked back and forth. Finally, by curling his stomach as tight as it could go, he managed to land a blow that struck, more by luck than judgment. It was only enough to fray the stout rope, but it spurred Smiley into landing a second blow, then a third.

There was a lurch, a snap, and Smiley was in free fall, landing painfully on the hard ground face first. After a moment lying in a painful, private world of his own, he reached beneath himself and began groping around, for he'd landed on something that was proving incredibly uncomfortable. Forcing himself onto his hands and knees, he pulled the mysterious object out from under his belly. It was a boot.

His boot, Smiley realized with a rising sense of dread. His boot and a very, very angry snake.

"Hurry up!" said Rathbone, for the fifth time in as many minutes. "I thought you said you could pick the lock!" He was pacing, agitated, trying to keep watch on all possible entrances at once while Shan crouched in the icy water and fumbled at the door of the cage. The merfolk within stared impassively as he stamped back and forth.

"I did say that," Shan agreed, his speech rather slurred thanks to the selection of slender metal implements clenched between his teeth. "But the thing about this lock . . . the main thing about this lock, right, is . . ."

"Is what!"

"Is that I can't pick it." Shan admitted, spitting his tools back into his hand and clambering out of the pool. "Not without the rest of my tools. I don't suppose—"

"No," said Rathbone firmly. "We'd never make it to the ship and back before that Douglas and his thugs caught up to us." He swore and shook his head in disbelief. "Merfolk! I mean, you always heard the stories, but never expect to see them in the flesh!"

Shan had to admit that Rathbone was right; the two creatures were captivating. Their faces were mostly human, with features that suggested one was male and the other female, though a few thin lines here and there hinted at the existence of gills and fins somewhere in their heritage. Their skin looked tough, like flattened scales, and seemed to be slightly pearlescent, shifting between white and silver depending on how you looked at them.

Much of their bodies were wrapped in a strange, smooth material that looked like nothing he'd ever seen before and seemed to flow effortlessly in water. The coverings extended all the way down past their waists and tied together neatly in a point, making it impossible to tell with any certainty whether they were disguising something approaching a pair of human legs or, like the legends promised, an enormous fishlike tail. The two mer had been watching the two men intently with large and doleful expressions, but so far they'd given no indication that they understood anything that was being said.

Forcing himself to think less about the cage's occupants and more about the current predicament, Shan began to join Rathbone in pacing around the cave. "So we can't pick the lock. Can't smash the bars. Reckon all four of us could carry the cage?"

"No," Rathbone said, curtly. "Even if we could, who knows if merfolk can survive out of the water? We need the key, and somehow I doubt Douglas is just going to hand it over."

"You know, I think he might."

Rathbone's hand went to his pistol, for Douglas's looming form had appeared at the entrance to the cave, but the voice was Ramsey's. He came in close behind the furious pirate, holding him at sword point. "Personally I was hoping he'd have swallowed it for safekeeping, so I'd have the pleasure of cutting it out of him, but young Smiley tells me it's on a chain around his neck."

"Ye've no business coming here and meddling in my affairs, ye' self-righteous prig!" Douglas snarled. "Just 'cos ye' got here first doesn't mean ye' run the whole damn ocean."

"Not yet," Ramsey muttered, and there was a glint in his eye as he spoke those words. "But I know more about being a pirate than you ever will, boy, and what separates us from kings and queens is *we* don't treat people like things. Not out here, not even if we hate 'em more than anything in the world. People aren't *property*."

He practically spat the last word as he reached for the key to the cage. It was rare for Ramsey not to be the tallest in the room, but he almost had to stand on tiptoe to grasp the silver chain around his captive's neck. He made no effort to lift the key away, but merely gave a savage yank so that Douglas choked and the necklace snapped.

Ramsey tossed the key to Shan, who caught it ably and began to fumble with the cage's lock while the merfolk looked on, silent as ever. There were quiet footsteps behind him, and he turned to address Mercia as she entered. "Did you find the rest of his little gang?"

"All awake, but tied up tight," she confirmed. "And a bit singed." No wonder, she reflected, considering the amount of gunpowder she and Ramsey had tipped over Douglas and his crew as they'd reentered the camp, covering them in a thick gray coat. The expression on

Ramsey's face as he dropped a burning torch down onto the group was one she wouldn't forget in a hurry.

Mercia stepped forward, giving a little smile in the direction of the merfolk. They all watched in anticipatory silence as Shan slid the key into the cage's lock, though Douglas still shook in barely suppressed rage. The door swung wide open, and that was when everything happened at once.

Smiley, who had snuck back into the camp just in time to witness Douglas's capture, decided that this was his opportunity to make amends. He leapt down from the dark ledges overhead with a loaded blunderbuss in his hands, but as he landed, his leg—bloodied and swollen by a dozen snakebites—gave out from under him. Smiley lost his footing, tumbling into the rock pool and bashing his head against the cage.

The ambush seemed to finally startle the merfolk into motion, and they fled from their prison, diving into the waiting river with two great splashes. What happened to them next no one could say for sure, as Smiley's frantic thrashing sent water cascading in all directions, extinguishing the hideout's campfire and casting the cave into darkness. Seizing his chance in the confusion, Douglas stepped forward, turning to swing a vicious punch at the captain who'd cost him his prisoners.

Ramsey, feeling the bulk of the man shifting away from him in the darkness, was faster. His sword came down sharply against Douglas's ribs, tearing through his tunic with ease—and yet, to his surprise, the blade seemed to bounce away as harmlessly as if he'd struck stone. He had just enough time to land a second, equally ineffectual strike against the man's leg before being lifted clean off his feet as Douglas's fist connected. It felt like being hit by a sack full of broken bricks.

Ramsey flew backward, crashing into the boar's head and dislodging it from its place atop the altar. Disturbing the remains appeared to trigger some kind of ancient mechanism, possibly a trap left behind to protect the shrine, for the ground immediately began to quake.

A ghostly blue light flooded the cave as the entire monument began to glow. It illuminated Douglas, who was standing over the fallen Ramsey with a large boulder held high above his head, meaning to crush him. He might very well have succeeded had Shan not scrambled for the blunderbuss lying next to Smiley's stricken form and unloaded its contents into the giant's back. Douglas staggered, but did not fall, and as he shrugged off the shredded remains of his coat, the others could finally see why.

Almost half of Douglas's swarthy body was calcified, his skin the texture of roughly hewn stone. "Caught myself a little curse a while back," he roared gleefully as he caught their astounded expressions. "Must've stolen something what didn't want stealing." Behind him, a fine trickle of sand began to pour from the ceiling. "Reckon I don't have long left but I'll last longer'n ye' curs!"

He brought the rock down against the altar with enough force that the stone plinth actually cracked, but Ramsey was no longer upon it, having disentangled himself and rolled aside just in time. More dirt was cascading down now, and the cave's exit was already half blocked by rubble. Whatever the purpose of the shrine had once been, its desecration had triggered an avalanche that looked set to entomb them all.

Ramsey ducked another of Douglas's blows, searching wildly for a weapon that might pierce that unnaturally thick hide—but a large slab of stone crashing down an inch to his left made him reconsider the wisdom of fighting a rock-skinned behemoth in a rapidly collapsing cave. The merfolk, he realized, were nowhere to be seen, and he realized what that must mean.

"Into the water!" he bellowed at the others, staggering as a rocky fist grazed his cheek and left a deep cut across it. "Before we're buried alive!" One by one, his crew threw themselves into the raging river, and Ramsey ducked under Douglas's outstretched arms to do the same.

"Ye'll not get away!" Douglas howled, leaping into the river after Ramsey as if to grab him in a great bear hug. Only when he hit the water did his beady eyes widen in fear and understanding, for while

Ramsey was buoyed along on the river's foamy surface, Douglas himself was far less fortunate. The curse of his stony flesh bore him helplessly down to the riverbed, and while he tenaciously tried to take a few faltering steps after the fleeing pirates, it was clear that he'd never be able to hold his breath long enough to escape.

After a moment, Douglas was forced to scramble back onto the riverbank, buckling under blows from tumbling rocks as he scrabbled uselessly against the rubble in search of an exit. There was an almighty crack, more enormous stones crashed down into the cave, and a billowing curtain of dust took him at last from Ramsey's sight.

The river carried them carelessly outside, bumping and scraping them all off rocky outcroppings and, once, plunging them over a small waterfall. They were all bruised and battered as they finally staggered back onto dry land, finding themselves only a short distance from the *Magpie's Wing*. Exhausted, they stumbled back up the gangplank and would have fallen asleep then and there if not for a strange keening sound that seemed to take up all around the ship.

Looking over the railings, the four pirates saw that they were flanked on every side by at least a hundred merfolk—it was hard to tell exactly, for they were all cavorting in celebration, diving and flipping and spiraling around one another.

"What's this?" Rathbone asked, bemused but curious. "Have they come to thank us?"

"More than that," said Ramsey cheerfully, clapping Rathbone on his aching back and making him wince. "They've come to keep up their part of the bargain."

LARINNA

Once the distant lights of Sanctuary Outpost had faded from sight, Adelheid and the crew took their places at the map table and spread the parchment out in front of them. Larinna wasn't entirely certain what form Simeon's memories would take, but she assumed some kind of map or chart would be involved. Rather, the parchment contained just two lines of spidery writing:

On strangled shores, my ship you seek
Begin your search at Tribute Peak.

Privately, Larinna didn't think that this was much to go on, and certainly not worth the grief they'd been through to obtain the information. The others seemed satisfied with what little they knew, though, and clustered around the table until they located Tribute Peak in a distant corner of the map. While Faizel and Ned headed above decks to set a course, Adelheid asked Larinna to linger for a moment.

"I'm sure you must think this is all just a wild goose chase," she said, preemptively. Surprised, Larinna nodded. "Oh, don't look so startled! You don't hide your emotions that well."

"Well, I expected something a little less cryptic," Larinna retorted, indicating the parchment. "It barely tells us anything, assuming it can even be trusted."

"It can," Adelheid said firmly. "Memories aren't always easy to interpret, but they don't lie. Besides, I knew Captain Simeon. Back when he was alive, I mean. I was a deckhand on his crew when I was young."

"You were?" Larinna stared. "That didn't stop you from pulling his head clean off."

Adelheid merely shrugged. "Better to be properly at rest than rattling around as a pile of bones for all eternity. He'd have thanked me." She gave Larinna a look. "Or are you saying you wouldn't want me to do the same for you, if it came to it?"

"It won't. Are you saying you know for sure that these memories of Simeon's are going to lead us to something good?"

Adelheid moved to the *Unforgiven*'s tiny kitchen and began to fish around in cupboards and cabinets until she produced a bottle of dark red wine and two tankards. "He ran a tight ship, did Simeon. As far as he was concerned, the captain's word was law. So he never used to tell the crew much."

"How terrible to be kept out of the loop like that," Larinna said, dryly, which earned her a scowl along with a proffered share of the wine. She took both with good humor.

"One night, I was up late." Adelheid took a deep swig of her drink and looked vaguely embarrassed. "Truth was I was stealing food from the galley, so when old Steel-Eye came in, I hid. I still don't really know why I did it. Perhaps I was already fed up of following orders. Anyway, him and his first mate started talking, and Simeon told her that he was sure he'd found it this time. Sure that he'd found a clue to Athena's Fortune."

It took all Larinna's self-control not to choke on her wine, and she was glad that the tankard obscured her shocked expression. The *Unforgiven* had been in dock when she'd arrived. Was it possible that Adelheid had been somehow goading her all this time, attempting to influence her actions with those stupid handwritten notes? This was a hell of a way to reveal her trickery if so.

No, she decided after a moment. This was no prank, for there was no trace of mischief on Adelheid's face, and she'd have been unable to disguise her glee at a successful joke. Larinna decided to play dumb. "What's Athena's Fortune?" she asked disinterestedly, reaching for the wine and topping up their glasses as though they were discussing any old trinket.

She expected Adelheid to scoff at the question, but the captain seemed happy enough to answer. "I didn't know either, not back then. Whatever it was sounded very important, anyway. Important enough for Simeon to risk life and limb going after it. I might have learned more, but at that point a rat bit my ear, I yelped, and they found me. Flogged me, of course, and put me off the ship at the next port. But I kept hunting for clues, and eventually I found an old fiddle player in a tavern who told me that Athena's Fortune is what they call the most valuable treasure of the Pirate Lord."

"And then," Larinna said slowly, finally starting to put the pieces of the puzzle together, "you learned that Simeon had died. Or undied, or whatever the term is. Became a skeleton, I mean." She didn't know what a Pirate Lord was, but it sounded important.

"Yes, and I knew that the Order of Souls was bound to put a bounty out on him sooner or later. Whatever memories they were able to get from him, I was sure they'd help lead to Athena's Fortune, assuming he ever found it." Adelheid set her empty mug down on the table with a satisfied burp. "The most prized treasure of the greatest pirate who ever lived . . . that's got to be worth chasing, don't you think?" Adelheid moved to say more but was interrupted as Ned stuck his head through the hatchway. "What is it?"

"Trouble," Ned said simply. The two women shared a glance and rose swiftly, jogging up the stairs to the upper deck where Faizel was standing, spyglass in hand, gazing out at the horizon.

"It would appear that we are being followed," he informed them, with none of his usual playfulness. "We have changed course twice and they have matched our heading both times."

"Is it the Order?" Larinna asked, squinting as if she could somehow make out the other ship through sheer force of will.

"Unlikely," said Adelheid. "They're a bunch of hocus-pocus merchants who normally rely on pirates to do their fighting for them. I suppose it's *possible* they've put a bounty on us, but I've never heard of them doing that for anyone who wasn't a skellie."

"I've never heard of anyone stealing their wares," Faizel suggested, grimly. "We did make quite a commotion leaving town, however, so it could be that other pirates know we have something worth taking. I think that they must be faster than us, but for now they seem content to keep their distance and let us know that we are being followed."

"That, or they want to work out where we might be heading before they try and sink us." Adelheid retorted. "Any bad weather around? Somewhere we can lose them? I'm not keen for them to know our destination."

"It might be too late for that," Larinna reminded her. "Occulia looked at the parchment, too. If we spend time hiding or trying to throw this ship off the scent, we might find their friends have had time to set up an ambush at Tribute Peak."

"We could take 'em head on," Ned offered. "They might not expect us to hit first."

Adelheid pondered for a moment. "Faster is better," she said, finally. "I want us to see if we can outrun them. If they can't see us they might give up and turn tail, and at the very least it'll give us a chance to hide."

The crew went about their business, tilting the ship's great sails to catch all the wind they could, but even as they tore across the waves

Faizel reported that the other ship continued to gain on them. They could see it with the naked eye, now, a dark and ominous smudge on the horizon growing steadily larger.

Finally, a frustrated Adelheid ordered all nonessential supplies be thrown overboard in an effort to lighten the load. Barrels of fruit and dried meat, crates packed with plundered weapons and ammunition, even the bed from the captain's cabin—it all went overboard, one item at a time, along with the spare sails and boxes of gold the crew had built up over the months.

Faizel made a point of marking the position on the map in case they one day had a chance to come back, but abandoning all of their treasure left them in a somber mood indeed. Even Larinna felt curiously glum about having no belongings of her own to surrender, save for the single golden coin tucked safely in her boot.

Even with all of these sacrifices, though, the other ship continued to bear down upon them. They could see her clearly through the spyglass now; she was a modified galleon that Faizel recognized as the *Black Gauntlet*, reportedly now under the command of a fearsome captain with a reputation for taking home some of the Order's most notable bounties. The *Black Gauntlet* herself was equally formidable; her hull had been reinforced with steel bands that Larinna supposed might help brace against cannon fire. Piles of powder kegs had been piled on the deck so that they could be thrown overboard, acting as floating time bombs that could damage and destroy any ship that might pursue them. They could see harpoon guns, too, capable of launching vicious spears that could tether two ships together if used effectively—not to mention skewer her crew.

Larinna lowered the spyglass, momentarily dazzling herself as the hot sun caught the lens. As she blinked furiously in an effort to clear the purple spots out of her vision, the first vestiges of a plan began to form in her head. She stood for a few moments, pondering. There was a good chance something could go wrong, she knew. But was there also a chance everything could go right?

"Faizel!" she called across. "What do you know about the captain of that ship?"

"If you are thinking that you can appeal to his better nature, I am not certain that he remembers where he buried it!" Faizel shouted back over the roar of the waves. "All I know is that his name is Quince, and that he is a military man. Strong as an ox, they say!"

So he's a soldier but not a tactician, Larinna thought to herself. Out loud, she asked, "If he was a soldier, would he know about flags and signals, things like that?"

"I would suppose?" Faizel looked at her, curiously. "Do you have a plan?"

"If it works, I'll let you know!" she called, already halfway up to the ship's wheel. "Adelheid, I think I've got us a way out of this, but you're not going to like it."

"I'm glad you're a pirate and not a politician, because that was a terrible speech." Adelheid grumbled. "What won't I like about it?"

"Well," Larinna hesitated, but she'd come this far. "All of it, honestly. Oh, and I'm going to have to borrow Ned."

"Captain Quince, sir!" Quince, who had been inspecting the newly installed cannons that ran along the deck of the *Black Gauntlet*, harrumphed at the sound of his name and glanced upward. To his surprise, he saw that the scruffy little ship they were pursuing was beginning to turn so that its own relatively meager arsenal was aiming directly at their prow.

"So, they've decided to make a fight of it, have they?" he barked. "Lucky us, eh? I was starting to get bored of the whole bloody cat and mouse game, after all. Prepare to fire!"

"Er," said a nearby deckhand, meekly. "I believe the plan was to bring them in alive, sir." He flinched as Quince rounded on him, for the captain was a great bull of a man—not tall, but as solid as a slab of beef with a great whiskery moustache that bristled when he was angry, which was often. Two piercing blue eyes bored into the deckhand, who was already regretting ever having spoken.

"Don't be a bloody idiot, boy!" the captain snapped. "Bringing prisoners aboard is a fool's game. No, they deserve to be scuppered and scuppered they shall be! Can't have the Companies thinking pirates can't get the job done or that'll be the end of the contracts. D'you want to spend the rest of your life digging up crusty old boxes on a godforsaken beach, lad?"

"Well, no, sir, but—"

"Precisely!" Quince patted the hull of the *Black Gauntlet*, his pride and joy. Back home, he'd diligently saved up all his wages from over twenty years of naval service and never managed to afford himself more than a creaky little sloop. Out here on the Sea of Thieves, free from the grasping fingers of the taxman and his cronies, he'd managed to afford himself a fine and distinguished vessel by handing in bounty after bounty. He was not, he vowed, about to let anyone take that away from him.

As he glared at the rapidly approaching vessel, Quince noticed something strange—a flashing burst of bright light, visible even in the daylight, winking at them with a regular pattern. Feeling for the ornate spyglass at his belt and peering down its length, he could see a hulking man with a great mirror clutched in his outspread arms, tilting it up and down to the instruction of a dark-haired woman at his side.

"It's a signal!" he declared out loud, after a moment. "They're trying to get our attention, I'd wager."

"Does that mean they want to talk to us, sir?" the deckhand inquired, cautiously. This was his first voyage, and he'd been hoping for nothing more exciting than a few skeletal bounties that might bring him to the Order's attention. Sparring with a crew of living, breathing pirates was another matter entirely, especially given the chaos their targets had already caused.

"Course it does, laddie! They probably want to surrender like the lily-livered filchers they are." Quince harrumphed. "Let's give these cowards our answer, eh? Fire the cannons!" He watched in satisfaction as his own ship began to turn, cutting across the *Unforgiven*'s path and striking her twice on her port side.

The instant the first blows hit home, the woman sprinted down the steps to the cannons on her own vessel, and Quince barked with laughter at the sight of the large man still dumbly holding the glittering mirror. "Oaf!" he barked, before ordering his crew to brace for impact. A single cannonball arced through the air from the *Unforgiven*, striking the hull of the *Black Gauntlet* and causing a small shudder.

"Only minor damage, sir!" someone shouted. "We'll have it repaired in a moment."

Quince sneered. "One cannon? Pathetic!" he called, hoping that his voice might carry across the waves somehow. "Is that the best you can do?" He coughed, wheezily, and then ordered a second volley. This time, three of the *Black Gauntlet*'s shots hit their mark, her crew shouting and jeering as the *Unforgiven* came close to rolling just from the impact. "It's almost too easy," Quince laughed, though this again gave way to a second coughing fit that nearly doubled him over.

"Right," he thundered, staring down at the crew with red-rimmed eyes. "Which one of you idiots is smoking while we've got powder on the deck?" All he got in return was a sea of blank expressions, however, and he turned slowly in place, trying to find the source of the acrid smell that was washing over him. Finally, Quince's eyes settled on the piled-up powder kegs stacked next to the bow of the ship, close to where he was standing.

The powder kegs were smoking and smoldering, becoming extremely hot—thanks to the focused sunlight directed by a large, curved mirror. One or two of them had begun to pop and sputter dangerously.

Captain Quince was not a young man, but he impressed his crew that day by executing an acrobatic dive over the railings, a few short seconds before the powder kegs exploded in a chain reaction that sent fire across the deck of the *Black Gauntlet*. Smaller fires erupted in the sails, but no one was left to extinguish them, for many of the crew had followed their captain into the sea—either hurled overboard by the blast or attempting to escape the roaring flames.

Larinna, watching the chaos from afar, was tempted to reload the cannons and exact some very satisfying revenge against the crippled ship. A lurch from below reminded her that the *Unforgiven* was in no shape to pick a fight, however, even if her opponent couldn't retaliate.

Instead, she called to Little Ned, who insisted on returning the mirror to the captain's cabin before returning to the sails, and Larinna swiftly set a course that would carry them out of sight. She didn't know whether or not they'd been able to inflict a fatal blow to the *Black Gauntlet* or not, but she was convinced that she'd bought them enough time to reach Tribute Peak unchallenged.

Sure enough, they soon left the other ship far behind, though Larinna still felt unsettled about fleeing from a half-finished fight. The *Unforgiven* felt sluggish and slow in the water, and although Adelheid and Faizel had been below to repair the damage, Larinna was starting to get concerned about how badly they'd been hit.

"Ned!" she called, unable to completely mask the unease in her voice. "I think we're safe for now. Why don't you head below decks and see if you can help the others finish making..."

She trailed off as Adelheid staggered up the stairs, grunting with exertion, for she was struggling under the weight of Faizel's motionless form. Ned moaned softly and was at her side in an instant, lifting the smaller man effortlessly and laying him out across the deck on a tarpaulin. Larinna could see a nasty purple bruise across Faizel's head where something had struck him, and his breathing was shallow and rapid.

"I've used up every last scrap of wood and cloth we have left to patch the leaks," Adelheid panted, looking pale and exhausted herself. "They hit us too hard, and we're still taking on water from half a dozen places. The ship is sinking, and there's not a damn thing we can do to stop it."

11

RAMSEY

The sky was the deep blue of a sapphire as the *Magpie's Wing* sluiced across the waves, surrounded by a veritable armada of merfolk who darted and danced around and under her hull. The lower decks were filled with their strange, keening wail that Mercia assured the others was harmless. She imagined it must have made the ship look like a mother whale surrounded by its young, although the mood aboard was rather tenser than the playful scene might have suggested.

Rathbone, naturally, demanded that she and Ramsey finally sit down and supply them with some explanation of everything to which he and Shan had been unwitting accomplices in the last few days. Ramsey refused to linger on details and insisted that they get under way at once.

Rathbone also wanted to raid the remains of Douglas's hideout for anything that might have survived the cave-in and could fetch a pretty penny. Any gang of pirates that size surely hoarded some valuable treasures, he insisted, until Mercia reminded him that at least two of the objects had been cursed in some way. The prospect of winding up with a petrified arm of his own seemed to have quieted him, at least for now.

Their destination was distant, and Ramsey wasn't sure how slowly they would have to travel, lest they risk leaving the merfolk behind.

As it turned out, they needn't have worried—they left the island at a crawl, with but a single sail unfurled, and their new companions surged ahead of them almost immediately, flipping and waving. *Is that the best you can do*, they seemed to say, and they increased their speed until the *Magpie's Wing* was sailing along at a tidy clip. Only when the horizon was free of both land and ship alike did Ramsey allow the others to go below as he kept watch at the helm, giving Mercia a chance to explain the truth behind their journey.

No sooner had the three sat themselves around the map table than Rathbone demanded to know all about their destination and what their reward might be, given that they'd risked life and limb to free the prisoners. Shan, by contrast, was rather more interested in the merfolk themselves and how it was that they'd come to ally themselves with the crew of the *Magpie's Wing*.

Mercia decided to start at the beginning—the very beginning, in fact, explaining how Ramsey had become taken with the idea of somehow possessing, or at least controlling, the magic that seemed to permeate the Sea of Thieves. How the ransacking of their hideout had made him eager to find any kind of trick, some advantage over anyone else who might seek to steal from him or challenge his authority.

She told them of the many fruitless hours she'd spent in taverns listening to prattle and nonsense before finally stumbling upon the old woman, and of the real reason for her trip down into the shipwreck. Finally, savoring the thrill of a good story, she explained in great detail their descent into the network of underwater passages. She was gratified to see their eyes widen as she described the grand hall that lay forgotten under the waves. "It was when I put the earrings on that everything suddenly became so . . . clear," she finished. "Like when you remember a dream."

"I don't dream," Rathbone said, curtly. "So you can understand that racket they're making out there, then? What are they saying? Nothing about what we might taste like, I hope."

"Their song is about, well, anything. And everything," Mercia shrugged. "I know that doesn't make sense, but it's their identity, it's their art, it's what they did a thousand years ago and will do tomorrow, all carried on the music. It's not like they can write anything down, after all."

"Interesting," Shan mused. "If it's anything as powerful as whale song, they must be able to talk to each other across huge distances. Could be a useful way of sending messages."

Rathbone rolled his eyes. "You two make quite the team, one of you pulling the world apart so the other can patch it back together again. So you put the earrings in. What happened next?"

Mercia took a deep draft of water as she considered how to arrange the story in her mind. Only when the last of the drops had passed her lips did she rest her chin thoughtfully on her fist and begin to speak.

Ramsey's hand, Mercia told them, went to the hilt of his sword when the water in the chamber's central pool began to churn, though she herself was far too enraptured to pay much attention to his actions. Her mind was filled with a sudden understanding that threatened to overwhelm her, and it was all she could do to stay on her feet.

That changed when the first of the figures erupted from the water with a great splash that soaked the floor in every direction, for the song had reduced to a muted, wordless hum. It was as if the singers themselves were waiting to see what would happen next.

The two pirates had found themselves staring at what they both knew had to be a mermaid. A living, breathing mermaid of the kind that Mercia had read about in storybooks when she was a child, now floating serenely before them and studying them much as they were studying her.

Her large eyes, sparkling with both interest and intellect, were the color of fossilized amber. Her skin wasn't blue, lavender, or silver—rather, it was some shimmering combination that seemed to shift and swirl from moment to moment, like oil on water. Her slender face with its strong jaw was framed by a mass of pale green hair, tied sensibly back into a delicate ponytail that seemed braided to intertwine with the flowing fabric that wreathed much of her body.

After a moment, two more mer broke the surface of the water to float slightly behind her, though they performed nothing as ostentatious as a backflip. Mercia guessed, correctly, that the two pirates were looking at some kind of leader or nobility. A mermaid queen, perhaps? Ramsey had evidently been thinking the same thing, for much to Mercia's surprise, he took a step forward, removed his hat with a great sweeping gesture, and bowed as low as his great frame would allow.

It was a gesture that seemed to please the merfolk, for their song started up again—not a chorus, this time, but a single voice calling out from the darkness. Mercia had no way of knowing if the words she was hearing belonged somehow to the mermaid in front of them, but a lone singer was far easier to understand, and after a few seconds her face split into a broad smile. "Yes! Yes, I can!"

Ramsey looked at her in confusion then, and she attempted rather clumsily to explain that the merfolk were trying to communicate with them. With her. Not through speech as humans understood it, but by changing the meaning and tone of the song—one that they seemed to sing at all times and that seemed to unite them, no matter how far apart they were.

To begin with, the song had been filled with a mixture of curiosity and uncertainty. The merfolk were, unsurprisingly, aware of the many humans who had recently come to the Sea of Thieves. (They used a strange and complicated word to refer to anyone who dwelled on land—a word that Mercia first tried to translate to "sand-swimmer," then "two-tail," before she finally gave up.)

What Ramsey and the others saw as discovery, however, the merfolk viewed as a homecoming. They expected to be met in the old ways of their people and were surprised and a little alarmed when the humans not only seemed unfamiliar with the merfolk, but also had begun warring with one another. "They think we're the same as the people who built this place," Mercia explained to Ramsey, finally. "Or at least, that we're somehow their descendants. They expected us to *remember* them! No wonder they've been so wary of us until now."

It took some time, but Mercia managed to explain to the merfolk that she and everyone else who sailed above had come from far away, where the idea of a sea-dwelling people was considered nothing more than a myth. Their song took on a mournful tone at this point, though when she expressed a desire to learn all about the mer and the ancient inhabitants of the Sea of Thieves, the sadness was replaced by a wistful refrain. She sat cross-legged on the floor and listened, Ramsey standing patiently behind her.

Long ago, she learned, what humans now thought of as the Sea of Thieves had been home to a nameless people whose civilization flourished and thrived. There were ships back then, too, and even a few pirates. There were also artisans and sculptors, philosophers and painters—men and women who the mer had no name for but whose understanding of the world around them had led them to harness great power.

It was while describing this power that Mercia had first, reluctantly, use the term *magic* for herself. There were special places in the world, it seemed, certain spots where magic would manifest itself in a variety of ways. The ancient humans marked these special locations not with words, which could be forgotten, but with paintings on the rocks and stones whose meaning would endure beyond any written language.

Across the centuries, temples and altars were created at these special locations to harness the power and gain some understanding of its potential. Eventually that understanding grew into reverence, and reverence led to ritual. The temples became sacred ground.

Over time, this ancient people was able to channel this magical power well enough to imbue the objects and belongings they had created with special properties. Through their knowledge and efforts, all kinds of strange and magnificent artifacts were brought into being.

Some granted great boons to whoever possessed them, such as an unnaturally long life or the ability to withstand burning heat. Other artifacts, most often ones that the owners wished to protect, were imbued with terrible curses that could freeze the soul to ice, or worse, if they were removed from their resting places. Mercia had been unable to translate a lot of what the song had to say about the dark nature of these curses, for which she was privately grateful.

As the people up above worked to master magic, so too did they strive to cultivate a relationship with the mer below. Using their wisdom and their craft, they took the purest pearls and transformed them into magical earrings with which they might hear the merfolk song and be understood in kind. They constructed great undersea chambers to act as meeting places, pointing the way with more of the eye-catching paintings, and the two civilizations began to live in harmony.

While both races were largely content to leave one another in peace, they would occasionally have reason to cooperate. The mer would uncover precious stones and gems in the very deepest parts of the ocean that the humans seemed to value, and it was but a little effort for them to be excavated and taken up to one of the meeting places as a gift. In return, the humans would use their weapons and their magic to help the merfolk deal with the problems they faced below the waves, like Old Mother or the Whispering Plague.

It had seemed like a union that could last forever, and yet—here the song filled with sorrow—the merfolk's song had begun to go unanswered. Jewels left in the chambers went unclaimed. The shadows of ships passed overhead no longer, and the merfolk had no understanding as to why. Saddened and concerned, they gathered together great search parties of their strongest and fastest, intending to swim beyond the boundaries of their kingdom in search of their land-dwelling friends.

Those who returned spoke sadly of a choking mist and poisoned ocean that they had encountered far beyond the waters they called home, forcing them to retreat. Perhaps the humans had managed to brave the fog somehow and sail to the lands beyond, but there was no way to know for sure.

Anguished by the loss of their friends, the merfolk kept the memory of those above alive within their song. They took the earrings and scattered them across the land in deep caves and rock pools where they would be safe and, one day, a human might stumble upon them. More years passed, and eventually, they became accustomed to being alone.

"They told you all that in a *song*," Rathbone said skeptically. "No wonder you were away so long."

"Well, they were excited to see us," Mercia said defensively. "As I said, they had no real clue of what humans get up to on land. No idea how long we live, or that we have to try to pass on what we've learned to our children as best we can. They have their song, after all. It was hard to get them to understand the idea of forgetting something, or not knowing what others of your kind are up to."

"Well, at least now we know what happened to Douglas," Shan said, thoughtfully. "Their curses, I mean. The idea that any random treasure you find could turn you into a pigeon or make your legs drop off is enough to turn a man honest."

Rathbone snorted. "Speaking of that oversized oaf..."

Mercia nodded. "That was the next thing we learned, yes. When we first arrived in the Sea of Thieves, the merfolk caught wind of us soon after we made it through the Devil's Shroud—that's the poisoned water they mentioned. They all swarmed to the ancient meeting places and waited for us to arrive, which of course we never did. So they started following us, keeping their distance for the most part. But a couple of them got too curious..."

"... and decided to pop out of the sea and say hello to Douglas and his men," Rathbone concluded. "Who not only couldn't understand them, but didn't see them as anything other than a sea monster to be paraded around back home. So they got themselves captured instead. Idiots."

"Those idiots, as you call them, would have had every right to take Ramsey and me hostage in retaliation," Mercia said, hotly. "As far as they knew, all pirates are one and the same. They asked for our help anyway. They knew where the two mer that had been captured had been taken, but they rarely go far inland unless they have to."

"And so you agreed to rescue them," Rathbone sighed. "Tell me that Ramsey, with his bleeding heart, remembered that we're *pirates*, not philanthropists, and has now commanded them to lead us to the hoard of long-lost treasure and jewels we so richly deserve. After all, they are in our debt."

"It seems to me," Shan said slowly, "that there's a lot more that these merfolk can do for us than offer up another chest full of gold pieces just to fritter away in the pub. If what Mercia says is true and they never forget anything on account of their song, that means they must know the location of sunken shipwrecks, and more of those old temples, not to mention places we want to be avoiding so we don't end up cursed ourselves."

"You're both right," Mercia said, diplomatically. "Although," She paused, tipping her head this way and that as she listened to the singing that surrounded them. "Come on," she said, standing suddenly and slapping her palms onto the table. "We're here."

They could sense the change in the air as soon as they made their way above deck. This region of the Sea of Thieves was a dour and gloomy place that Shan had heard referred to as the Wilds, and it was easy to see why. The islands here were a far cry from the gently curving beaches and lush greenery of Thieves' Haven, with straggling vegetation clinging to cruel, rough-hewn rocks that jutted out of the water at odd angles and made sailing treacherous. The air smelled of sulfur, and the water below them was cloudy and discolored as it reflected the murky sky. The breeze felt like a musky, fetid breath on their skin as they took in their surroundings.

Almost at once, they spotted their destination. It would have been hard to miss.

The view ahead was filled with enormous bones, monstrous in their scale and yet unmistakable as anything other than the remains of some great creature. When it was alive, however long ago that must have been, it would have been larger than any outpost. The *Magpie's Wing*, under Ramsey's command, was already sailing smoothly down what remained of its rib cage with room to spare.

Even though he knew it was an irrational fear, Rathbone couldn't help but feel uneasy. Every pirate had heard legends of those ships that had been swallowed up by enormous whales or other similarly massive sea creatures. Now here they were in the belly of the beast, or at least where its belly used to be. "What *was* this thing?" he breathed, not daring to speak too loudly.

"Old Mother!" Ramsey called, cheerfully, not the least bit intimidated by the macabre surroundings. In fact, he rather seemed to be enjoying himself, adjusting course so that their ship emerged from between two bones and began to trace a route alongside the behemoth's skull. The top part of the skull jutted sharply out of the water, and an immense eye socket stared at them accusingly as they sailed past.

"Funny," said Shan, "that's almost what I'd have called it. Mercia mentioned that name just now. Was she something to do with the merfolk?"

Ramsey nodded. "It used to eat 'em. Quite a lot of them from the sounds of it, waking up every century or so to feed and then settling back down to sleep again. Of course, they tried to fight it, but what good's a blade going to be against the hide of a beast this big?"

"Eventually, the merfolk went to the humans and begged them for help," Mercia continued, gesturing over the deck at the swimmers. There was no frolicking or playing around now; the waterborne figures all looked deadly serious as they moved in pairs through the remains. "But not even the most powerful magical weapons would have been enough to deal a mortal blow to Old Mother, even if you could get close enough. Instead, the humans forged great chains to bind her and placed a curse on them. The links could never be broken, and the locks could never be picked. A thousand years could pass and you'd never see a single speck of rust."

"They snuck up to Old Mother while she slept on this very spot," Ramsey cut in, swinging the ship around so they could take in the view. "And they ran the chains around her body and through her tentacles, looping them through all the caverns and caves they could find down below. Chained her up, good and proper, so she could never chase 'em down again! They say it took another hundred years before she stopped thrashing about, and every night her roars would shake the sea. When she finally died, her young left her and went their separate ways, heading out to every corner of the sea."

"Young?" Rathbone snorted. "Say the word, Ramsey. I doubt there's anything left I'm not prepared to believe today."

"Krakens, then," Ramsey said mildly. "Well, Old Mother's feasting days are over now, and that's why we're here." He rested his hands on the wheel and took a deep breath, as if the words he was searching for had to be dredged up from deep inside him.

"Maybe it was wishful thinking to believe the Sea of Thieves would be ours forever, and maybe it's better that it's not. It's a place that pirates were destined to find. There's adventure and plunder enough for all of us here, enough to last a lifetime, and we shouldn't need to steal from each other. But if that's the way it's going to be, if there's going to be a pecking order, then I'm the one who's going to be doing the pecking!"

Leaving the wheel to spin idly, Ramsey strode past the others and placed one gloved hand upon the capstan. "The ones who used to live here learned how to make magic work for them, and I reckon I can too. That starts today." With a flourish, he allowed the anchor of the *Magpie's Wing* to drop, bringing them to an abrupt halt.

As Shan and Mercia moved to furl the sails, there was a sudden commotion all around them, a splashing and crashing so tumultuous that the ship rocked back and forth slightly. The merfolk were diving now, forming neat formations that darted into the watery deep with a sleek efficiency that presented a stark contrast to their earlier playfulness. Far below, they could see the silvery figures rushing this way and that.

After a few moments with his mouth moving silently, Shan worked out why they'd come all this way. "They're unchaining Old Mother," he said, slowly. "It's the chains, isn't it? That's what you're after. That's why we came all the way out here. Iron that never ages, and locks that can't be broken."

Ramsey grinned at him, then hauled himself onto the ship's ladder and down toward the water's edge. As the others watched in bewilderment, a procession of merfolk made its way toward him, each handling a length of silvery metal that looked as shiny and newly forged now as it had when it was made, all those years before. Grasping a few links in his hand, Ramsey hefted himself back up the ladder with a grunt of effort until he was back aboard, at which point he began to haul. "Don't just stand there, you lot!" he snapped, and together they began to heave more of the cursed metal aboard.

Finally, with the *Magpie's Wing* now noticeably lower in the water, they stood around great coils of hastily piled chain, all of which was still icy cold from the centuries it had spent beneath the waves. Looking heartily satisfied with his unusual cargo, Ramsey moved to the prow of the ship and gave another solemn bow to the waiting merfolk, who were now arranged respectfully behind their leader. At once the song began anew, though only Mercia could discern the words, and even she was uncertain as to its meaning:

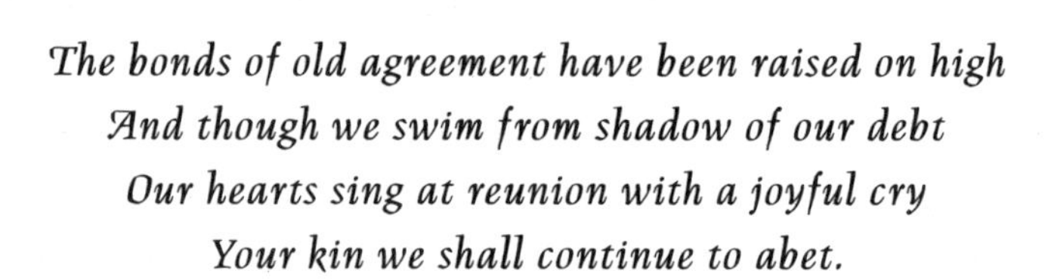

The bonds of old agreement have been raised on high
And though we swim from shadow of our debt
Our hearts sing at reunion with a joyful cry
Your kin we shall continue to abet.

And that seemed to be the end of it, for a deafening series of splashes marked dozens of figures diving back into the water and making for friendlier seas. Within moments, the merfolk's song had faded into the distance, and the crew was alone once more.

"Locks and chains," Rathbone said, dully, his voice hollow as he broke the sudden silence. "All this work for locks and chains." He turned as if sleepwalking, moving stiffly and sightlessly, and went below decks without a word.

"We are sure they're really unbreakable, aren't we?" Mercia asked. "I mean, I know they chained up an entire kraken, but are we sure that the magic hasn't, I don't know, faded or something?"

"They look fine enough, but we won't know for sure until we get back to Thieves' Haven and I can get 'em nice and hot on the forge," said Shan, thoughtfully. "I can already think of a few uses, though, as long as I can reshape the metal. I mean, the *Wing*'s anchor—"

"No," said Ramsey, forcefully. "You'll have your chance to tinker, Shan, but I've got plans for this little lot. By the time we're finished, no pirate will ever be able to steal from us again."

With the heavy chains stowed in Ramsey's cabin for safekeeping, as no one particularly wanted to drag them down all the way to the hold, the *Magpie's Wing* set sail with her most unique plunder yet. The ship cast a long shadow over the ancient bones as it sped across the waves, the sound of a celebratory shanty washing around what was left of the ancient beast.

It was a merry tune, and it carried down to the deepest, darkest crevices in the seabed, where a lone form lurking in Old Mother's shadow had woken. The merfolk had disturbed the slumber of ages, and now one wrathful, golden eye, milky and crusted with barnacles, watched the little ship keenly as it moved away.

The sound of the music, the scent of the wood in the water, and the heat of the bodies were considered carefully. All were remembered. There had been too much time spent sleeping to give chase just yet, but the ship would not be forgotten. Smaller prey would do for now, and then, once its strength had returned . . .

Down in the blackness, the one-eyed form began to stir.

LARINNA

Larinna's back burned so furiously as she pelted up the stairs with a bucket in either hand, she was surprised the water she was hauling hadn't already started to bubble. The buckets' contents were sloshed over the side of the ship, and she was on the move again, ducking past Ned, who had abandoned his own buckets and was now bailing using an enormous wooden cask. His eyes were glazed and his muscles bulged as he staggered up the stairs with gallons of water in his arms. She'd never known one man could be that strong.

Even with Ned's herculean efforts, though, they were losing the battle to save the *Unforgiven*. Water was still pouring into the ship's lower deck through a handful of breaches in the hull, and without the supplies to permanently repair the damage, there was no way to stem the tide for long.

Larinna had stuffed everything she could think of into the gaps, including one of Faizel's gaudy shirts, but if they were going to save the *Unforgiven*, they needed decent wooden planks to do a proper job of it. In the meantime, all she and Ned could do was run an endless, Sisyphean loop up and down between the decks, scooping up all the water they could carry and sending it back into the sea where it belonged.

With Faizel still out cold from the blow he'd received, Adelheid was attempting to sail the ship on her own. She was clinging grimly to the helm, trying to avoid contact with the larger waves that would send yet more water into the hold and hasten their demise. She hadn't said where they were heading, and although Larinna was vaguely aware of some high cliffs coming into view, she was too focused on bailing to care much about their destination.

Once again, she staggered below to where the water was waiting to meet her, filling up her buckets to their brims before hauling them up to the deck. Again. And again. And again. She was back below deck, noting grimly that the lapping water had crept up farther and was starting to slop across the floor of the map room when the ship lurched so savagely that she stumbled, spilling all the water she'd scooped up back into the flooded room. Recovering herself and swearing, Larinna scrambled to refill them, wondering if Adelheid had beached the ship deliberately.

As soon as she reached the stairs, she knew that something had changed drastically. She had staggered above decks not into the warmth of the afternoon sun but into the clammy dampness of a large cavern. In the few moments she'd been below, Adelheid had sailed them into some sort of shelter, and the impact she'd felt was the prow of the *Unforgiven* as it struck the rocky wall, bringing them to a sudden stop.

Adelheid herself was already wrestling with the gangplank, creating a causeway to a rocky ledge on which junk and detritus had been piled. "You keep bailing, Ned!" she bellowed with all her might, her voice echoing around the high cave and disturbing a pair of nesting bats, who squeaked and flittered away in irritation. "Larinna, with me!"

Though she felt about ready to collapse, Larinna obeyed, moving rather less steadily than she'd like across the gangplank. Adelheid was already rooting through the old barrels and crates that littered the smooth rocks, and Larinna joined her in a search for the supplies.

"Found nails!" she gasped, feeling the cold metal sliding between her questing fingers as she groped around at the bottom of a barrel, seizing a handful and caring not that a few stuck painfully into her palm. Cuts would heal.

"Not much good by themselves," Adelheid grumbled. Upon discovering a stout, if rusty, ax leaning against the cave wall, she rounded on the crate she'd just finished searching and attacked it savagely in the hope she might fashion it into the sturdy planks they so desperately needed. Instead, the wet and rather ancient wood simply collapsed in on itself, briefly eclipsing her in a cloud of dust and mold.

There was an ominous creak from behind as the *Unforgiven* began to list dangerously. Frantic now, the pair joined forces, tugging with all of their might at an old tarpaulin. Beneath it laid the supplies they needed, left behind by some unknown adventurer whose loss would most certainly be their gain. The question now would be whether they could act quickly enough to save the *Unforgiven* before the water she'd already taken on sent her broaching sideways, at which point this island would be her final resting place.

Larinna didn't think she'd ever run so fast as on the journey back to the ship, and she hurled herself bodily into the water that now flooded the bottom deck with her share of the planks. Working in tandem for as long as they could hold their breaths, she and Adelheid moved methodically through the belly of the stricken ship, looking for the telltale air bubbles that indicated a hull breach.

Whenever they spotted a stream, they laid a plank across it, pounding in the nails that would hold the wood in place and stop the flow. Every time they sealed one of the *Unforgiven*'s wounds, they'd erupt from the water, take a deep gulp of air, and move on to the next. Before long, the heat of physical exertion was washed from Larinna's body, and she felt frozen to her very core by the icy liquid.

Through it all, Ned kept bailing, and when Larinna came up for another gulp of air she was immensely relieved to see that the water level was back below the hatchway. By the time she'd patched a few more holes it was lower still, and now she felt confident enough to leave the rest of the breaches to Adelheid and rejoin the bailing effort. Before long, they formed an exhausted bucket chain, scooping up water with one hand and accepting empty pails with the other until, at long last, the *Unforgiven* righted herself. She was whole again.

They showered Ned with praise, but he simply gave a little smile and went to sit indoors beside Faizel, who was lying under Ned's jacket in the captain's cabin. Between their flight, the fight, and the flooding, the ship barely had anything left inside her save for the map table and other shipboard essentials. Even most of their food and grog, which was stored down on the lower deck, had been lost to the seawater.

Adelheid gave out a long, irritable yawn, seemingly annoyed by her own fatigue, when she caught the others looking at her. "We might as well stay tonight and make camp," she admitted. "And we may be facing another ambush or a fight, so let's scavenge anything and everything we can take from here."

Larinna nodded, looking around. "Where is 'here' anyway? It seems pretty well protected."

"This old place?" Adelheid grinned, weariness visible in her eyes. "It's been a refuge for the lost and lonely as long as anyone can remember. Used to be a pirate hideout way back when. Thieves' Haven, they called it."

Larinna sniffed. "Daft name."

"Well, it was the olden days," Adelheid informed her. "They did things differently back then."

They took their ease around an ancient campfire in one of the many offshoots from the central cavern, dining on the fruit that grew on the island's upper peaks and a pungent jar of pickled fish that had somehow survived the day's trials intact. No one could remember purchasing it, and Adelheid suggested wafting it under Faizel's nose to see if it might act like smelling salts. They were still soaked to the bone, and so elected to spend the night around the warmth of the flames rather than in the damp underbelly of the *Unforgiven*.

"I remember the first time I found this place," Adelheid commented, her voice unnaturally nasally as she gulped down one of the fish with her nose pinched tightly shut. "I'd found an old treasure map and was climbing around on top of the cliffs looking for a place to dig. Stepped right through one of the gaps in the ceiling and just dropped like a stone into the sea."

They laughed, and Ned replied, "Well, there was one time I was wiv Faizel, right, this was before we met you, captain, and we was out at Shipwreck Bay explorin' some ol' galleon, the *Blackwyche*."

Adelheid smirked, laying down with her arms folded behind her head and her eyes closed to take full advantage of the fire's warmth. "Let me guess—hunting for the Captain's Soul? You shouldn't believe everything you read, even out here."

"Yeah, well, Faizel says, 'Ned, you go on up the main mast and see what might be up in the crow's nest,' and so muggins 'ere agrees," Ned continued, stabbing his finger into his own chest. Larinna couldn't remember ever hearing him talk this much. "And there ain't no ladder, so I has to wrap my arms around it and slowly make my way up, an' I'm almost at the top when I hears this crack ..." Ned raised one arm and mimed the felling of some great tree or other. "Took 'em three hours to dig me out of the sand!"

"Ned, my friend, you do so love to exaggerate," Faizel murmured weakly from his prized position by the fire. "It was only two... hours..." He lapsed back into silence once more, but Larinna could tell that it was the sleep of the exhausted rather than the unconsciousness of the unwell.

They all relaxed a little more after that and drifted off one by one, not even bothering to keep watch. Nothing disturbed them that night, however, save in those few fleeting dreams that visited them as the moon slid across the sky on some voyage of its own.

They awoke with the dawn, and though it was a gray and misty morning, everyone felt fresher and more optimistic now that their crew and their ship were whole once again. The fog would make traveling at speed difficult, and Faizel suggested they wait for the morning sun to wash it away and spend that time scouring every nook and cranny of Thieves' Haven.

Adelheid agreed, though she insisted they focus their search on supplies they sorely needed. "We're out of anything and everything," she reminded them. "Though if someone manages to find me a new bed, something gorgeously soft and fit for an empress, I'll buy them a drink once we're rich."

They spread out and moved through the caves, poking and prodding into nooks and crannies, though Larinna wondered aloud why they were expecting to find anything at all. Why, she inquired, had this place not been picked clean long ago?

"Sometimes it is a matter of practicality, I think," Faizel explained, pottering around quite readily now that the bruise on his head was almost gone. "Let us say you set out on a long voyage loaded with food and supplies, and you come across another ship loaded with treasure. You fight, and of course you win because you are a mighty pirate, but what is this? Your hold is full of bananas. You need the space, so you leave them behind in a place like this, or perhaps throw them overboard to be washed up somewhere. The Sea of Thieves gives and takes in equal measure."

"And sometimes it's a matter of drink," Adelheid added, rather more pragmatically. "There've been plenty of pirates who've forgotten where they stashed their cargo or buried a treasure chest because they were too busy raising a glass." To emphasize her point, she wrenched the lid off a barrel and pulled out a sample of the provisions inside, smirking.

"Either way," Faizel continued, "it always pays to be thorough. Sometimes even skeletons will ferry things from place to place. Perhaps they remember the days when they were pirates, or perhaps—"

He was interrupted by a loud crashing sound from the depths of the cave and an angry bellow from Ned a moment later. Sprinting through the caves in search of the sound, they eventually traced the racket to a large, bowl-shaped room filled with leaves and detritus, with an open roof and a large square pit in the floor.

There was a grunt, and Ned squeezed himself back through, covered in a thick layer of dust. "Fell inna hole," he explained. "Wood's all rotten, see. There's stuff down there, though. Books and fings."

"I have enough to read," Adelheid said blithely, for her meager library was now at the bottom of the sea.

Larinna lit her lantern and moved over to what remained of the trap door. "We should be thorough, remember? You never know what might be down there," she said.

There was a rope ladder leading into the chamber below, she could see, but time and woodworm had taken their toll, and it looked as rotten as the trapdoor itself had been. Instead, she procured a length of abandoned guide rope she'd spotted during their search, tied several sizable knots in it, and secured it against a large stone pillar. The knots provided small but viable handholds, and Larinna was able to climb deftly down into the hole.

Much to her surprise, Faizel joined her a moment later. He shrugged when he caught her quizzical expression. "This is more interesting than loading up the ship, yes?" He picked up a pile of parchments at random and began to peer at them by the light of the lantern. "Some of these are old, I think, very old indeed ... *hah*!"

Larinna started slightly at his bark of laughter. "What's so funny?" she demanded, moving deeper into the little room and peeking into boxes to examine their contents.

"Listen to this," Faizel cleared his throat and began, somewhat haltingly, to read the unfamiliar scrawl. "New cannon design was a success. Metal from cursed objects seems to keep its special properties and can be used as barrel—M. helped lots!—but still had to coat with two layers of primer. Should be able to handle even larger pirates. Hope to see design made popular, will sell to shipwright for high price."

He looked up at Larinna, his eyes twinkling with mischief. "I think this was an inventor's workshop, or something very much like it, and of course his design did indeed become popular in time. What a tinkerer he must have been!"

Larinna was still puzzling over Faizel's words. "Are you saying he invented magical cannons that could fit *pirates*?" she said, incredulously. "And you lot launch yourselves out of them?"

"Of course not," Faizel said, reproachfully. "That would be foolish."

Larinna flushed. "Well that's what I thought."

"It is much better to get someone else to launch you, if possible, so that they can aim."

"Yes, but," Larinna raised her hands in an exasperated gesture, "doesn't it hurt?"

"Only if you miss. Now *these* ..." Faizel exclaimed, pulling away a large waterproof sheet and examining the weapons underneath it. "These could be worth getting excited about, perhaps?" He pulled out a large rifle with a very long barrel and squinted down its sight. "Yes, I think these will be very useful indeed if our adversaries really have made it to Tribute Peak ahead of us."

Larinna, moving to appreciate a gilded sword hanging on a rack, couldn't help but agree, especially when she considered the chipped and blunted offering from Wilbur that currently hung at her side. "They're in superb condition, yes."

"Fashioned back when the world was new," Faizel mused. "The others will be very pleased, I think."

Working together, they carefully removed all of the weapons they could find from the dusty old workshop, along with a healthy supply of lead shot. With a gem-studded pistol at her side and the weight of a gleaming cutlass in her hand, Larinna felt far more confident about taking on any other crews who dared to stand in their way. As an afterthought, she carefully wrapped Wilbur's old sword in an oilcloth and placed it in a barrel for some down-on-their-luck wanderer to find in the future. *Give and take*, she thought with satisfaction.

They piled the rest into a large weapon chest and carried it gingerly to the gangplank, expecting to be met with congratulations for their find. The minute they saw Adelheid standing at the stern of the *Unforgiven*, however, they knew that something was wrong.

"We've got company," she said grimly as they approached. From this angle, the cave's opening gave them a narrow view of the ocean; by following Adelheid's outstretched finger, they spied the forbidding silhouette of another ship threading its way through the morning's mist. Larinna's eyes widened. "Don't tell me. Is that..."

"The *Black Gauntlet*," Adelheid said, grimly. "Scorched but not scuppered, it would seem." She kicked irritably at a chunk of driftwood, watching it skip across the water below. "We lingered too long."

"Assuming they know we're here," Faizel offered. "Perhaps they came to Thieves' Haven to lick their wounds, just as we did?"

Adelheid shook her head. "They'd likely have sailed straight inside if that was the case. Instead, they've been circling. No, they've got us trapped, and they know it. We'll have to—"

"Ned, *no*!"

The cry rang out with such ferocity that Ned actually jumped, poking his head up above deck as Faizel tore across the gangplank and snatched at whatever he was carrying. He held it at arm's length as he carried it well away from the *Unforgiven*, moving with such caution that the box might as well have been a fizzing powder keg. Larinna couldn't quite understand the reason for his alarm, though, for what he'd confiscated seemed to be just another treasure chest, albeit one with a very unusual design on its lid. It reminded her of something, but she wasn't certain what.

"What's wrong, Faizel?" Ned had moved to stand behind them, looking upset. "I couldn't find a way to open it, so I thought I'd bring it aboard for later."

"Well-intentioned as ever, my friend," Faizel said consolingly. "But with our luck so far, we scarcely need to be bringing a cursed chest with us on our voyage."

"Cursed?" Adelheid, who was a moment away from brushing the lid of the strange box with her fingers, jerked her hand away immediately. "What's wrong with it?"

"It is known as a Chest of Sorrow, though I have only seen one like it before," Faizel proclaimed. "If it is disturbed, it will begin to cry at intervals, normally when you least wish it to do so, until the box is opened. If we wait a moment, I'm sure you will see for yourselves..."

As they watched in horrified fascination, the design upon the box ran thick with moisture, and Larinna recognized what she was looking at: the face of a mer, at least as she'd heard them described, twisted in misery. Great rivulets of water began to gush from its large, mournful eyes, and a forlorn sobbing echoed throughout the cavern. In moments, a small waterfall was trickling over the edge of the walkway and into the seawater basin below.

"Anyone who unwittingly carries a chest such as this as cargo will soon find themselves quite flooded out," Faizel commented. "It is better for us to leave the wretched thing behind for some more desperate soul to take as a prize."

"Faizel," Larinna murmured, thoughtfully. "About those modified cannons you mentioned, I don't suppose you've seen any around Thieves' Haven? Any form of defense?"

"Only one, on the north face of the island, and one is not enough. You would get one surprise shot off, perhaps two, and then whoever is working the cannon risks being blown to pieces because they are a stationary target. We pirates are somewhat harder to patch back together than our ships, I am sad to say."

"You sound like you've got another plan," Adelheid challenged her. "May I remind you that your last scheme nearly cost us the bloody ship?"

Larinna scowled. "At least give me a chance to explain what I have in mind before you tell me I'm crazy . . ."

"You're crazy," Adelheid told Larinna for the fourth time, watching the taller woman slide herself awkwardly into the barrel of the cannon. "Insane, even. Have you any idea how difficult this will be?"

"You wanted me to trust you," Larinna grunted, squeezing her arms up in front of her so that she could reach out and accept the cursed chest from Faizel. She hoped fervently that the wretched thing wouldn't start sobbing while it was inside the cannon with her. "That's why I'm letting you take the shot."

"Yes, and since I first laid eyes on you, there have been plenty of times I've wanted to launch you into the sea. I just never imagined our lives would depend on it." Adelheid moved around to the back of the cannon and gave it an experimental tug, shifting the little circle that currently provided Larinna's only window into the world so that it pointed down toward the water. Far below, she could see the imposing form of the *Black Gauntlet*, its deck blistered and burned from the fire they'd started, several of its sails singed, but armed and ready for a fight. She could just about make out Captain Quince, motionless at the prow of the ship like a hunter watching a foxhole.

"Maybe a bit to the left," she said nervously. "And watch the angle, I don't want to skim like a stone. Oh, and did you remember to the factor in—"

Adelheid, with no small amount of pleasure evident on her face, fired the cannon.

Larinna's world exploded with a shockwave that started at her boots and ricocheted up through her body like a tsunami, rattling her from toes to teeth as she was flung through the air. She clutched the Chest of Sorrow like a lifeline, wearing an expression that somewhat resembled the design on its lid as the stinging wind brought tears to her eyes. Her hair whipped madly across her face, both ears still rang with the cannon's roar, and for a moment Larinna sailed helplessly across the sky, blind and deaf to everything.

She reached the apex of her flight and she blinked furiously as her stomach gave a lurch, forcing her eyes open a crack so that she could peer downward and work out where she was going to land. Worried that she might fall short of her destination, Larinna concentrated on bringing her knees up snugly against the bottom of the silver box and tucking in her elbows so that she was as small a target as possible.

Behind her, a second shot rang out, then a third as Adelheid put the second phase of their plan into motion. The cannon fire was designed to distract attention from Larinna—to make it seem like she was just another shot that had missed its mark and struck the water. Hopefully, no one would pay her the slightest bit of notice. If she was spotted, she was as good as dead.

The *Black Gauntlet* was directly underneath her now, her crow's nest so close Larinna felt like she could almost touch it. Fortunately, the crew were squabbling among themselves as they searched for the source of Adelheid's ambush, and no one thought to check the skies for flying pirates.

Now Larinna was level with the balcony that wrapped around the captain's cabin, and she had only a second to suck in a deep breath before the waves closed over her head. Her momentum carried her deep underwater, and she kicked out and up, turning as sharply as she dared. A few determined seconds of swimming saw her break the surface once more, alongside the bottom of a thin ladder that ran up the side of the *Black Gauntlet*.

Now comes the hard part, she thought, grimly, tucking the box under her arm as she grabbed the lowest of the rungs. The chest had started crying again, and she hoped that the wailing sound it made would be drowned out by the general commotion above deck, for Quince and his crew had begun peppering Thieves' Haven with cannon fire of their own.

Hauling herself halfway up the side of a moving ship with the soaking chest braced against her body was only half the battle. Next, Larinna was forced to awkwardly stretch her form as far from the ladder as it would go, allowing the soggy chest to dangle in her free hand before taking a one-armed leap toward the railings that bordered the captain's private deck.

She missed.

The *Black Gauntlet* had turned at the last second, sending the carved wood out of Larinna's reach as they swung, about to deliver another volley, causing her to splash gracelessly into the sea for a second time. Spluttering and swearing under her breath, Larinna was forced to climb the ladder once more. She was all too aware that sooner or later, someone was bound to peer over the side and spot her clinging to the ship like an unwanted barnacle to be disposed of.

Her second attempt to leap from the ladder to the railings, powered largely by a rising sense of panic, was more successful. Her outstretched fingers wrapped around a handhold, and Larinna swung herself forward, using her motion to toss the cursed chest aboard. It fell onto the balcony with a dull thud, and she followed it, hooking her legs around the bannisters so that she could topple onto the polished wooden planks on which the ship's captain might normally stand to enjoy the view.

Not the most elegant way to board a ship, Larinna considered, hoping that the others weren't watching her through a spyglass. She allowed herself a moment to catch her breath, keeping low against the polished wood, then tried the little side door that led to the captain's cabin from the balcony. Not only was the door open to the cool sea air, but the key was still in the lock, for Quince's hubris had blinded him to the possibility that anyone might dare sneak aboard his beloved vessel, and she was able to sidle easily inside.

As she'd expected, the level of opulence in the room was almost obscene. A thick carpet and numerous works of art added splashes of vivid color to the room, while feather pillows and silken sheets served to muffle her footsteps. She longed to steal a trinket or two as a memento, but she knew she had work to do and little time in which to do it. Dragging the captain's heavy desk up against the door that led to the main deck to block the entrance, she wedged the Chest of Sorrow beneath it. As if on cue, it had begun to sob furiously once again, and she hoped the *Black Gauntlet*'s cannons were loud enough to muffle the sound.

Larinna returned to the balcony, this time locking the cabin's side door for good measure in case any of the crew attempted to break into the cabin the same way she herself had, and consigning the key to the bottom of the ocean floor. She cast one final look through the windows, noting with satisfaction that the room was already partially flooded. Before long, she knew, the water would find its way through cracks and rivulets in the floor, dripping down and flooding the unheeded lower decks while the crew was struggling with the cannons above.

She dove overboard, then, staying far below the surface of the waves and out of sight until she was back at the entrance of Thieves' Haven. As she'd hoped, Ned and the others had finished their preparations and were waiting to cast off, the grin on Larinna's face telling them everything they needed to know about the success of her plan.

As the *Unforgiven*'s prow slid into the sunlight and the sails began to billow, her crew got a good look at the *Black Gauntlet*. She was drifting nearby and listing dangerously, her cannons silent as the crew splashed around inside her in search of a hull breach they'd never find. Only Captain Quince seemed to have guessed the true nature of the subterfuge, for he was slamming his stout form repeatedly and uselessly against the door of his cabin, crimson with exertion and fury.

Adelheid's crew favored Quince with a mocking salute as they passed, and each of them raised a tankard of grog, drinking cheerfully in a toast to his vessel's demise. If looks could kill, Quince's expression as salt water began to slosh into his boots would surely have blown them all to smithereens. They savored his rage until the *Black Gauntlet* dropped out of sight, lost beneath the crest of a wave, and the sea belonged to them once more.

RAMSEY

Rowenna,

How many months has it been since we last raised a glass together? Too long since you upbraided me for the mud and straw tracked upon your nice clean floor. To write to you is a poor substitute for standing in the warm light of your tavern. Do you still save a stool for me at the bar?

Truthfully, I would find no anger in my heart if you did not. Too many times now I have broken my promise to visit home. To visit her, if she will even see me. It is this place, Rowenna, this Sea of Thieves! Every day I wake to yet more wondrous sights and sounds, and every night I take my rest with the thrill of an adventure riding high in my heart. I cannot abandon it.

I finally have your present, a dueling pistol to hang above your bar. This is no ordinary pistol, though I shall wait until I am able to see your face in person before I say anything more. I wish I could say when that will be, for this night, the night on which I write to you at last, may be the most important night of my life.

What does it mean to be a pirate? Are we, as those back home would declare, mere thugs and criminals who seek to gain from the honest labor of others? Or is there more to the life than greed? Is it ambition that drives us or a desire to shape our own destiny? Tonight, I shall—

Ramsey, muttering under his breath as he always did when trying to grapple with the intricacies of the written word, paused midsentence as Mercia knocked on the door of his cabin. "The last ship just dropped anchor, captain. It's time we were going."

"Already?" Startled, Ramsey checked his pocket watch and realized that over an hour had passed since he'd settled at his desk to put his thoughts down on parchment. Grumbling, he got to his feet and fumbled with his greatcoat. Mercia couldn't help but notice he was dressed rather more finely than normal, but that was to be expected given what was about to happen.

Parley!

Even thinking the world sent a shiver of excitement through Mercia. To call so many pirates together in one place was a risky business, she knew. The odds were high that many of them would be nursing grudges against one another, whether from chance encounters on the high seas, long-standing rivalries that had hardened into bitter feuds over the years, or simply old-fashioned jealousy coming to the fore. Even pirates who had no quarrel could enter a parley with a handshake and leave with their fists swinging once the beer started to flow, decks of cards started to appear, and the first coins began to clatter down on tables. She'd only heard of a couple of such gatherings in her life, and most had ended in bloodshed.

Yes, a parley was a risky business, and though she had some inkling of what their captain was planning for the night, Mercia and the others had still spoken out about the need to be cautious. Shan had suggested holding several smaller meetings on neutral ground, but Ramsey stood firm. This, he said, would be the culmination of his plans, an all-or-nothing wager on the future of the Sea of Thieves.

In the end, they'd settled on inviting three crews to join them at a newly formed outpost known as Golden Sands, though the gathering was certain to attract a number of hangers-on, curious shopkeepers, and assorted ne'er-do-wells who'd turn up regardless. Each of the captains Ramsey had finally settled upon had made both a reputation and a fortune for themselves since their arrival at the Sea of Thieves, and all had expressed a desire to meet with Ramsey in person.

The first to arrive was Eli Slate, a brusque and straight-talking fellow with whom Ramsey had apparently had prior dealings. Mercia knew very little about him, but his ship was as sleek as they came, shining and polished with crimson sails and a brown bear figurehead. Ramsey had informed her that the vessel was named the *Morningstar*. Out of everyone at the parley, Mercia imagined that Slate would be the most easily convinced by Ramsey's proposition.

Nobody aboard the *Magpie's Wing* knew very much about Ramsey's second choice, though nobody could deny that he'd certainly made a name for himself. Captain Gideon Graymarrow was a wild and fearsome figure with a long coat and wild, unkempt hair that hung limply around his lanky frame. It was said that he demanded nothing less than utter loyalty from his crew and that his word was absolute—an unusual attitude for pirates on the Sea of Thieves, who tended to treat their crews as equals.

Graymarrow's crew was granted shore leave only rarely, and he himself set foot on land only when absolutely required. Shan expressed surprise that Graymarrow had bothered to respond to Ramsey's invitation at all, let alone accept. The enigmatic captain came ashore alone, leaving his ship—a stern and joyless vessel known as the *The Twisted Horn*—with its sails unfurled and its cannons primed, ready for the first sign of treachery.

The third invitee was something of a wild card, and certainly the most unpredictable guest. She was known only as Briggsy, a nickname she'd acquired thanks to an almost superhuman talent for breaking out of cells and jails of all kinds; she was considered something of a maverick even by pirate standards. She'd disappear for weeks on end and return with wild tales of huge creatures lurking in jungles, ancient stone golems springing to life to protect their treasure, and battles against entire fleets of enemy pirates who'd taken a dislike to her charm and obvious success.

Briggsy also seemed to change her crew when the fancy took her, sometimes leaving her own ship adrift while she sailed under someone else's flag. Nobody really knew what to make of her, but almost everyone *did* know of her, so clearly she was doing something right. Her ship, or at least the ship she'd arrived in, was a two-person sloop called the *Homeward Dove*.

Rathbone had volunteered to keep watch, but Ramsey wanted to show his crew at full strength, so together they locked down the *Magpie's Wing* and made their way to the tavern where the parley was to be held. They walked slowly, for each was laden with a number of valuables that would shortly become the primary topic of conversation for miles around. The culmination of Ramsey's plans, or so he hoped.

There were a few light cheers as Ramsey squeezed his bulk through the door of the tavern, for the drink was already flowing and pirates all around them were gambling, bickering, or singing the shanties whose words they could all agree on. Graymarrow and Slate were not drinking, however, merely standing at opposite ends of the tavern, stiff as statues, gazing levelly at one another and at the crowd without a flicker of emotion.

Ramsey grabbed a table in both hands, moving it into the middle of the tavern where everyone could see it, and on it he placed the box he'd carried with him from the ship. The others did the same, leaving a pile of gilded boxes in the center of the room.

These, as expected, drew the crowd's attention almost immediately, for they were of a design that none of the assembled pirates had ever seen before. Ramsey knew this with absolute certainty, because the chests had been created by his own hands, shaped with hammer and tongs at the forge until his hands blistered and sweat dripped from his brow. It had taken months of toil, brooding in the depths of Thieves' Haven among the husks of his failed attempts, but finally Ramsey was ready to return to the Sea of Thieves and claim his rightful place.

"My friends!" Ramsey bellowed, banging two tankards noisily together and quelling the conversation. People were already beginning to shuffle into a loose circle so they could get a look at the enticing treasures atop the table. "The last time I addressed a crowd in this way, it was on the eve of our return through the Devil's Shroud. We brought with us what we believed to be great treasures—fine rubies and emeralds, golden crowns and silver bracelets for all to see!" The crowd cheered at this, and several mugs were drained.

"The truth of it," Ramsey continued, "was that we had not yet begun to comprehend the real treasures that awaited us here. Since then, we have all sailed out upon these vast and untamed waters. Sometimes we have been allies, sometimes we have been opponents. All of us have learned that the world is stranger and more dangerous, more alive and fantastic than we ever could have dreamed. Ours is a world of great power and terrible curses! Of vast riches and ancient knowledge that lurks beneath the waves. It is a world so full of mystery and wonder that we could journey for a hundred years and every day it would bring us something new.

"They call this place a Sea of Thieves. But if that is all we are, if we allow our greed to consume us, if we continue to prey upon one another and to steal from a fellow pirate's pockets instead of celebrating their glory and achievements, then thieves is all we shall ever be. I say to you tonight—rogues and rascals, scoundrels and scallywags alike—that there *can* be a better way for all of us."

"The strong prey upon the weak." It was a hoarse, croaking rasp of derision and it was coming from Graymarrow, who had yet to move from his spot in the corner. "That is not folly, Ramsey, that is fact. A fool who can't hold his tongue will feel a fist upon his lip, and a pirate who cannot hold on to his gold will wave it goodbye. Who are you, so high and mighty, to tell us that we should be ashamed to think that way, eh? You, who lost his fortune when his hideout was turned over not one year ago!"

This last comment drew a laugh, but also a few jeers and calls of derision—mostly, Mercia noticed, from a gang loitering in the shadows at the back of the room. There was something vaguely familiar about them, though she didn't recognize their outfits.

"Too right!" called a voice from the crowd. "I came here to get away from Trading Companies and soldiers trying to tell me what I can and can't do! It's my life and I'll live it how I want. Take what I want!" This, too, got a cheer from the back of the crowd.

Captain Slate, who had lit his pipe during the exchange, blew a gently smoking O across the tavern and coughed, lightly. "I agree, at least in principle," he stated to the room at large. "We're alone out here, and that gives us our freedom, but these are strange shores. If we keep blowing each other to pieces, squabbling over the same handful of coins, there'll come a day when none of us can afford to patch up our ships or buy a barrel of grog for our crew. But what are you suggesting, Ramsey?" He turned to face the man he was addressing. "Some kind of treaty? *Rules*?" More jeers, louder this time.

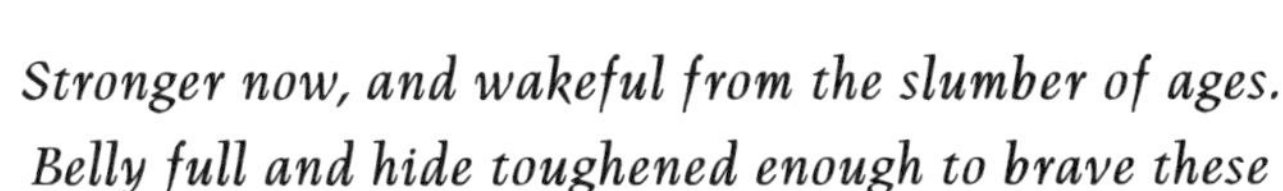

Stronger now, and wakeful from the slumber of ages.
Belly full and hide toughened enough to brave these
unfamiliar waters. Searching and seeking . . .

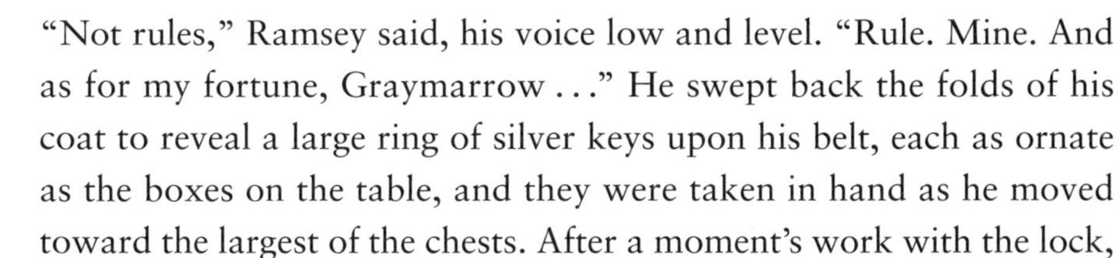

"Not rules," Ramsey said, his voice low and level. "Rule. Mine. And as for my fortune, Graymarrow . . ." He swept back the folds of his coat to reveal a large ring of silver keys upon his belt, each as ornate as the boxes on the table, and they were taken in hand as he moved toward the largest of the chests. After a moment's work with the lock, the lid swung open and every pirate in the place leaned forward greedily. Ramsey had chosen carefully, arranging eye-catching gems and his shiniest gold pieces in a way that practically begged to be sifted and run through grasping fingers.

He let the crowd drink in the sight, just for a moment, and then shut the lid firmly, locking the chest again and slipping the keys back out of sight. "All that I lost in my hideout that day, everything that those cowards took from me, that was barely a day's plunder!" he boasted. "This is just a fraction of my fortune, and I'll give it to the first person that can open this chest." He hefted the box as he spoke and placed it in the middle of the floor, stepping deliberately away.

The room was silent for a moment as more than a dozen pirates stood staring at the little box, as if trying to work out what trick Ramsey might be playing on them. Finally, Briggsy hopped up onto her table and used it as a stepping-stone to leap nimbly over the crowd and land theatrically next to the box. "I shall be your first volunteer, Captain Ramsey," she declared, sinking down beside the box and drawing an oilskin pouch from a pocket on her breeches. This, it soon became apparent, was filled with a number of slender tools designed to pick and jimmy: the arsenal of a born burglar.

As Briggsy set to work, a number of coin purses began to appear, and soon wagers on how long it would take her to pick the lock were being tossed back and forth. Shan seemed to ingratiate himself into the crowd with remarkable speed at that point, spitting into his hand and shaking in any number of bets with half a dozen different pirates. More beer was served, and the conversation begin to swell once again as Briggsy, tongue poking impishly between her lips, probed and poked at the chest with practiced ease.

As a full five minutes passed, however, then another ten, the good humor began to sour. Pirate after pirate lost their bets, handing over gold to Shan with reluctance. Finally, Briggsy gave a little grunt, and there was a click, a snap, and her broken tools dropped to the floor next to the firmly locked chest. She swore, scowled at Ramsey, and made a very particular gesture at the box before skulking to the bar to drown her embarrassment in a tankard of grog. There were a few boos and hisses in her direction, but those were quickly silenced when people saw the furious look on her face.

"You put on a fine show, Ramsey," Slate said wryly, "but I'd wager brute strength'll succeed where skill fell short." He accepted a large sledgehammer from one of his crewmen, who'd been sent to procure it from the outpost's shipwright. He too had come to watch the show, and was now leaning his burly frame against the door in bemusement.

Slate approached the box, getting a feel for the weight of the hammer in his hands and taking a couple of practice swings. At last he gave a grunt of effort and the great metal oblong descended, striking the lock once, twice, three times. On the fourth blow, the head of the hammer came away from its wooden handle, arced neatly through the air, and landed on the foot of a nearby pirate, much to the amusement of his crewmates. Slate, panting, stooped down to glare balefully at the lock, which hadn't been so much as scuffed by his efforts.

More pirates came forward then, one after another, goaded into action by their crewmates and emboldened by drink. One plied the lock with a red-hot poker; the next took a stout woodcutter's ax to the lid itself. Another insisted on placing the chest in the tavern's fireplace until it glowed red-hot, but it came no closer to catching aflame. Even when it was cooled in the rain barrel outside, it remained as pristine as the moment Ramsey had first presented it.

Finally, the box was returned to the table by a luckless and exasperated Graymarrow, who'd unloaded the contents of his pistol against the hinges and succeeded only in burning his own fingers. Crews muttered among themselves with more and more outlandish ideas, but no one else came forward. The box, it seemed, had defeated the lot of them.

Gliding through current and tide, letting the pull of hunger light a path to the distant prey, their scent diminished by time but not forgotten . . .

Finally, Ramsey got to his feet once more. "All that I have claimed from across the Sea of Thieves is now secured in chests like this one. A chest whose lock cannot be picked," he announced, his eyes gleaming. "A lock no shipwright can force open, and whose contents cannot be spilled by the blow of an ax or the ravages of time. A chest that can only be opened by someone with a suitable key."

"You're forgetting one thing, Ramsey," Slate cut in. "Just because I can't open this box of yours doesn't mean I can't take it from you. Hide it somewhere you'll never find it, or cast it to the bottom of the ocean."

"A pirate never forgets." Ramsey was smirking now. "I have another chest here, as you can see." He patted the lid of it, fondly, before pushing it forward so they could all make out the crudely carved etching atop the lid. It looked like two tankards clinking. "There's a fair bit of gold in this one, too. Who among you would like to try and carry it back to their ship?"

This time, no one seemed to want to be the first to volunteer, and almost a full minute passed before someone stepped forward. To everyone's surprise, it was the shipwright. "I may not be much of a pirate," he said thoughtfully, "but I reckon I can haul that box back to my workshop easily enough. And if I do, Cap'n, will you hold up your end of the bargain and open it with those fancy keys of yours?"

"Certainly I shall," Ramsey agreed, and the assembled crews began to flood outside, shivering and stamping their feet in the cool night air. Groups of onlookers lined the path between the tavern and the shipwright's premises, with excited whispering as to what effects this second box might have upon the unsuspecting craftsman.

The shipwright himself looked a little uncertain as he approached the chest, grasping its handles firmly. He stood for a moment as if waiting for some nasty surprise or other, then turned and marched smartly toward the exit. He reached the tavern door at a brisk pace but suddenly staggered hard into the wall. Rebounding unsteadily, he bumped against the doorframe before finally making it outside, for his legs seemed determined to move in opposing directions.

"Hell's bells!" he uttered, stumbling this way and that, crashing noisily into a pile of barrels as he lurched about. "I've not touched a drop in five years, but I feel dizzier than a bellboy in a brewery!" The crowd doubled over with laughter at every stagger and crash the shipwright made as he swayed along the path, but he managed to take step after faltering step, making it as far as the dock before the chest's effects finally overcame him. The box slipped from his grasp, his eyes rolled up into his head, and he tipped sideways into the water. There was a great round of applause, and a few kinder souls moved to help the stricken man back to dry land.

Graymarrow faced Ramsey now, but he wasn't laughing. "So it's sorcery you've turned your hand to, is it?" he demanded. "Going to trade your captain's hat for an alchemist's robe, perhaps? How many nights did you spend working on that box of tricks when you could have been out with your crew, drinking and fighting and looting like the rest of us?" Some sixth sense made Mercia glance across at Rathbone just then, but his expression was inscrutable.

Ramsey raised his voice so he was addressing the crowd rather than Graymarrow. "Magic is alive and well on the Sea of Thieves. There's no point denying it. I see a couple of you in the crowd with golden fingers from handling forbidden coins, or a cursed bracelet you can't seem to take off. I say we shouldn't fear what we can't understand. Not when we can use it to our advantage, as I have."

Closer still to the little shapes that flit where the world ends.
There are so many different sizes and smells and tastes.
Soon it will be time to feast ...

Ramsey planted one booted foot on the cursed chest as he continued. "I called you here today to extend an invitation: membership in a union of pirates under my command. An alliance, if you prefer. One that agrees never to steal from one another, to come to each other's aid when needed, and to keep the pirate ways alive out here. To guard the secrets of this place, and to share what we learn amongst ourselves.

"In return, you'll get your own chests, just like mine, to store the vast fortune we'll be finding. Chests that'll curse any pirate who tries to steal them, and chests that only you'll be able to open—because you'll have one of my special keys."

The whole outpost seemed to erupt in a storm at Ramsey's words; no one seemed to know quite how to react to the enormity of what he was proposing. Staring across at his crew, Ramsey could see similarly conflicted expressions on their faces. The alliance was a part of his plan that he hadn't dared speak of to them, not even while Shan worked to shape the cursed metal into functioning locks and Mercia carefully applied the devious curses she'd devised.

Graymarrow began to move, and as he did, a strange silence fell upon the crowd. He strode so close to Ramsey that their noses were practically touching, and his raspy voice shook with fury as he spoke. "Those words," he snarled, "are an insult to every pirate here. To pirates everywhere. Ye dare suggest that we all should dance to the tune you're whistling and follow your orders just because you've dreamt up a piece of hocus-pocus or two!" He spat at the chest, contemptuously, a wad of tobacco striking Ramsey's boot. "To have us sail out in your name while you tell us how to think, how to live, like some kind of Pirate Lord!"

His rage was echoed in a number of angry shouts from around the outpost, and Graymarrow pushed rudely past Ramsey, up to the dock where his ship was moored. "Well hear me well, Ramsey. I'll be damned before I ever strike a bargain with you!" He strode out of sight, and a few moments later the *The Twisted Horn* vanished into the gloom.

Barely anyone saw the ship leave, however, because those final words had ignited sudden quarrels between groups of formerly friendly pirates. Slate in particular was in a heated conversation with his crew, though whether or not he'd been swayed by Ramsey's offer was impossible to say.

Ramsey let out a great sigh, turning to find Mercia at his side. She had quietly reclaimed the sealed chest from its spot in the tavern and was now watching the arguments blaze around them, her face blank. "What did you think?" he asked her, finding himself oddly keen to seek her approval.

"I think you should have been completely honest with your crew," she said coldly, though her expression softened a little when she saw his shoulders sag. "Some will never agree to an alliance, Ramsey, but a few might. Once they've had chance to sober up and think it through without worrying about their pride, perhaps." She laid a hand on his arm. "Rathbone and Shan are already heading back to the *Wing*, and I think we should join them."

Ramsey looked older than Mercia had ever seen him as he nodded wordlessly, stooping to pick up the chest at his feet. They'd barely made it halfway along the boardwalk, however, when a loud warning bell rang out from one of the docked ships. Another joined it, and another, forming a jangling cacophony that echoed around the outpost and caught everyone's attention. Shan was bellowing over to them, screaming a word from the deck of the *Magpie's Wing*, but there was no way to hear him over the sudden panic.

Pirates all around them were breaking into sprints, racing back to their ships to deal with whatever might be happening. Ramsey and Mercia did likewise, uncertain as to what could rattle such a huge number of experienced pirates.

They were almost home when the sea itself seemed to explode, showering the outpost with mist and spray and violently rocking every ship that was docked there. Suddenly, they understood what Shan had been trying so desperately to tell them.

Kraken.

LARINNA

Nobody was trying to kill them, and that made Larinna very nervous indeed.

Just as they had feared, the crew of the *Unforgiven* had arrived at Tribute Peak—a squat and gloomy island located at the heart of what Faizel had referred to as the Wilds—to find that another crew of pirates had gotten there first. There had been no roar of gunfire by way of a welcome, however, and the mercenary ship hardly seemed ready to launch an ambush. Her sails were furled, her cannons silent, and—when Adelheid cautiously had them pull alongside—her decks were empty.

"This is a very strange way to behave, yes?" Faizel commented, unnecessarily, as they boarded, moving below decks with their swords drawn and pistols at the ready. "To leave the ship unguarded like this?"

"Well, they were expecting us yesterday," Adelheid reminded him. "Perhaps they assumed we'd been sunk and went ashore to get the treasure for themselves."

"If Athena's Fortune really is here, it would be a tempting prize for any crew," Faizel agreed, then pouted slightly as he saw Adelheid's glare. "Please do not be angry, Captain. You talk in your sleep, that is all."

Adelheid harrumphed, but said, "Very well, so we all know what we're looking for. First things first, though, we secure this ship and moor the *Unforgiven* somewhere out of sight. I don't want anyone stealing away with her while we're ashore." Though they searched the abandoned vessel from end to end and back again, the only signs of life turned out to be a couple of scurrying weevils.

Ned offered to transport a few of the ship's furnishings back to Adelheid's cabin and restore some of its former glory, but she shook her head. "If all goes well, we'll need every last inch of room for the plunder we'll be bringing home," she assured him.

"Yeah, but . . ." Ned protested. "What if all doesn't go well?"

"We'll be dead."

"Oh." Ned seemed satisfied enough with that answer, and together they nestled the *Unforgiven* beneath a rocky outcropping that hid her from view before heading ashore, crunching across a barren coastline made of glassy, volcanic rock.

"*On strangled shores, my ship you seek*," Larinna recited from memory, "*Begin your search at Tribute Peak*. . . . Well, here we are. Now what?"

"It is like a riddle, you see," Faizel explained as they picked their way across the uneven stones. "Every mind is different, so we must think of it like a puzzle to be solved. The word *shores* means we are more likely to find what we are seeking along the coast than inland, for example."

"Fair enough, but *strangled*? What is there that strangles?"

"Snakes?" Ned offered, helpfully.

"Badly fitted shirts?"

"A gallows?"

"Vines!" Adelheid said, confidently, pointing forward with her sword. Ahead of them the craggy shoreline curved sharply outward, and they could see that the rocks and outcroppings up ahead were coated in a thick latticework of brambles, sickly green with blood-red thorns peppering their length. In the very center of the twisting forest, they could just about discern the remains of a small sloop that had been consumed by the crawling creepers, its rotting hull barely visible within the overgrowth.

"I'd say that more or less describes a ship if we're being generous," Larinna said dryly. "Simeon must have been caught up by a storm or a tidal wave of some kind. What do we do next?"

"We still need to get closer." Adelheid drew her sword once more, as did the others, and little by little they hacked their way toward the beached wreck. Even with the fresh blades they'd acquired at Thieves' Haven, it was hard work, and Larinna swore once or twice that a few of the brambles she chopped away regrew themselves shortly after.

Eventually, they reached the remains of the sad little sloop. As Adelheid held the riddle up for the others to inspect, more words seemed to flow across the page as if penned by the hand of some ghostly author. *That's why we had to steal the original parchment*, Larinna realized. *The riddle only reveals itself in stages.*

Once the words had settled down, four more lines had appeared on the scroll. Adelheid flipped it over in her fingers so that she could read the new directions out loud.

I joined the birds atop their roost
And once inside I soon deduced
My place below the tumbling sands
With light and shadow 'neath my hands.

The four of them mused on this for a moment. "Well, we have to start somewhere," Adelheid said. "I assume there must be some birds somewhere on this wretched island. Does anyone have any idea how we'd go about finding where they like to sleep?"

A thunderous blast made them all jump out of their skin, and they turned to glare at Ned, whose smoking pistol was still aiming into the sky. As they watched, he pointed to the distant hilltop where a startled flock of seagulls were circling, having been startled by the sound. After a few moments, they disappeared back into the shadow of a large cave mouth high on the hillside. "Up there, maybe?"

"Very good, Ned my friend," Faizel said happily, patting him on the back, or at least as far up it as he could reach. "Although perhaps a little warning next time will help keep my gray hairs at bay for a few years longer, hmm?"

Larinna was staring at the distant cave. "That's a long way up," she said, doubtfully. "D'you think there's a pathway?"

"Only one way to find out." Adelheid took the lead, chopping and slicing once more until they were clear of the vines and could move more freely toward the base of the hill. There did seem to be a path of sorts: a narrow trail that zigzagged its way through more of the jagged rocks. It was narrow, and one side dropped treacherously away into a tangled, thorny jungle down below, but it was the only way they could see to reach the bird-filled cave.

They picked their way up the hillside single file, taking their time and stopping to fill their flasks at a shallow pool. The water was cloudy here and tasted slightly sour, but they choked it down regardless, for the day was sticky and deceptively warm. Little by little they ascended and were almost to the summit when Larinna felt the hairs on the back of her neck rise.

She couldn't explain which slight sound or shifting of shadows first gave her the clue that something was wrong, or what survival instinct it was that compelled her to scream, "Get *down*!" before flattening herself against the rocky wall with her arms spread. There was a tremendous series of crashes and booms as huge boulders tumbled down from overhead, carrying dust and smaller stones in their wake. Larinna scrabbled around, blinded for a moment by clouds of grit and dirt, trying to get a sense of the others. She wondered helplessly if they'd had time to avoid the deadly avalanche, or if the rocks had carried them helplessly down the hillside.

She heard a bellow of pure rage; a voice so deep and loud it just had to be Ned. As the dust settled, Larinna saw that he'd thrown his bulk across both Faizel and Adelheid to protect them and was now bleeding from a dozen places, though this didn't seem to slow him down. He began to leap from rock to rock, climbing with remarkable speed.

Overhead, Larinna could make out the crew of the ship they'd discovered, all of whom were scrambling for their weapons. Clearly, they hadn't expected any survivors of their little ambush, least of all ones who were now lunging toward them with murder in their hearts.

Larinna got to her feet and took the longer way around, sprinting around another bend in the path and arriving just in time to flatten another one of their assailants with a roundhouse punch that sent her tumbling over the cliff with a scream. Ned, who'd reached the high ledge a moment before, had grabbed two more of the pirates and was robbing them of their will to fight by repeatedly banging their heads together.

That left one, who was already backing away down the trail until the point of Adelheid's sword in his kidneys convinced him that it would be a really, really good idea to stop moving.

"That was a dirty trick," Adelheid hissed viciously into the pirate's ear, "and it might almost have been a clever one except for one thing: *You missed.*" She watched as Ned released his two opponents, tossing their limp forms into the sticker bush below. "Luckily for you I want some answers, so that gives you a few more minutes to enjoy walking and talking."

"Do your worst," the pirate growled, yellowing teeth bared in a snarl of defiance. "I've got nothing to say to the likes of you!"

"Oh." Adelheid looked a little crestfallen for a moment, and then shot him.

The pirate's mouth was an O of surprise as he slumped downward, his prone form tumbling along the steep path before vanishing over the edge, but Adelheid was already striding onward toward the looming cave mouth. The others had no choice but to pursue her, hands moving to their lanterns as they pressed on into the darkness of the cave.

Far below, in the jungle, the fallen pirate's body began to fade, outlined in an ethereal fire. After a moment, it was as if he'd never been.

"That's creepy."

Staring down the long canyon ahead of them, Larinna found herself agreeing with Ned. The cave had eventually given way to a narrow gully, one in which the sky could be glimpsed high overhead. It was tall and imposing, and both walls were lined with hundreds of roosting seagulls.

They could feel pair after pair of beady black eyes staring down at them as they walked in single file, keeping conversation to a minimum and trying very hard not to think about what they were treading in. No one wanted to risk causing another panic that would result in a whirlwind of beating wings, scrabbling talons, and above all, lots of very *nervous* birds over their heads.

Fortunately, the canyon soon opened out and they left the squawking birds behind, stepping into a large chamber lit only by shafts of weak sunlight that made it through the cracked ceiling. It was manmade, clearly, though it looked far more ancient even than the fort at which they'd encountered Simeon.

Huge square panels coated the walls, each adorned with a single symbol, while four braziers marked the corners of a raised stone dais at the far end of the room.

The centerpiece of the whole chamber, however, had to be a large, bowl-like shape forged from bronze and suspended near the ceiling. It was filled with a fine golden powder, and the stopper wedged at its lowest point suggested that, should someone give the dangling rope a good tug, its contents would swiftly pour out and into a small aperture below.

"Tumbling sands, indeed," Faizel remarked. "Though I see nothing to suggest a light or a shadow. Do you think we are perhaps supposed to wait until nightfall?"

"Not a chance," Adelheid said, firmly. "Not when there could be more pirates on the way." She reached past Faizel, grabbed the rope connected to the bowl's huge cork, and yanked on it as hard as she could.

As the first grains of sand tumbled through the air and vanished into the darkness, the chamber seemed to transform itself around them. The wall panels, which had previously been little more than unremarkable slabs of stone, began to shine brightly with a number of luminous symbols. Larinna moved swiftly to the center of the chamber along with the others, trying to take it all in as the hiss of the pouring sand intensified. *A mountain. A tree. Some sort of lizard. A swirl that could be anything.*

Faizel had moved to a stand by a panel with a crown on it, tracing his fingers across the glowing shape to discover that it moved beneath his fingers. He pushed experimentally, and the stone recessed into the wall only to slide back into place the instant he relieved the pressure.

Larinna kept searching the walls, cursing Adelheid's impatience. Already, the sand had dipped below the rim of the bowl and they were no closer to understanding the meaning of the riddle. If they ran out of time here, she suspected there'd be no second chances. Their quest would come to an abrupt end, and they'd be sailing home shamefaced and empty-handed.

A bird, a wave, a flower, she thought desperately. *An eye, a sun, a skull . . . wait.*

"I think I've got it," she called, vaulting over the dais to stand by the panel that bore the sun's likeness. "This symbolizes light, right?" She pushed against the stone, feeling it slide back into the wall with a satisfying click. "Now what about shadow?"

Now it was Adelheid's turn to stare around at the walls as the last of the sand began to trickle away. Finally, she spotted what she was looking for—a circle divided by a curving crescent, which she could only hope symbolized the moon to whoever had devised this strange test. She lunged across the chamber, almost tripping, and her hands struck the panel just as the last grains of sand dropped out of sight.

All at once, the symbols winked out, and the stone was nothing but stone once more. Larinna didn't dare speak, let alone move her hands away from the panel she was pushing against. Had they been too late? Was their answer even correct?

There were four low pops, and the braziers around the central dais came to life one by one, their flames precisely matching the colored symbols. Only then did the dais itself begin to glow with the same bright lines as they'd seen on the panels, only far more intricate. Sweeping curves wrapped around complicated squiggles etched in stone, while wavy lines forked and forked again before disappearing.

"It's a map!" Faizel exclaimed, triumphantly. "A map of this island! *Hah!* How much more elegant than a piece of parchment! Have you ever seen anything like this, Adelheid?" He began to trace his fingers over the lines and contours, scrutinizing the dais intently.

"Never," she admitted, "but then this is no mere treasure box we're going after. This is Athena's Fortune! It makes sense that it would be well protected."

"And possibly well guarded," Faizel mused. "What does the riddle say?"

Adelheid blinked, clearly having forgotten the parchment in her possession. New words were already forming, and she spread the parchment so they could all read the newly added verse.

A fallen titan lies alone
Glory waits upon her throne
To reach the sanctum will require
A gift to match his heart's desire.

No sooner had Adelheid finished reading this out loud than the images upon the dais began to fade, growing dimmer and dimmer until the detailed map was quite unreadable. Finally, even the braziers snuffed themselves out, and the chamber was quiet and still once more, perhaps forever.

"Wonderful," said Adelheid, bitterly. "Now we'll have to scour the entire island, and who knows how many more hidden passages this place has in store?"

"Scour? I think not," Faizel replied, a mischievous grin on his face. "I shall lead the way, yes?"

"You worked out the riddle already?" Larinna asked, dubiously, dusting off her hands and settling in at the rear of the group. Faizel would not be drawn as to their next destination, however, clearly enjoying being in charge for once. Larinna felt tempted to shake an explanation out of him, given how serious their situation was, but Adelheid seemed content to let him have his fun.

They passed back through the gully of slumbering seagulls and emerged from the cave atop the rocky hillside. They couldn't see any new sails on the horizon and dared to hope that the other ships might finally have given up their pursuit of the *Unforgiven* and her crew. But they kept a wary lookout just to be safe having come too far and sacrificed too much to let complacency prove their undoing.

They followed the coastline for a full hour under Faizel's direction, edging along rocky outcroppings and hopping nimbly from stone to stone to cross a frothing river rapid. Finally, the pathway opened out onto a vast plateau, and the sight was nothing short of breathtaking. Ten enormous statues rose before them, easily over a hundred feet high, carved from the same glassy rock that formed the island's shores. Each was of a human figure, some male, some female, and each was seated in a high-backed chair with an expression of stern, blank-eyed benevolence on its face.

"Are they kings and queens?" Larinna asked. She had learned very little about royalty growing up. Anyone who might have arrived on her home island wearing a big gold crown and declaring they were in charge would have soon been sent on their way again, only without the crown and whatever else they'd arrived with.

She had to admit that the enormous statues resembled what she'd imagine a king or a queen to look like, though. Even the statue at the far end of the line, which had toppled from its perch at some point in the long distant past, had an untarnished nobility about its weather-worn features. "Wait, this is the fallen titan, isn't it, Faizel?"

"I should say so, yes!" Faizel clapped his hands expectantly. "And how impressive she is! I would say that they look like gods and goddesses, myself, but I suppose it doesn't matter one way or the other." They were standing in the shadow of the statue now. It rose like a high cliff overhead, huge enough that they could have lit a campfire in her palm.

"Athena was a Goddess..." Adelheid mused. "But you're right, Faizel. What was the second line? Something about glory upon the throne?"

One by one, they looked up at the gigantic monument on which the statue had once been seated—a vast lump of rock that rose imposingly into the sky. They made a complete circuit, hoping to find some handholds or other means of purchase, but the edifice was as smooth as glass, sheer and unclimbable.

"We could try the cannon trick again," Larinna said doubtfully, but Adelheid shook her head. "There's no way to get the *Unforgiven* close enough, and even if we could, it'd be like firing you at a wall—funny but wasteful." She smirked at Larinna's expression, and added, "Maybe we're looking at this the wrong way. What if this is about width rather than height?" To illustrate her point, she stood in the gap between the base of the throne and the cracked torso of the statue and spread her arms out wide.

Faizel clearly understood what their captain was implying, for his eyebrows shot up in surprise. "I know that you have always been the most nimble of us all, Adelheid, but this strikes me as foolhardy even by your unparalleled standards of recklessness. Surely you have not forgotten that unfortunate incident at Devil's Ridge?"

"Nor have I forgotten that you still owe me five gold pieces," Adelheid snapped. "I can do this. I'm probably the only one who *can* do this, unless any of you has a better idea." She looked from one to the other as if challenging them to speak up, then began to fiddle with the buckles of her coat. Once divested of her heavy outer garments, her feathered hat, and anything else that might weigh her down, Adelheid seemed suddenly a lot smaller and quite a lot younger.

She gave a sardonic bow, for pirates never curtsied, and turned to face the statue. "Be nice to me, lady," she told it sternly, then stepped right up toward the huge face and began to climb. The statue's carving, not to mention its collapse, had left a series of small cracks and grooves here and there. Adelheid used these to ascend, wedging her stockinged toes into gaps and clinging stubbornly to the stone with numb fingers. It was slow going, even so, and at one point she had to reverse her course and seek a different route when a promising handhold crumbled away.

At last, she stood atop the statue's shoulder and took the opportunity for a brief rest, waving merrily down at her crew far below before setting off once again, tracing the outline of one immense limb. Larinna and the others kept pace with her on the ground, losing sight of the distant figure from time to time as it was obscured by a curve of the arm or a sharp fold of the great stone cloak.

Finally, Adelheid reached the point where the body of the broken statue came to an abrupt halt, leaving empty air between her and the throne's enormous seat. The wind whipped at her hair as she assessed the distance. *It can't be more than ten feet or so*, she told herself crossly. *You've managed that before. You can make this easily. It's definitely possible. Definitely probable, anyway. Maybe. And a little scary. But everyone's watching…*

"Oh, what the hell," she muttered, and leapt.

There hadn't been space for much of a run-up, but a life spent leaping about the rigging, bounding between ships during raids, and outrunning anyone who might want their money back had served Adelheid well. Even so, her outstretched fingers were barely able to grasp the ledge that formed the seat of the throne, and she struggled to keep her purchase on the smooth stone as her legs scrabbled.

Inch by inch, muscles screaming in protest, she brought her hands farther and farther onto safe ground, then her forearms, and finally she hauled herself to safety, rolling onto her back and offering silent thanks as she stared up at the reddening sky.

"You alive, Captain?" Ned's voice echoed up, and Adelheid peered over the side of the throne at the distant figures, giving another wave before clambering to her feet and looking around. There wasn't much to see, for the plateau was largely featureless save for some sort of raised plinth tucked away in the corner. She ambled over for a closer look, rubbing her fingers to work the feeling back.

It reminded her of the ship's capstan, and as she got closer she could see that it turned in much the same way. Bracing herself, as the rock beneath her was slippery, she began to spin the contraption clockwise, wondering if anything would happen and how she'd know when it did. She found perspective suddenly shifting, for each turn seemed to lower her down into the stone…

Larinna, who was leaning against the base of the throne far below, jumped and spun around as the monument suddenly came to life beneath her shoulders. An imperceptible crack was beginning to widen in what had seemed like a featureless surface, and an entire section of the throne's base was retracting, swinging open by degrees as Adelheid worked the mechanism far above.

Before long, a wide entranceway revealed itself, and light flared as the pirates peered into the darkness. It was Adelheid's lantern, for she was perched atop the capstan inside, the mechanism having descended fully into the throne. "Miss me?" she asked glibly, before insisting that they wait for her while she retrieved and replaced her clothing and accoutrements. "Better," she admitted, adjusting her hat. "Now I feel like a pirate again."

The passageway beneath the huge throne descended sharply, with flight after flight of stairs spiraling around a treacherous gap. Faizel could not resist dropping a stone down into the shaft, counting the seconds in a low voice and waiting for the echo to come. It didn't.

They took each step cautiously, for a few were beginning to crumble, and the deeper they went, the more perilous their route became. Before long they were being forced to take exaggerated strides over gaps in the stairway, and finally small leaps to get from step to step.

They were all very grateful when the stairs finally came to an end and another passageway beckoned, for it seemed far more navigable and they were already exhausted. They moved through the gloom for only a few hundred yards, however, before they came across the door.

It was sturdy, made from two huge slabs of carved stone covered from floor to ceiling in yet more markings. It was ornate, with a pattern of diamonds around a large golden key with a hole in its center. And it was, much as Ned heaved and strained against it in an effort to force the stones apart, most definitely locked.

"What now?" Adelheid asked, impatiently. "There has to be some way through, now that we've come all this way. Another puzzle, perhaps?" She traced her fingers across the metal of the key shape as if she could somehow force her brain to comprehend it.

Faizel, who had been studying the door for a long while, coughed. "I cannot say for sure, of course, but take a step back. Does the design not seem at all familiar to you?"

Adelheid did as she was asked, pursing her lips and looking for all the world like she was assessing a piece of fine art. "I suppose," she said slowly. "It looks similar to the crest of the Gold Hoarders. Not that that helps us in any way."

Larinna had no clue who the Gold Hoarders were, though she vaguely remembered hearing their name mentioned once before, but that didn't matter. She was running the final lines of the riddle over and over in her mind. Finally, she stepped forward. "Does anyone have any money?"

Adelheid gave her a strange look. "No, because it's all on the other side of that door," she snapped, then her expression grew curious. "What are you up to now?"

"I just need a coin," Larinna persisted. "You mean to say we haven't got a single gold piece between us?" Looking at the shame-faced expressions of the others, she sighed deeply and reached into her own pockets, finding only a handful of coppers left over from her trade with Wilbur. It felt like a lifetime ago.

Sighing, she sank to the floor and began to tug at her boot, feeling the familiar weight of her last gold piece in its usual resting spot, and tugged it free from between her toes. She held it up for a moment, inspecting it somewhat sadly, before moving forward and placing it in the hole at the very center of the key. *This has to work*, she thought. *What else would be a gold hoarder's desire?*

To her relief, the coin seemed to do the trick. The two stone slabs slid slowly apart with a deep grinding noise, startling a few beetles and revealing yet another passageway. No more words of wisdom from Simeon appeared on the parchment this time, though they stared at it intently. It seemed as though their journey had reached its end.

"Well now," Adelheid said finally, folding up the parchment for the final time and drawing her sword. "This is where things get exciting."

RAMSEY

Every pirate knew about krakens. More precisely, every pirate knew another pirate who knew *another* pirate who swore they'd had a close encounter with one. The descriptions varied wildly depending on the story and who was doing the telling of it, but a few things were always the same.

Krakens were huge behemoths, made even larger by the mass of writhing, squid-like tentacles that surrounded their bodies, with great maws that gaped open at the end of each tentacle. Krakens were ferocious, seeking out passing vessels and the tasty morsels that crewed them in order to drag them down into the deep and feast. Krakens were patient; they would lie in wait for weeks or even months and sleep for so long, incautious sailors would often mistake them for small islands.

For all that Ramsey knew about krakens, and that included sailing his ship through the bones of Old Mother, seeing a living, breathing specimen was like nothing he'd ever imagined. It reared up out of the water, casting its long shadow over the shops and stalls that clustered around the dock. While the beast was only a fraction of the size of Old Mother, whose beak would have been enough to swallow a ship whole, it was still far larger than any of the ships it seemed to be sizing up.

Probably deciding how it wants to tackle the menu, Ramsey thought grimly. He bounded up the gangplank with Mercia in his wake and was gratified to see Rathbone and Shan already loading the cannons. There was no use attempting to outrun the creature, not when the wind was so unpredictable. Besides, if they fled, the beast would surely turn its attention to the outpost, raining down destruction on the boardwalks and buildings and leaving the place in utter ruin. Given how many people Ramsey had invited here tonight, he knew he had to stay and fight—at least, long enough for everyone else to get away.

And if I win, he thought grimly, *I'll hang its skull from my wall. As soon as I've built a big enough wall, that is.*

Ramsey lumbered up to the helm, the *Magpie's Wing* still rocking fiercely beneath him as the kraken churned up the water and sent heavy waves crashing toward the dock. Once they'd weighed anchor, Ramsey tugged hard at the wheel, bringing the ship into a defensive position that cut a path between the outpost and the first approaching tentacles. If he could get the kraken's attention, he hoped, he might be able to lure it out into the deeper water.

Another ship cut across their bow, moving at speed, and Ramsey recognized the distinctive bearlike figurehead of Slate's ship, the *Morningstar*. Her deck was busy, thronged with not just the crew but also several of the outpost's regulars, including the shipwright who'd tangled with the cursed chest. They were ferrying supplies and hefting cannonballs, eager to help defend their livelihoods in any way they could. The two captains locked gazes for just a moment, and Ramsey found himself grinning. He hadn't expected aid in this fight, but he was grateful indeed to receive it.

The kraken was closer now, more details visible in the gloom. It looked old, Ramsey realized, and littered with ancient scars, bite marks, and deep cuts from long-forgotten battles; its coloring was blotchy, and only one of its saucerlike eyes seemed to have any sight to it. The other was scabbed and healed over, or perhaps even missing entirely beneath the wound.

Just because it was old, Ramsey knew, was no reason to take the beast lightly. Age just meant experience, after all, and since he doubted any pirate on the Sea of Thieves had fought a kraken before, the creature would have no trouble dealing with them. Given all that, there was no reason not to strike first.

"*Fire!*" he roared, and the starboard cannons sang as they unleashed four shots directly at the looming behemoth. Almost reflexively, two of its huge tentacles lashed out, absorbing three of the blows with their thick and scaly suckers. The fourth cannonball struck home against the mountain of flesh, but the impact seemed to do little. The *Morningstar* had better luck, cutting in at a steep angle and managing to score two hits of its own against the creature's side.

The kraken's rubbery limbs slammed down against the water in retaliation, perilously close to the prow of the *Magpie's Wing*. The ship was tossed backward, landing heavily in the waves with a blow that staggered everyone aboard and made her rock violently. For a moment, Ramsey feared that the flailing appendage might crash down again and cleave his ship neatly in two, but the leviathan's attention was diverted by another volley from the *Morningstar*'s guns.

"All we're doing is making it angrier," Mercia screamed. "We can't keep this up forever!" Already, one of the mighty tentacles was snaking beneath the surface of the waves, gliding with a terrible grace to curl up and behind the hull of Slate's ship.

The great limb erupted from the water, soaking everyone aboard, and suckers the size of barrels latched onto the deck while the very tip of the tentacle began to wrap around the main mast. Even at this distance, there was an audible creak as the kraken began to squeeze.

Scrambling to reload while the *Morningstar*'s crew and passengers began to hack frantically at the tentacle that had snared them, Shan and Mercia concentrated their fire on the same outstretched limb, hoping to cause the kraken to withdraw. The more their shots struck home, however, the more the kraken seemed determined to crush the life out of the little ship.

This isn't working, Ramsey realized. *But it has to have a vulnerable point somewhere; everything does.* His hand went to his spyglass, wishing he could get a clearer look at the fate of the *Morningstar* through the spray and the darkness, and that was when he realized. *Its eyes. Something's already claimed one*, he thought. *If we can finish the job, it'll be blind.*

"Shan!" he called, hoping his voice would carry through the chaos. "I've got an idea, but I'll need some time to pull it all together! Can you keep the beast busy for me?"

Shan nodded. "I've got a little snack in mind that should keep it occupied for a while." Ramsey gave a grim smile of satisfaction before thundering down the stairs and disappearing from sight below decks.

As Rathbone reluctantly seized control of the helm, Shan likewise left his post with a plan of his own. He delved into the captain's cabin and emerged a moment later, a small silver box clutched tightly in both hands. He muttered a few of the words Mercia had taught him and closed the lid before calling out to Rathbone. "Take us in closer! I'm only going to get one shot at this!"

"A shot at what? Isn't that a treasure chest?" Rathbone snapped, irritably. "What are you going to do, bribe the kraken to death?"

"It's cursed," Shan called back, already halfway up the ladder that led to the crow's nest. "It's one that cries! I'm going to toss it right into the belly of the beast, give it a stomachache it won't forget in a hurry." He leapt onto the ship's rigging with the chest in hand, balancing precariously as the *Magpie's Wing* tipped this way and that.

The others looked decidedly unconvinced by the plan, but Rathbone reluctantly steered the ship toward the hulking mass of the kraken's body, weaving to port and starboard at random in a bid to evade the thrashing tentacles. It was a risky maneuver, made even more dangerous by the thudding of yet more cannon fire, for the kraken had moved within range of Golden Sands Outpost, and those on land were doing everything they could to keep it at bay.

In the distance, there was a terrible splintering sound as the power of its tentacle finally proved more than the *Morningstar* could bear. Her great masts snapped first, sending a colossal mess of sails and rigging down into the sea, and then the hull began to splinter and buckle under the pressure, caving in beam after beam, crushing the wood inward, and finally splitting the entire ship in two.

Those aboard her were forced to hurl themselves overboard to avoid being dragged down along with their luckless vessel. They paddled amid the wreckage, helpless and terrified, for they were too far out to swim for safety, but the kraken ignored them for now. It had brought its attention to bear on the *Magpie's Wing*, the impetuous little ship whose actions had disturbed Old Mother's remains and that now bobbed tantalizingly before it like a mouse that had strolled into a lion's waiting jaws.

The huge arms engulfed the vessel in a stench of rotten meat so strong Mercia had to fight down the impulse to be sick, and the kraken let out a shrill, deafening screech quite unlike anything they'd heard before.

Shan, trusting his instincts, chose that moment to hurl the chest at the looming creature from his vantage point, a motion that sent him tumbling back to the deck with a loud thud and a grunt of discomfort. Had it been packed with treasure, the little box would surely have fallen pointlessly overboard, but Shan's aim was true and his arms were strong—they sent the cursed container directly into one of the gaping maws at the end of the creature's tentacle. Shan let out a triumphant shout, but it died half-formed, for he'd been a second too slow.

Rather than the chest sailing effortlessly down the creature's gullet and into its stomach as he'd hoped, the box had stuck and caught awkwardly in the kraken's tentacle maw and temporarily wedged in place. Confused, the kraken began to shake the tentacle this way and that, flaying the surface of the sea. It was certainly preoccupied, but its powerful tentacles would only take a moment to crunch down upon the little box and reduce it to nothing more than splinters.

Mercia turned to Shan to console him for his near miss, and found him cramming his elderly frame into one of the ship's cannons. "What are you doing, you idiot!" she gasped, moving forward and intending to yank him forcefully out of the barrel.

"Finishing what I started," Shan said stubbornly, glowering up at the stricken kraken. "We haven't got long, Mercia. Launch me. Please."

Realizing that every second they spent arguing made the idea more dangerous, Mercia reluctantly lit the cannon's fuse and hauled the heavy barrel upward until she was sure Shan wouldn't simply hurtle helplessly into the sea. *This is insane*, she thought, *I'm firing my friend straight into the clutches of a thing that wants to eat him.* Still, there was something about Shan's quiet confidence that told her this wasn't their final moment together.

The blast sent Shan hurtling through the air, his arms and legs splaying as he landed just below the beast's struggling maw. He'd already drawn his sword, and now he plunged it deep into the ruddy flesh so he had something to cling onto as he pounded at the stubborn box. The kraken paused momentarily, confused and irritated. It wasn't used to its food volunteering to be eaten, and certainly not to finding it fighting back.

The Chest of Sorrow bawled with even greater intensity, and suddenly, the repeated impacts dislodged the gushing chest, and it disappeared down the kraken's maw, unleashing a great burp of putrid air. If anything, this only seemed to enrage the creature further.

Shan had already let go of his blade and was somersaulting backward through the air; even so, the snapping tentacles missed him by mere inches as the kraken lunged toward the infuriating little morsel that dangled before it. He landed hard, the wind knocked out of him as he struck the water, and Mercia could do nothing to intervene as the monster bore down upon him with a flurry of enraged tentacles.

As Mercia opened her mouth to scream Shan's name, she realized she could hear another sound—a song that had gone almost unnoticed beneath the beast's thrashing but was now getting steadily louder.

Much to her relief, she could make out silvery shapes darting nimbly just underneath the waves, easily dodging the clumsy tentacles as they made their way toward the vulnerable man in the water.

She couldn't help but cheer as Shan was taken in strong, scaly hands, spirited away from the kraken, and carried safely back toward land at a speed not even the *Magpie's Wing* could match. In the distance, she spotted yet more merfolk coming to the aid of those who still floundered amid the wreckage of the *Morningstar*. That left...

Just us, she realized. "Rathbone, we need to get out of here, now!" As if to underscore her point, the kraken's tentacles were closing in on them from all directions, for they were now the only thing standing between it and Golden Sands. Skilled though Rathbone was at the ship's wheel, they were being besieged on every side by curling, grasping limbs, and every strike seemed to be coming closer. "Ramsey," she howled at the silent stairwell, "We are *running out of time*!"

Their salvation came not from their captain, who was still working feverishly below decks, but from a hail of harpoons that soared over the *Wing*'s prow. They struck a thrashing tentacle that lay directly in their path, causing it to retreat below the waves and clearing a way for the ship to escape the creature's clutches.

Twisting around to stare behind her, Mercia spotted Briggsy almost at once. She would have been hard to miss. The young pirate was whooping and howling, standing on the prow of the *Homeward Dove* and calling the kraken every rude word Mercia had ever heard, along with quite a few she hadn't. Briggsy seemed to be sailing solo aboard the little sloop, allowing the wind to carry her freely while she focused on skewering her foe.

Rathbone wasted no time in using this new distraction to their advantage, finally freeing the *Magpie's Wing* from the tangle of tentacles and pulling up alongside the sloop. "I could use a little help at the helm," Briggsy called up when they were within range. "I feel like I'm going in circles right now."

Mercia shot a questioning look over her shoulder at Rathbone, unwilling to leave him steering the ship alone. "Go!" he shouted. "It's not like our cannons are hurting it anyway!" Nodding silently, Mercia dropped over the railings and landed on the upper deck of the *Homeward Dove.*

The sloop was small and swift; together, she and Briggsy darted here and there to make their marks, Mercia deftly steering them away through the danger while Briggsy stuck spike after spike into the kraken's hide. The beast itself seemed to be suffering now, both from the stings they'd inflicted and from the effects of the cursed chest in its belly. Its movements were becoming more erratic, as it had lost all interest in the outpost and was now fixated on the *Magpie's Wing*, which it seemed to consider the cause of its discomfort.

Rathbone was fleeing into open water now, leaving Mercia and the outpost far behind as the *Wing* became the kraken's sole target once more. Even with the ship at full tilt, the huge creature was gaining. The largest of its tentacles was once again drawing level with the stern when Ramsey finally reappeared on deck. In his arms, he cradled a large cask of the sort used to store supplies, its lid nailed shut and its contents a mystery.

"Sure I used to have more of a crew than this," he grumbled. "Get us in closer, Rathbone! I need to stare that thing right in its eye." Without waiting for a response, he moved to the cannon and began to load the barrel inside.

Rathbone's lip curled in a sneer. "You're going to hit it with a wooden barrel? It'll shatter in a second!"

Ramsey had finally had enough of Rathbone's attitude. "Obey my orders for once in your wretched life!" he thundered. "Get us in closer, I said!"

Rathbone's lips pursed into a thin line, and his shaking hands gripped the wheel so tightly he half expected to snap it in two, but he spun the wheel nonetheless. The *Magpie's Wing* turned as sharply as it could manage in the gusting winds, moving closer and closer toward the sopping beak as tentacles bore down upon them from every angle. Ramsey stood with his hands braced upon the cannon he'd primed, glaring at the beast as if they were lifelong foes.

The kraken roared, and Ramsey stood firm as the great creature advanced on him. He waited until they were close enough that he could see himself reflected in the creature's hate-filled eye, and only then did he fire the cannon.

The force of the blast reduced the barrel and its contents to an expanding cloud of hot shrapnel, which was precisely what Ramsey had been hoping for. He'd packed the cask with all the gunpowder they had left, then thrown in shards of broken bottles, old nails—even salt and pepper from the tiny kitchen. Everything aboard that could sting, burn, or blind was striking the monster's unprotected eye with the speed of a cannon's fury, and the response was as violent as it was impressive.

The kraken screamed, each of its tentacles going rigid at once, and then it began to thrash wildly, for it could no longer see beyond a searing fog of crimson pain. Deprived of its vision, with its belly swollen fit to burst with water and a hundred aches and pains from where the cannons were striking home, it had finally had enough.

The leviathan lowered its huge body into the sea, sinking back into the safety of the waters where fire couldn't burn its eyes and little boxes couldn't choke it, out of reach of the stinging ships. It released great clouds of murky ink, clouding the waters so that its great bulk was obscured and no more harm could come to it, for today's battle had nearly been its last.

Beaten as it was, however, the wounded creature did not retreat quietly. Its tentacles were still looming over the *Magpie's Wing*, bobbing her this way and that as they were dragged back below the surface. The flailing limbs smashed down toward the little ship that had proved impossible to devour, and their final, sightless blow struck home.

Hundreds of pounds of blubbery flesh smashed into the deck, crashing directly onto the cannons where Ramsey was standing in triumph. He attempted to leap out of the way, but the ship tipped wildly under his feet. He stumbled and fell, and the tentacle's great weight came down upon his left leg.

Now it was Ramsey's turn to roar in pain, and to scrabble at the deck as the departing tentacle ripped away the railings. One by one, the cannons tumbled overboard, and Ramsey followed them. Had the ship not righted itself at the last minute, he would have been lost. As it was, he was left clinging to the shattered woodwork with one white-knuckled hand. He dangled and swore, his leg hanging uselessly below him, unable to find purchase for his free hand. His grip on the slimy wood was slipping inch by inch, and his boots kicked out at empty air.

With a yelp, Ramsey fell—and there was Rathbone, grabbing Ramsey's wrist tightly and lying spread-eagled on the deck. They stared at each other, eyes locked, but Rathbone made no move to pull the larger man back aboard. After a moment of staring into Rathbone's pitiless eyes, the helpless Ramsey realized that his crewmember had no intention of doing so.

"See what your grand alliance has brought you, Ramsey?" he hissed. "A broken ship, a missing crew, and an empty hold! Haven't got a magic chest to get you out of this one, have you?"

Ramsey's eyes burned like black coals, but his voice was calm. "I don't need a lecture from the likes of you, Rathbone. If you're going to drop me, be quick about it."

"Oh no, 'Captain.'" Rathbone leaned farther forward so that their faces were barely a foot apart. Down below them, foamy water rushed past, for the wounded ship was still speeding along unguided. "You're finally going to listen to me, just like you should have been doing for the past two years instead of letting the others fill your head with nonsense."

The *Magpie's Wing* tilted and Rathbone grunted, readjusting his grip so that Ramsey's weight didn't send them both sliding overboard. "Mercia and her mermaids!" he continued. "Shan and his crackpot inventions! Your very own *pirate paradise*! It's a delusion, all of it, because nothing matters but the gold! And when the gold runs out, it's time to move on."

"Gold can't watch your back," Ramsey growled. "You think you can make it out here alone?"

Rathbone laughed loud and long at this. "I'm not alone, you old fool!" he chortled. "I've never been alone, not since I gave my friends their map to the Sea of Thieves. Oh, they struggled out here at first, but they were able to set themselves up quite nicely once I told them how to find Thieves' Haven. I made sure they took my belongings along with everyone else's, of course, so that you didn't get suspicious. We've been doing quite well for ourselves these last few months, though of course you were so busy with your magic boxes you didn't even realize I was gone for days at a time!"

Rathbone's tone was bitter now. "But why should I have expected anything else? You've kept secrets from me ever since we found this place. Me, a member of your crew! Luring me out here with promises of incredible wealth and then demanding I kick my heels in a filthy hideout because you fancy yourself some trumped up Pirate Lord! Well, that claptrap about an alliance was the last straw. You want to rule the Sea of Thieves, Ramsey? You don't *deserve* her! Not one coin."

Rathbone reached forward with an outstretched hand, and Ramsey was powerless to stop him from curling his fingers around the chain that held the set of silver keys. He yanked, hard, pulling his prize greedily toward him. "Everything you've ever plundered, sealed away in unbreakable chests that only these keys can open," he mused, in a singsong voice. "That is what you were boasting about, isn't it? Well, it may take a while for my friends and me to find them all again, but you can consider them a long-overdue payment for my services! I'm resigning my position, by the way, not that you need a crew anymore."

For a moment it looked like Rathbone was ready to fling Ramsey into the sea, and then something about the hand he was clutching caught his eye. "A black diamond ring," he commented. "Oh, but that's your *wedding* ring, isn't it? I'd quite forgotten you had someone special back home."

Greedily, his fingers prized the thin band from around Ramsey's bloodstained digit, pulling it free and slipping it onto his own index finger. "Perhaps you should have stayed at home with your feet under the kitchen table instead of getting in my way all these years. Though I suppose she can't have been that special, not if you left her behind to come and play at being a pirate." He tutted. "I wondered if she knew how little you really cared about her."

At this, a wordless, primal snarl shook Ramsey's whole body, and he leapt forward like a predator springing for the kill. Had Rathbone not smartly released his grip and cast the captain disdainfully overboard at that moment, Ramsey would surely have ripped the man apart.

As it was, his bearlike form simply plummeted, hands clutching uselessly at thin air, and Ramsey briefly struck the hull of the *Magpie's Wing* with a dismal crunch before disappearing under the waves.

16

LARINNA

Sword in one hand and lantern in the other, Adelheid strode confidently down the newly opened corridor, though she'd taken fewer than a dozen paces when she felt something plucking at her sleeve. To her surprise, she realized it was Faizel. His face, what she could see of it in the lamplight, displayed none of his usual confidence. Rather, she could see something was bothering him greatly, and she slowed to a halt. "What is it?"

"I, ah, that is to say," Faizel shifted from one foot to the other, miserably. "While it is undeniably true that we have overcome many obstacles already, are we really absolutely certain that we want to be poking our noses into a room with *that* symbol on the door? The riddle did declare these ruins to be a sanctum of some kind, after all."

"Who are the Gold Hoarders, anyway?" Larinna put in, eager to be on the same page as the rest of her crew for once. "Is this their hideout?"

Adelheid looked from one to the other. "Fine," she said finally. "Let's talk about it. And no, the Gold Hoarders as we know them today are just another Trading Company. Probably the oldest Trading

Company out here on the Sea of Thieves, now that I come to think about it, but this place is far older."

"They sound more like a gang than a business," Larinna commented. "What do they trade in?"

"Gold." Adelheid caught Larinna's expression and huffed. "Look, most of the treasure you can dig up around these parts is sealed away in chests, right? They won't open and there's no point trying to break into them. Well, the Gold Hoarders have a special set of skeleton keys that are the only way to get the chests open."

"So *they* say, at least," Faizel added. "But if you ever find such a chest, you can take it to one of the Gold Hoarders and they will give you a cut of what's inside it. It is said that back in the day they used to sail the Sea of Thieves themselves, but as their fortunes have grown and their interests in the wider world have expanded, they've become little more than merchants. They prefer to send pirates to collect any chests they hear about, and such information normally comes from..."

"The Order of Souls," Larinna finished, understanding beginning to dawn. "Well it doesn't sound like they're much to worry about, so what's the problem here?"

Faizel looked uncomfortable again. "The problem, as you put it, is that the Gold Hoarders took their name, and their crest, from the group's founder, and *he* is said to still walk the earth to this day in an endless search for treasure. If Athena's Fortune ever did exist, then this first 'Gold Hoarder' would surely be the one to possess it. Even after death, he, by all accounts, is a fearsome fighter and not to be taken lightly. So you see, we may well be walking into great danger."

"Yeah, but that's what pirates do, innit?" Ned said. "'Sides, ain't no skellie ever gotten the best of us. Why should this one be any different?"

"I agree with Ned," Larinna said hotly. "There's four of us, and this place was clearly built to protect something good. I want to know what it is."

Adelheid held up a hand. "All right, all right. We agree this is a risk, and we're all tired. Let's press on until we can find somewhere to make camp, then have a rest and some provisions. Whatever's waiting for us, we might as well face it with our bellies full."

The prospect of a hot meal was enough to quell their doubts, and they resumed their descent into the ruins. There was life even this far underground—strange, blobby mushrooms that pulsed unnervingly to the touch, and even areas where ancient tree roots had forced their way between the stones in search of water, bringing with them patches of moss and fungus.

The deeper they traveled, the more evidence they discovered of a much older expedition: piles of old rope and chain, discarded swords, and even an old notebook. Someone had gone to the trouble of chopping logs for firewood, and now they were stacked neatly in a corner, grayed by dust and time. Faizel pointed out that if people had been here, skeletons could also linger, but although the crew kept their weapons at the ready, no rattle of bones disturbed them.

Eventually the passage widened out, and they found themselves staring across the width of a deep fissure that had created an underground ravine. The splashing of distant waterfalls echoed around them as they contemplated their next obstacle—an old wooden rope bridge that spanned the chasm. It was ancient, it was rickety, and it appeared to be the only way across.

"That," said Ned, "is the kind of bridge you need a spare set of breeches on the other side for."

"Poetic as ever, Ned, my friend." Faizel gave one of the two ropes that served as handrails an experimental tug. "But I do not think this bridge will be the end of us. It has spanned this chasm for a hundred years, why should today be any different?"

"Today it's got me walking on it, that's why," Ned said stubbornly. "And what about when we has to come back wiv all the 'eavy treasure?"

"One problem at a time," Adelheid said firmly. "And one pirate at a time. That's how we'll cross, and we'll keep both our hands on the rails and never put both feet on the same plank." She placed her first booted foot on the bridge, as if daring it to defy her by collapsing, and began a series of slow, measured steps out over nothingness. Watching her traverse the swaying bridge was the longest two minutes of Larinna's life, but the antique craftsmanship had stood the test of ages, and eventually Adelheid stood on the far side of the ravine, beckoning them over.

"I should go last," Ned said miserably, staring down into the abyss. "That way you'll all be on the other side when it collapses under me."

"Don't talk that way," Larinna said, sternly. "Besides, you need to be on the other side, so that you can grab my hand when the damn thing collapses under *me*." This earned her a little smile, and Ned inched his bulk out onto the bridge. It creaked and swayed with each one of his huge steps, and once or twice he froze in place as a board buckled beneath his feet, but by cajoling and coaxing him, the rest of the crew managed to talk him safely across. Faizel went next, rather more confidently now that he'd seen the bridge carry Ned safely across the ravine, and lastly it was Larinna's turn.

She was almost halfway across, easing her foot onto the next plank, when it suddenly surrendered to gravity and fell away into the chasm. She teetered, caught in the act of shifting her weight onto thin air, and was forced to throw herself forward across the gap, clinging onto the rest of the planks for grim death while her legs flailed over empty space and the others shouted her name in alarm.

Slowly, barely daring to breathe, Larinna tensed her stomach and dragged her legs up onto the precarious walkway one at a time until she was resting on all fours, staring down into the blackness. It took several deep breaths before she could bring herself to pull her hand away and reach blindly for the handrail, but finally she was able to raise herself off her knees and back to a standing position. She gritted her teeth and stared straight ahead, crossing the rest of the way without incident until she was able to sag against the comforting stone of the far wall, the others clustering around her in concern. "Never again," she said firmly. "I'm just going to live down here forever, all right?"

"Be careful what you wish for," Adelheid remarked, and then added: "There's a chamber up ahead that's as good as any to rest in. There's even a spot for a fire. We'll all feel better with some grub inside us."

She was quite correct, for Larinna found her spirits somewhat restored after just a few mouthfuls of the thick stew Faizel somehow prepared at a moment's notice. He seemed to be back to his chatty old self, too, and while they were eating, he asked everyone what they intended to do with Athena's Fortune, should it truly be waiting for them somewhere down below.

"I'd spend it," Adelheid said firmly. "On the sleekest, fastest, ship I could find. Hand-stitched sails, a custom-made figurehead. I'd want everyone to know when Captain Adelheid has arrived, and to run to the tavern so they could hear all about my adventures. And no one would dare cross me on the waves, either, because my cannons would always be loaded and my sword would always be sharp. The Order of Souls would be coming to *me* for work. What about you, Larinna?"

"The first thing I'd do is pay a team of craftsmen to come down here and fix that bloody bridge," she replied, wryly. "And then find somewhere to stash it until I needed it, I suppose. Use it to buy a ship and go sail out to the places no one's been yet. Be the first. Faizel?"

"I would use it to make the tavern keepers of the world very happy," Faizel said promptly. "Everyone would have a friend in Faizel, yes indeed, and there would be no end of shanties to sing and jokes to tell. Living well and eating heartily with a smile on my face until I am old and gray."

"Well, I like things just as they are," said Ned, a trace of stubbornness in his voice. "So you can all have my share if it means we can still be a crew and fight skellies and things." The others laughed at this, but not unkindly, and shortly after, Adelheid declared it was time for them to move on.

Snuffing out the fire and packing up their belongings, they set off once again, wondering what trials awaited them farther below. It took Larinna a few moments to realize she'd forgotten her own lantern, which still sat on the ledge where she'd been reclining back at the camp, and she hoped there were no more trials ahead that might require it.

The ancient ruins seemed to have given up putting the pirates through their paces, however, and no more puzzles or traps lay before them. Before long, the darkness began to ease gently away, and soon they could see well enough to hood their lamps, though the light spilling out from the room ahead had a strange tint to it. As they entered the final chamber, it was easy to see why, for Simeon's memories had proven their worth after all.

The room was vast, larger than any they'd seen so far on their quest; it could easily have accommodated the fallen statue they'd seen above ground. Its true dimensions were impossible to determine, however, for every corner was piled high with veritable mountains of gold and jewels. Almost all of the heaps were larger than they; great mounds of treasure piled up with no rhyme or reason that they could see. All of it sparkled peacefully in the flickering glow of a hundred burning torches that lined the walls.

Wordlessly, jaws agape, the pirates spread out across the room and began a closer examination of the treasures. Circlets lined with rubies, golden chalices studded with sapphires, ornamental knives, and totems of forgotten gods—if it was made of precious metal, it was here, all surrounded by innumerable golden pieces.

Now that Larinna's eyes had adjusted, she could see that the walls of the room had been augmented with scaffolding that seemed to stretch, haphazardly, all the way up to the ceiling. Large wooden planks had been nailed down to create a series of broad platforms bridged by walkways, and these were loaded with treasure chests of all shapes and sizes. She had the sneaking suspicion that the great piles of gold had been plundered from these chests, the boxes themselves stored like trophies that loomed precariously overhead, ready to come crashing down upon their heads.

Adelheid broke the silence, giving voice to what each of them was thinking. "This is impossible," she croaked. "It would take ten lifetimes to carry this back to the surface."

"And if you did, you would also need a fleet to transport it," Faizel said softly. "More than a fleet, a whole navy, perhaps. Is this Athena's Fortune, then? The great treasure of the Pirate Lord? Something does not sit right with me about all of this, Adelheid! What if it is cursed in some way?"

"Then we'll be the richest cursed pirates anyone has ever seen," she snapped. "Ned, you can help me look for the stuff that's worth the most. Faizel, get some of those chests down here, we'll use those to haul our pickings back to the ship. Larinna, see if you can find another way out of here. There must be a back door to this place, somewhere."

Larinna nodded, making her way between the piles of gold and checking every corner carefully. Knowing the predilection of whoever had built this place, she suspected that any shortcut to the surface would most likely be a secret passage locked away behind a stone panel or shifting door. She hoped it hadn't been buried underneath yet another mountain of treasure and forgotten about.

She rounded a corner and stopped, for her instincts told her that something here was different, and after a moment's reflection she realized what it was. One of the torches was streaming slightly, its flame angling slightly to the side. When she reached up in front of the flame, Larinna could feel the light breeze that was disturbing it, a coolness that raised goose bumps on the back of her hand.

She traced the source of the draft to a large piece of stonework that, sure enough, turned out to be a secret panel—one that had been prevented from closing properly by a discarded silver goblet. She suspected that the tunnel led all the way to the surface, though she wasn't about to venture into the darkness without her lantern to find out, and so decided to rejoin the others and let them know what she'd discovered.

Larinna was halfway across the length of the chamber when she saw it happen. Ned had spotted a large golden tankard, its surface studded with iridescent gems, half-buried under yet another mound of riches so that only part of it was visible. He clearly believed it was worth salvaging, for he grasped the glittering handle and tugged as hard as he could.

The tankard came free from the treasure in which it had been buried, but so did the skeleton that had been holding it, apparently slumbering under the golden pile. It yanked its prized possession out of Ned's grasp in irritation before tilting back its head and preparing to take a mighty swig of some long-forgotten grog.

For a moment, everyone stood transfixed as a single dust-colored spider tumbled out of the empty tankard and scurried away, for its contents had long ago drained dry. The skeleton appeared to stare in fury from Ned to the tankard and back again, as if Ned were somehow to blame for the situation, before letting out a rattling cry.

Many more of the piles began to shake, and Larinna realized that the room had been occupied all along, its undead inhabitants slumbering underneath the treasure just as they had been content to bury themselves within the rubble back at the skeleton fort. She let out a cry of alarm, for Adelheid was standing in front of the largest pile of all, staring across at Ned in shock, and hadn't noticed that the riches behind her were also tumbling away and spilling across the floor.

The figure, slowly revealed by the collapsing treasure, was lounging obscenely on a golden throne. Much like the other skeletons Larinna had seen, parts of his body had fallen or rotted away—but the hulking cadaver appeared to have found a unique if macabre solution to the ravages of time. His lower jaw and many of his missing teeth had been replaced by a facsimile made of shaped gold. His eye sockets held two large emeralds that seemed to burn with a mysterious energy all their own, and a large crack in his forehead had been crudely patched with a large golden medallion.

If there was any doubt that this terrifying amalgamation of bone and bullion was the Gold Hoarder, the medallion's crest—which matched the symbol on the door—confirmed it. Even now, he was reaching slowly toward the unwary Adelheid with a sharp-fingered golden claw that had supplanted his right hand.

Larinna made to shout a warning, but with her attention so focused on the others, she'd forgotten that she, too, was standing amid vast mounds of treasure. A skeletal hand burst forth from a pile to her left, then another, wrapping around her arm and tugging at her. She stumbled, her feet slipping on the coins at her feet, and slammed into the hoard with a yelp. The impact was enough to send the whole thing cascading down to the ground, leaving her sprawled next to another skeleton, which snapped angrily at her until she took its lower jaw clean off with a vicious right hook.

Fighting a shiver of repulsion, Larinna rolled on top of the skeleton she was grappling with and did as she had seen Adelheid do, grasping what remained of its head and heaving until the bones went still beneath her. She threw the disembodied skull as hard as she could across the room and against the wall where, to her deep satisfaction, it smashed. There was no time to gloat, though, not while the others were still under attack by the rest of the undead sentinels.

As the one who'd disturbed their slumber, Ned seemed to have drawn the bulk of the skeletons' ire, and three of them were currently clinging to him as he staggered around the chamber. One of them wrapped its bony arms around his neck from behind and began to choke him, forcing Ned to stagger backward and slam repeatedly into the wall with all of his might. There was a series of deeply unpleasant crunching noises, and the bony body turned limp, toppling to the floor as Ned pulled away. The others were flung aside, buried under yet more collapsing treasure.

Faizel, high up on the maze of walkways, was also struggling. The skeletons were leaping nimbly from platform to platform with practiced ease to assail him from all sides, and Larinna knew he was the least practiced fighter among them. Faizel was forced to duck a sweeping sword attack, swinging around the heavy chest he was holding in a move that, mostly by pure luck, took his opponent's head clean off.

But it was Adelheid who seemed to be in the most danger, for she was facing off against the Gold Hoarder himself, having spotted him looming above her at the last possible second. Her sword was drawn, but the intimidating figure was easily parrying her attacks using a stout shovel that was almost as long as Larinna was tall. Whatever the Gold Hoarder chose to use it for—digging up yet more treasure, she supposed—it was clearly able to double as a weapon, and now its long handle whirled like a staff, its sharp blade slicing closer and closer to Adelheid with each passing second.

Larinna broke into a sprint, drawing both her cutlass and the pistol she'd claimed from Thieves' Haven, but more skeletons were bursting forth from the sea of treasure that surrounded her, many with weapons of their own. She found herself forced to fight, lashing out with her cutlass in between potshots at the skellies threatening Faizel overhead.

The onslaught was relentless, and Larinna found herself forced backward away from her crew, scrambling onto a pile of casks at the rear of the chamber. Holding the high ground kept her safe from the approaching skeletons, hacking and slashing at any who dared get too close, but it meant that she was stranded, left separated from the others.

It also meant to she got to see every little detail of what happened next.

One of the skeletons advancing up the walkways toward Faizel swung its sword in a lazy arc that the pirate barely managed to dodge. It was a heavy blow, strong enough to reduce several wooden beams to matchsticks, and as it passed Faizel, it ripped savagely through the precarious scaffolding. The chests on the platform above began to spill and tumble as the remaining supports gave way, and as one in particular struck the floor it began to tremble ominously. A *cursed chest*, Larinna realized, and a powerful one by the looks of things. The rumbling intensified and a moment later the box exploded like a powder keg.

The blast was enough to trigger a landslide of silver and gold. More and more of the precariously packed chests were tumbling now, supports giving way one after another like dominoes. At last the whole thing gave way, collapsing with an almighty thud that shook the chamber and sending Faizel and his attackers out of sight.

Adelheid shrieked out Faizel's name, and in that instant the Gold Hoarder was upon her, eager to claim the life of the woman who'd come to plunder his hoard. He picked the struggling pirate up with his solid gold claw and slammed her down against the treasure-strewn floor with all of his considerable might. All Larinna could do was watch helplessly as he pinned Adelheid down beneath one booted foot, raised his shovel high in the air and brought it down with a savage strike aimed directly at her heart.

The last she saw of Adelheid was her motionless form upon the floor of the treasure chamber as the Gold Hoarder stalked away, and then the rest of the chests came crashing down, trapping Larinna behind a mountain of masonry and stealing her captain from her for good.

RAMSEY

It was a sunny day, which would once have pleased Rathbone endlessly. He had lamps enough to see by, of course, and a fine coat to drape around his shoulders for warmth, but the sunlight had a way of gleaming on the mahogany of the table where he did his business and tended to create a wonderful first impression upon his guests.

The entire room had been constructed to Rathbone's exacting specifications by the finest masons he'd been able to contact. Some of them had traveled for weeks for the honor of coming and plying their trade for him. All had been handsomely compensated and sailed back to their homes significantly wealthier thanks to the handful of uncut gems they now possessed.

In fact, Rathbone reflected as he padded down the length of the soft green carpet and took his customary place at the head of the table, it had been quite the shock to come home and remember what just one gold coin could buy you. Compared to the Sea of Thieves, where gold and jewels flowed freely from hand to hand, a single treasure chest out here in the wider world could set a man up for life. He had far more than a single treasure chest ... and yet it had rankled him to give away even one box in exchange for the creation of his estate.

It was a necessity, he admitted, casting his mind back to the earliest days of his new life—which was, in its way, a warped reflection of his old one. It began shortly after he managed to sail the stricken *Magpie's Wing* back to Golden Sands on his own, which had given him time to dream up a suitably tragic tale to explain Ramsey's disappearance.

Rathbone had never considered himself a storyteller in the way that the others were, but the crowd hung on his every word as he forged a fable in which Ramsey, sword in his hand, had been plucked from the deck of his own ship by the blinded kraken and dragged down beneath the waves to his doom. He suspected those who remained at the outposts would swallow anything he said, for everyone wanted to shake the hands of those valiant pirates who'd faced the monster and put themselves in jeopardy for the sake of those back on land.

The only people who didn't seemed to see Rathbone as a returning champion were his former crew, who were utterly unconvinced by the "facts" of Ramsey's death. Rathbone had been canny enough to don a pair of thick gloves and hide the black diamond ring, at least, for he suspected that if Mercia spotted it on his hand she'd cut him down then and there.

The grateful shipwright had offered to repair the stricken *Magpie's Wing* for free, but Rathbone had no more need of that vessel other than to stealthily remove the sealed chest from its hold. Once the celebration reached its end, he was approached by Stitcher Jim and the others he'd helped find their footing in the Sea of Thieves, and together they traveled back to their camp at Smuggler's Bay.

It was there that he showed them the skeleton keys he'd snatched from Ramsey's grasp. His men had been lurking in the tavern for the demonstration, so each of them understood what the keys meant for their prospects. Feeling the lock of that first chest click open and running his fingers through the riches inside gave Rathbone a thrill he'd been missing in all those months spent chasing magic and merfolk. Here, at last, was his reward.

The other chests were more difficult to obtain, not just because Rathbone was forced to rely on memories of his travels to help locate and recover them, but also because news of his gang's newfound wealth seemed to be spreading faster than he'd ever imagined it would. They were being referred to colloquially as the Gold Hoarders and, like so many titles bestowed by the Sea of Thieves, the name seemed to stick. Unfortunately, that made their ship an attractive target, and barely any voyage went by without opportunistic pirates attempting to waylay and board them.

Nursing a black eye from one such encounter and reflecting bitterly that no amount of money in the world would help it heal any faster, Rathbone formed a new plan. Passage through the Devil's Shroud, while still an intimidating prospect for an inexperienced crew, was no longer the deadly gamble it had once been so long as you paid handsomely for the most recent charts. He and his crew began to ferry much of their plunder through the fog away from the Sea of Thieves, allowing banks and brokers to take it willingly into their vaults for safekeeping.

Back home, that amount of gold easily washed away the stain of Rathbone's former crimes, and he was able to establish the Gold Hoarders as a lawful business venture. He laid out plans for his estate, which would function both as his home and as their headquarters, and as his empire expanded, he found himself spending less and less time sailing the Sea of Thieves.

Unfortunately, the newfound legitimacy attracted even more ire from other pirates, many of whom still regarded the Trading Companies as old enemies. Without Rathbone's zeal and experience at the helm, the Gold Hoarders began losing ships and people almost every time they set out in search of Ramsey's treasures.

Privately, Rathbone suspected that Mercia was coordinating at least some part of the assault on his ventures, though the two of them had had no direct contact since he sailed away from Golden Sands.

Whoever was responsible, their repeated attacks on Gold Hoarder vessels saw the company's profits dry up almost overnight.

It was Stitcher Jim who had the chance encounter that transformed their fortunes. He was sitting in a tavern, licking his wounds after yet another voyage had ended in failure, when a grumbling pirate stormed up to his table carrying one of Ramsey's sealed chests. "I hears only you've got the keys what can open this," he'd growled, "so it's no use to me. Let's split her open and share the contents, eh?"

It revolutionized the way the Gold Hoarders did business. Rathbone saw to it that a company representative was instilled at every major outpost on the Sea of Thieves, armed with voyage contracts and one of his precious skeleton keys. Now it was pirates that brought the treasure to them, surrendering the chests in exchange for a cut of whatever happened to be inside. Many a new arrival got their start in the Sea of Thieves by cashing in a chest or two, and the rest of it came back to fill the pockets of the Gold Hoarders.

None of it was enough.

Rathbone was as rich as Croesus, by rights, but still he resented every golden coin, every traded trinket that left his vaults to pay a wage or help maintain the business. He found himself plagued by dreams in which he sailed on an endless sea of gold—*his* gold, shining and precious. Waves of gemstones were crashing against the diamond-studded prow of his ship, and he found he could count them all. He'd often wake up twisting the fine silken sheets between his fingers, grasping for the treasure.

Now, almost twenty years since he'd first taken the keys in his hand, Rathbone found himself surrendering the last of them to a slick-haired young man who was to be his latest representative on the Sea of Thieves. He sank moodily back into his seat, only half listening as his subordinates ground through the meeting's agenda at a glacial pace. The conversation turned to the prospect of purchasing treasure maps from an up-and-coming gang of soothsayers, but Rathbone was hardly listening, preoccupied with staring at his reflection in the polished surface of the table and fiddling with the black diamond ring upon his finger.

"Any other business?" he demanded as the meeting reached its end, already making to leave, but one of his advisers raised a plump hand into the air. With a sigh, Rathbone lowered himself back into his seat.

"Well, it's not strictly on the agenda, but a couple of our representatives have been hearing rumors about some treasure trove or other out in the Wilds. If tavern talk is to be believed, it would represent almost forty percent of our annual income." This caused a susurration of interest from the assorted committee members, not to mention rapt attention from their leader. "I had considered putting together some voyage contracts and getting some of the more reliable pirates to—"

"No!" Rathbone said, slightly too loudly. He looked around at their surprised expressions, and amended. "That is to say, you know what pirates are like. This'll be nothing more than a drunken embellishment or an outright fabrication, mark my words. No reason to waste our time."

The Gold Hoarders always had the best of everything, and the sloop Rathbone commanded was a fine vessel indeed. Nonetheless, it had been many months since he'd last taken to the sea, let alone attempted to navigate the Devil's Shroud. While making his return to the Sea of Thieves, he had a couple of close calls with tendrils of the ebbing, flowing fog that crept a little too close for comfort.

He was rusty, he knew, and the most sensible course of action would have been to bring a crew—*no*, he corrected himself, *it would have been never to have come at all*. He knew he was being irrational, and yet, imagining the sight of an unclaimed, uncounted hoard that was *his*, entirely his to tip from palm to palm ... it was irresistible. He had to have every last glittering gewgaw to himself, to savor the look and the touch and even the taste of the metal. He'd surrender it to no one, not even his own people.

And so Rathbone had set out alone, sidled into the only tavern he knew for sure still existed from the old days, and learned what he needed to know from its denizens. He was grateful that his long absence aided his anonymity, though he still had to shrink back into the shadows when a couple of Gold Hoarder representatives wandered in for a grog or two of their own.

Currently, he estimated, he was around halfway to his destination: a forbidding island that had only recently been released from the Shroud's grip. It was such a recent discovery that it didn't even have a name but could, if the rumors were true, be readily identified by the oversized statues on its coastline. He was sure Mercia would have found their origins fascinating, but as far as he was concerned, the ruins were nothing more than a landmark to help guide him toward whatever fortune lay in wait.

Sailing by oneself, he decided, was equal parts idyllic and infuriating. Even through his preoccupation with the prospect of treasure, he found that he was enjoying the feel of the ocean as it rocked his sloop this way and that. Perhaps later, he could explore—

No, he told himself sternly. *Only the gold matters. Everything else is . . . sentiment, and that's poison.*

The pirates back in the tavern had told Rathbone that the path to the treasure was long and winding, doubtless filled with puzzles and traps to overcome. Well, Rathbone had had his fill of ancient riddles and tests of character left behind by centuries-dead pirates. After twenty years getting used to the Sea of Thieves, he was prepared.

He made it to the unnamed island without incident, for which he was grateful, for his fencing practice had fallen by the wayside in recent years. Once there, he began a slow circuit of the shoreline, noting not just the statues but also every point of interest along the way. A summer squall came and went, but Rathbone continued his search regardless, traipsing through the blustery rain until he finally located a circle of rocks. Their arrangement seemed slightly too perfect, so it was here that Rathbone began to dig.

Just as he suspected, his shovel struck a hard surface while he was hacking away at the sickly vegetation; by clearing the vegetation away, he unearthed a carved stone slab set into the ground. It was far too heavy to move, but that wasn't going to be a problem for Rathbone. He returned to his sloop and trotted below decks, rummaging around until he found one of the explosive powder kegs he'd prepared for the journey.

Staggering back up to the beach, he placed the heavy cask directly atop the stone slab, added a good length of fuse wire, sparked his flint—and ran. There was a shuddering boom, and the ancient slab broke neatly in two, one half landing in the sand nearby and the other disappearing down into the deep hole it was covering. Once again, Rathbone returned to his ship, breaking into a light jog, returning this time with a length of knotted rope that he lowered into the hole until he felt it go slack and knew he'd reached the bottom.

Little by little, forcing himself to be patient and methodical, Rathbone broke his way into the ruins underneath the deserted isle. He was absolutely certain that his treasure was waiting for him down there, calling out to him as he worked his way deeper and deeper underground. Finally, another explosive barrel cracked the mortar around a decorative frieze, enough that he was able to lever it aside, and Rathbone forced his way into the enormous hall at the heart of the island.

It was a treasure chamber, though that term hardly seemed to do the room justice, for it was piled high with more riches than even Rathbone had dreamed of. Great mountains of gold, scores of rubies and sapphires, fine jewelry, and even plates and goblets. All of it had lain undisturbed in a room where heavy tapestries hung from unseen stones overhead. Rathbone spotted a brazier in the wall and quickly moved to light the torches so that he could get a proper look at his find.

The huge golden throne that dominated the scene suggested that this place might once have been a secret palace, or perhaps a treasure vault for some nameless king who liked to linger among his tribute. Rathbone, weak-kneed at the vision that sprawled before him, found himself sinking into that same chair as he gawked at his surroundings, and found that it suited him very well indeed. He placed one hand on the arm of the throne and found that the gold was warm beneath his palm, even though they were deep underground. *You belong here*, it seemed to say.

The largest heap of all was piled in front of the throne, and Rathbone leaned forward in his seat and ran his fingers through the pile of coins and precious stones that lay heaped before him. He had no idea how long he lingered in the forgotten vault, plunging his arms into the cold metal and feeling the coins sift between his fingertips. It could have been hours, or perhaps days. Had the need for food and water not overcome him, he might have remained below forever.

These ruins, he decided, would become his sanctuary. No more would he allow his fortune to be siphoned away by simpering lackeys and underlings who claimed to be faithful to him! Rather, he would continue to bring treasures here as he found them, adding more and more to the hidden hoard and ensuring he knew the whereabouts of every last precious stone in his collection.

I need supplies, he thought to himself, *but I won't be gone long.* Barely had he made it back above ground, however, before Rathbone found himself hesitating. Others knew about this place. What if pirates arrived while he was making his preparations and tried to take his fortune for themselves? He couldn't leave it unprotected. Finally, grudgingly, he settled for taking all that he could with him upon his tiny sloop so that he could personally keep watch over as many of his newfound riches as possible.

Filling two sacks and hauling them across his shoulders so that he was bent nearly double, he made journey after journey back into the vault to collect his fortune. The hold of the sloop was full before long, but Rathbone kept bringing treasures to the surface, stuffing them first under the table in the map room before discarding ammo chests and supplies to make space. Next, he stored what he could on the upper deck. Finally, there was nowhere left to store more gold—nowhere apart from on his own body.

He forced rings onto his fingers and anklets and bracelets onto his arms and legs. A golden crown that was slightly too large for him rested haphazardly atop his head. He was sweating, for the warmth of the throne had never left him, and it was only when he took a look at his hand in the light of day that he could see the yellowing sheen that now coated his palm.

A curse, he realized in alarm, but even this misfortune could not prevent him from weighing the anchor and setting sail, casting one final look back at the island and thinking of all the treasure he'd had to leave unprotected. *I'll be back soon enough*, he vowed.

His sloop was now riding so low in the water that even the smallest waves were within inches of breaking over the deck, but Rathbone barely noticed. He was focused solely on setting a course back through the Devil's Shroud and returning to his estate. *Once I'm home*, he thought feverishly, *I'll find someone who can fix my hand. You can do anything if you're rich enough.*

He fumbled clumsily with the sails, annoyed to find that the overburdened ship could barely make it above a crawl, even with the wind behind him. *I could lighten the load*, he thought, but the prospect of throwing even one coin overboard filled him with such intense revulsion that he forced the idea from his mind and set his gaze firmly on the waves ahead of him, ignoring the stiffness in his fingers.

An hour passed, and the island—his island—was barely over the horizon when ships appeared either side of him. They were both galleons sporting identical colors and trim, their crews staring impassively down at him from either side.

Rathbone swore, grunting as he raised his afflicted arm above his waist to clutch at the ship's wheel. Under ordinary circumstances, he'd have surged the sloop forward, making use of its maneuverability to dodge between rocks or into shallower waters and make his escape.

There was no hope of that now, however, for the little ship was simply too encumbered.

Suddenly, Rathbone understood the real peril of the situation. To see two ships cooperating was unusual enough, but that they had both appeared right when he was at his most vulnerable, with one arm useless and a boat on the verge of sinking... This, he realized, was no mere run of bad luck. This was an ambush.

His mind whirled as he thought back to the meeting where he'd first heard about the treasure, trying to work out who his nemesis might be. Could this whole affair be the machination of one the Gold Hoarders? Someone who was seeking to remove him from power? Or was he perhaps seeing conspiracies where none existed, and he'd simply been recognized in the tavern and followed?

The two ships had drawn even closer now, near enough that Rathbone could make out the individual faces peering down at him. He suddenly realized how foolish he must seem, standing at the helm with a crown upon his head, covered from head to toe in jewelry with a golden arm hanging uselessly at his side. No one had fired at him yet, fortunately, even though a single strike to the sloop's hull would be enough to sink it and its precious cargo. It might just be possible to talk his way out of this.

The captain of the leading ship certainly seemed willing to converse, for he had moved to the railing and cupped his hands to his mouth, but it was nothing Rathbone wanted to hear. "Drop anchor immediately and prepare to surrender!" he called. "You have until the count of ten. One... two..."

Rathbone growled wordlessly, but didn't see that he had much of a choice. Struggling over to the capstan, he let the anchor fall, discreetly leaving his sails unfurled so that he could try and effect an escape. He soon realized he wouldn't have the opportunity, however, for the galleons began to circle him like hungry sharks. Slowly and methodically, as if they had all the time in the world, one ship brought its port side across his bow and the other up against his stern, pinning the sloop in between their twin frames. A moment later, several powder kegs were tossed into the water, carried by the waves until they were scraping up and down against Rathbone's hull.

Rathbone's head was starting to swim as the first lances of pain shot up his arm, but he struck a defiant pose long enough to bellow up at the crews. "Sink me if you think you can, you wretches, but this is my treasure and I'll not give so much as a copper coin to the likes of you!"

"That treasure, Rathbone of the Gold Hoarders, is precisely what has gotten you into this mess," the captain replied, leaning forward over the railings to fix him with a steely glare. The more Rathbone thought about it, the more he was sure that something about the voice sounded familiar. He didn't know this man now, but what about twenty years ago?

His eyes widened with a jolt of recognition. "Slate!" he breathed. And sure enough, the figure looming over him was the same pirate who had lost his ship defending Golden Sands nearly twenty years before. A life on the sea had aged the man, tanning his skin the color of walnuts even as his hair had faded to silver.

Slate tilted his head very slightly at Rathbone's acknowledgment but continued speaking as if nothing had been said. "We suspected that news of an unclaimed treasure pile might be just what was needed to draw you out of hiding, but we never expected you'd be so foolhardy as to come back to the Sea of Thieves by yourself. Has your avarice really dragged your soul so deep that you can no longer see reason, man?"

Rathbone didn't respond to this. In truth, he was having trouble standing, such was the weight of his arm. Slate stared down at him with something akin to pity in his eyes, and continued. "Our demands are very simple. There are many of us who do not wish to see the Trading Companies encroaching upon the Sea of Thieves, siphoning away its riches and natural wonders to sell, piece by piece, for their own ends. If you surrender here and now, Rathbone, and agree to begin the withdrawal of your representatives from our waters, then we will agree to spare your life."

"I..." Rathbone growled. "What about my treasure?"

Slate scowled. "That treasure is consuming you! Look at what it's done to your arm, for pity's sake. Give it up and come aboard as my prisoner or I'll have my crewmen sink the whole bloody lot."

Rathbone stared up at Slate in amazement, utterly baffled at the idea that anyone could be so insane as to deliberately consign such glorious, beautiful wealth to the bottom of the sea. Sensing that the man was serious, he desperately began to stuff his pockets, cradling the wealth against him even as coin after coin slipped from his grip and began to tumble into the sea.

Slate had clearly had enough of watching his quarry scrabble helplessly at an impossible task, and impatiently gestured one of his crew forward. She held a large rifle in her hands, one of the more modern varieties, with a scope atop its barrel, and she steadied against the ship's railing as she sighted carefully. "Time's up, Rathbone."

Pausing in his futile efforts to gather up the treasure all around him, Rathbone stared up in shock at his would-be executioner. Time had put a white streak in her hair and a scar had taken one of her eyes, but there was no doubt who it was who was aiming the weapon at his helpless ship.

"The Pirate Lord sends his regards," Mercia informed him, then emptied her rifle into the bobbing powder kegs in three precise bursts. A trio of explosions tipped Rathbone's sloop viciously from side to side, sending water gushing into its lower deck, and the stricken ship's cargo began to tumble out through the newly ruptured hull down toward the seabed. With an anguished howl, Rathbone flung himself over the railing of the sloop with his golden arm outstretched, eyes fixed on the vanishing coins as they tumbled beneath the waves.

Water filled his lungs and burned his chest, but there was another burning there too: a yearning to claim every last one of the golden pieces followed by everything beyond. To have every gemstone and every treasure that there ever could be clutched safely in his fingers, to make it a part of him, so that he and he alone could possess it.

To squeeze the life out of anyone who might come between him and his ambitions. The thought of drowning no longer seemed to matter, not when there was still so much to do, so much to take.

He never noticed the wreck of his ship strike the seabed behind him, nor did he register that Slate and the others were sailing away across the waves high overhead. Rathbone, the Gold Hoarder, was already on his hands and knees in the inky darkness as his life ebbed away, scrabbling and searching for treasure to fill the void where his soul had been.

LARINNA

Scrambling down off her mountain of gold, Larinna pelted toward the huge blockade of fallen boxes and splintered walkways. A straggling skeleton that had somehow avoided the collapse reared up at her, and she peppered it with shots from her pistol until it fell apart.

Try as she might, however, she could find no way through the fallen debris and was left pounding her fists uselessly against the barricade that separated her from her crew. She was only vaguely aware that she was bellowing Adelheid's name, over and over again.

The wood was becoming hotter and hotter beneath her hands, and she realized that she could no longer see the roof of the chamber, for it was now obscured by a thick, roiling cloud of smoke. *The torches*, she thought in panic. All it would have taken was for some of the dry and ancient wood to topple onto a brazier during its collapse, and the whole pile would soon be one gigantic bonfire. Her funeral pyre, if she didn't escape. Gazing upward, she could see the fallen masonry beginning to singe as flames licked across its edges.

She pulled a handkerchief from her pocket, wetting it with water from her flask, and was tying it securely over her mouth and nose when she heard a noise. A loud crash echoed from the other side of the divide, then another, and a spark of hope flared within Larinna's heart. She imagined Little Ned on the far side, heaving away chests and clearing a passage for her so that they might escape together, and began to scrabble at the debris on her side, seeking where the commotion was loudest. "Ned!" she shouted. "Can you hear me? Is Faizel okay?"

A hand burst through the wreckage, reaching aimlessly for a moment before retracting, but Larinna could tell immediately that it didn't belong to Ned. Not unless he'd lost an awful lot of weight.

She staggered backward, torn by two conflicting desires, as the Gold Hoarder's face leered at her through the gap. Part of her wanted very much to avenge herself upon the monster that had killed her captain, but she knew that her pistol needed reloading, and besides, there was the little matter of the chamber being on fire. She doubted very much that smoke and flames would slow the Gold Hoarder, but she could already feel her lungs burning as they took in more of the acrid smoke.

Flight was her only option then, and quickly. She turned as the glittering skeleton began to heave himself through the gap in the burning barricade and sprinted back across the golden landscape. It was tough going, for the collapsed treasure spread across the floor to create a treacherously unstable surface where coins and gems shifted underfoot. Twice she stumbled, all too aware of the clattering from behind her as the Gold Hoarder dragged himself upright, and twice she scrambled to her feet.

She almost ran straight past the secret passage she'd found earlier, spotting it at the last second only to find an escape route denied her. Spilled coins had cascaded across the entrance and into the passageway itself, blocking it in a golden landslide. Even if she'd been left in peace, Larinna doubted she'd be able to dig her way out before the flames and fumes overcame her. As it was, with a crazed skeleton bearing down upon her in large, loping strides, escape through the passageway was not an option.

Wheezing, her eyes stinging, Larinna took a few clumsy swipes at the approaching Gold Hoarder with her sword, scooping up a handful of money and flinging it at his face to distract him while she darted under his arm and back the way she'd come. The hulking figure hissed angrily as she picked up the gold, his head darting backward and forward as he made a futile effort to track the flight of every last coin. By the time he turned to pursue, Larinna was already back at the blockade, diving through the gap the creature had dug for itself and tucking herself into a roll that ended rather painfully when she collided with yet another pile of treasure.

This side of the ruined chamber was both brighter and hotter, the fires burning more intensely. Rivulets of liquid gold were beginning to trickle out from the piles closest to the flames, and for a moment Larinna had a vision of the whole chamber acting as an cnormous melting pot, transforming every piece of treasure into part of a flowing, golden mass that would stream along the passageways and drop relentlessly into the abyss beyond. The greatest fortune ever known, lost forever due to a moment's misfortune. Shining . . .

Hold it together, she commanded herself, aware how light-headed she was feeling as she forced herself to focus. Adelheid's body, she noticed with a jolt, was gone. There was no sign of Faizel either, though to her relief Larinna spotted a scrap of his coat snagged on the very edge of the wreckage. She hoped that Ned had been able to pull him free and that the two of them were already well on their way to the surface.

A sudden movement caught her eye, and she realized that the last of the Gold Hoarder's minions still lingered, shambling around in a pack and making vain attempts to snuff out the flames with their feet. She took down the first while it was still intent on its task, knocking aside the arm of a second skeleton as it lunged toward her, still dripping flecks of the molten gold it had been carrying in its fleshless fingers.

The third took her by surprise, for it had been lurking out of sight behind the golden throne, and Larinna bellowed in alarm as it leapt upon her. She pitched forward, her face only inches away from a stream of boiling metal. Arcing backward to keep her face away from the floor, she wedged the barrel of her pistol underneath her own arm with the barrel facing backward, hoping there was one last shot left within its chamber. To her relief, she felt the heat of the shot against her and heard the splintering of old bones.

Rolling out from under the skeleton that had pinned her—which, she was pleased to see, was now missing its left arm—Larinna scrambled upright and lashed out with her foot. The kick carried her assailant backward into yet more of the fallen crates, which toppled down upon it with a satisfying crunch.

Larinna fumbled to reload her pistol, but that seemed to be the last of the undead underlings, and she backed cautiously toward the passageway they'd used to reach the chamber. She was almost to the exit when she spotted Adelheid's fallen knife, its dark handle a stark contrast to the gold coins on which it lay. She wasn't sure why she did it, but Larinna knelt down to retrieve the little blade, now perhaps the only memento of her fallen crewmate, and slipped it carefully into a loop on her belt.

As she stood, there was an almighty crash from behind her, and great chunks of the burning wreckage gave way, sending embers and splashes of gold across the room. Larinna felt the burning flecks land upon her skin and hair and quickly dropped to the ground, rolling uncomfortably back and forth across the flagstones until the last of the white-hot sparks were extinguished.

She looked up, and there was the Gold Hoarder, standing with its shovel raised atop the collapsed portion of the barricade. It gave one mighty leap and landed with a great crash in front of the chamber's exit while Larinna was still struggling upright. The green jewels in its eyes shone vindictively as it tilted its head this way and that, as if studying her.

Its jaw dropped open, but rather than the animalistic roar she'd been expecting, there were words. Slow and ponderous words, sibilant and dry as a crypt. "Treassssurreeee...," it hissed. "Thiiieeeveeessss..."

It can talk, Larinna thought, astonished. *If it can talk, maybe that means I can bargain with it.* "We didn't come here to steal from you!" she called, coughing from the smoke-filled air. "We thought this was Athena's Fortune! The treasure of the Pirate Lord!" She wasn't sure what she'd said wrong, but these words seemed to enrage the Gold Hoarder even further. The blade of its shovel lashed out, carving through one of the endless treasure piles, and she barely leapt backward in time.

Larinna responded by diving sideways and circling, trying to keep her distance as her pistol sang out. She needn't have bothered reloading, it seemed, for her first shot struck the creature's glittering lower jaw, but the Gold Hoarder took no notice. The second struck a glancing, harmless blow along its cheekbone. The third did nothing but leave a dent in the shovel's blade as the Gold Hoarder began to wield the tool like a shield.

Firearms, Larinna realized, weren't going to be enough. Whatever dreadful ambition had compelled the Gold Hoarder to amass its unimaginable fortune over the years seemed to give it far greater fortitude than the others of its kind. Even the rusty blunderbusses adorning the walls of Wilbur's weapon shop would struggle to slow it down, she thought grimly. Remembering the distant outpost and its denizens struck a fresh wellspring of rage within her, and all she could see reflected in the shovel was Adelheid's shocked expression in her final moments.

Now it was Larinna who went on the offensive, lashing out against the Gold Hoarder with blow after vicious blow. Her cutlass dented and sparks flew as its whirling blade struck against the skeleton's gem-studded body. "You killed my captain," she roared. "You belong dead!"

The Gold Hoarder threw its head back in an obscene parody of human laughter, the sound echoing throughout the ruins and filling the smoky air. With a single shove, it brought the handle of its shovel up to meet Larinna's cutlass, and her blade stuck fast in the wood. Wide-eyed, she released her grip on the sword just in time, for the cackling cadaver gave an almighty tug that would have wrenched her off her feet and tossed her effortlessly into the roaring flames.

That left Larinna unarmed save for her pistol, which she unloaded ineffectively at the grinning visage of the Gold Hoarder before finally resorting to throwing the weapon itself at his head. The undead monster delivered another mighty swing of its shovel, and Larinna dodged again, but her throat was raw now, her eyes puffy and swollen. If she didn't reach the safety of the passageway soon and seek refuge from the smoke and fumes, she was going to collapse and be lost beneath the rising tide of flowing gold, assuming the Gold Hoarder didn't rip her apart first. *At least Faizel and Ned will live on to tell everyone what happened*, she thought. And then she had an idea.

"It doesn't matter what you do to me!" she goaded, calling out to the Gold Hoarder though it hurt to speak. "My crew are on their way back to the surface right now with the rest of your treasure. They'll spend it in so many places, you'll never get it all back, and they're going to tell everyone what's left down here. Imagine that! Ten thousand thieves, all coming for their share of your fortune, and you'll never, *ever* be able to stop them all!"

Enraged, the Gold Hoarder raised its deadly shovel high overhead, assuming the same stance that had felled Adelheid. It brought the jagged blade down toward Larinna using every ounce of its strength—but she was no longer there, having flung herself forward between two bony legs. The shovel's blow struck the barricade, causing great piles of flaming wood to tumble down atop the Gold Hoarder, but his fury was such that he shrugged off the heavy blows and lumbered after his prey.

Coughing and spluttering as she sprinted toward the exit, Larinna paused only long enough to pluck up a length of wood and thrust it into the roaring flames. The result was a crude torch, her only defense against the all-consuming blackness that lay ahead. She had the unpleasant feeling that the Gold Hoarder would be able to see just fine in the dark.

She made it back to the room where they'd made camp just in time, driving the sputtering firewood like a stake into the ground and casting around for the lantern she'd left behind until, at last, her questing fingers curled around its familiar handle. The steady glow of its flame was a welcome relief, and as she clipped it to her belt and prepared to move on, she could hear the distant sound of booted feet advancing along the corridor behind her.

She also took hold of a stout woodcutter's ax that must have belonged to whoever had made camp here all those years ago, for it felt good to have a weapon clutched in her hands again as she sprinted through the gloom.

At last, Larinna came to the great ravine that they'd crossed before. To her relief, she saw that the decaying bridge was much as they'd left it, although one of the ropes they'd previously clung to seemed to have given way. She'd feared that Ned and Faizel's escape might have collapsed the entire thing, trapping her forever in the darkness with a murderous skeleton. Even so, she hesitated at the cliff's edge, shuddering at the memory of lying sprawled on those planks with nothing but a few lengths of rotten wood between her and howling oblivion.

It took another hiss from the Gold Hoarder, who sounded uncomfortably close behind her, to compel Larinna's feet onto the bridge. The first of the remaining planks held her securely as she inched forward, as did the second. She clung tightly to the handrail, barely daring to breathe as she took step after heavy step across the divide.

The third bowed under her weight, but held. The fourth plank gave way a few moments after she'd stepped on it, and a white-lipped Larinna increased her pace yet again, breaking into a trot when the far side of the ravine was just a few feet away. Finally, she gave one almighty bound for safety, dropping the ax as she landed roughly on the bare rock face. Her landing added to her cuts and bruises, but she didn't care.

She turned, and found she could make out the Gold Hoarder in the darkness, for its glittering jaw and hand shone in the light of her lantern. To her surprise, it had already stepped onto the furiously swaying bridge. She watched the monster's progress, certain that its footholds must surely collapse at any moment.

The alternative, that the vengeful skeleton might somehow make it across the ravine, was unthinkable. Larinna felt utterly drained, and knew that she'd never make it back to the surface before the creature caught up to her and brought its mighty shovel crashing down. This chasm might be the only chance she had to put an end to the pursuit once and for all.

The skeleton's boot struck heavily upon the second plank, which creaked alarmingly under the sudden weight. *Come on*, Larinna thought, staring intently at the bridge as if she could force it to collapse through sheer willpower. Just as she hoped, the third plank did indeed give way as the Gold Hoarder stepped closer.

Better still, the ravages of time seemed finally to have caught up with the decaying structure. One by one, the rest of the wood splintered and fell away, leaving the Gold Hoarder clinging to one last rope that spanned the ravine. She watched with some considerable pleasure as the skeleton struggled to keep a grip, its shovel crashing down into the darkness below.

The gleaming skull turned toward her as Larinna watched defiantly, and then back to the handrail. Taking the taut rope in its jaws, the Gold Hoarder bit down, severing the line to which it was clinging. Now it was no longer dangling helplessly, but swinging toward her side of the canyon in a large arc with its legs braced for the impact.

She heard, rather than saw, the creature strike the cliff with a loud clatter and a hiss. Peering down into the darkness, she could make out the skeletal form as it began to climb the rope, hauling itself up hand over hand and hissing more angrily than ever.

Larinna's hand flew to Adelheid's knife, and she knelt on the very edge of the cliff, back braced against the rocky pillar to which the rope had been anchored. Her only chance at survival, she knew, was to cut the cord and send the ghoulish creature into the abyss once and for all. Strand by strand began to peel away as she worked furiously with the little blade, but the enraged skeleton was getting closer by the second.

Now she was halfway through the rope, and the Gold Hoarder's hands were ten feet away from the edge of the cliff. Three quarters done ... almost there ... three strands left ...

The rope snapped.

The Gold Hoarder leapt.

Larinna screamed as a golden hand seized her leg, claws raking across her flesh as the skeleton dangled. The pain and pressure as it clung to her limb like a lifeline was intense, and she was forced to hook her other leg around the pillar, which was all that stopped her from sliding across the floor and being dragged into the ravine. She flailed around, desperately looking for something to hold on to, for the Gold Hoarder weighed far more than one might expect from a pile of bones and rags. *It's the gold*, she thought, fighting through the red fire of exhaustion. *Gold is a really heavy metal. Heavy ... but soft.*

Her hands closed around the woodcutter's ax, and Larinna brought it down upon the claw that held her leg, issuing a cry to rival the Gold Hoarder's own angered roar as the blow struck the creature mere inches from her own flesh. The creature scrabbled furiously at the cliff face with its other hand, realizing her intentions, and Larinna felt her grip on the rock give way.

She began to slide inexorably toward the cliff edge, inches away from their mutual doom, and panic swelled within her. Clamping down on the feeling, she summoned up the last of her strength and brought the ax down for one last live-or-die attempt. This time, the blade sliced, unstoppable, through the golden hand until it struck stone.

The Gold Hoarder had no expression to read, but its jaw hung open in surprise as it plummeted into the darkness, reaching for Larinna with the hand it no longer possessed. That hand was still squirming on the ground nearby, and she lashed out at it with a savage kick, consigning it to the void along with its owner. Only then did she slump fully to the floor, poking gingerly at her injured leg and wincing.

Her eyelids were heavy and she yearned for sleep, but not as badly as she yearned for daylight and for the smell of the sea. Larinna permitted herself to sit only for a moment before getting unsteadily to her feet, testing her weight on her wounded limb.

It was then that she noticed the ring, little more than a glimmer in the darkness, and pinched it up between her fingers to examine the black diamond set against the band. She pocketed it without much thought and staggered back through the ruins, taking the endless staircase at her own reduced pace. After some time, she no longer needed the lantern to see.

Stepping out of the shadow of the fallen statue and into the warmth of a sunny morning felt even better than she'd imagined it would, and Larinna wished for the shade of a palm tree so that she might sit and slumber for a while. *You can rest in a tavern when you're safely home*, she told herself. *Today's story ought to be good for a grog or two.*

She knew that the *Unforgiven* must be far away by now, Faizel and Ned having made their escape long before she escaped the Gold Hoarder's clutches. Quite how she was going to find her way home was a puzzle that stumped Larinna for a while, at least until she remembered that the pirate crew that had ambushed the crew of the *Unforgiven* had come here in a ship of their own.

She limped along the coastline until she could see the sails of the mercenaries' galleon, still bobbing peacefully off the coast, at which point she waded out to sea. The salt water stung the cuts on her leg where the Gold Hoarder had grabbed her, and once she was aboard she shrugged off her coat, tugged at her breeches, and tended to the wound properly.

Next, she raided the ship's supplies until she found something she could eat that wouldn't kill her, which turned out to be bananas. After hours underground fighting for her life, they were the sweetest thing she'd ever tasted.

Working a galleon meant for a crew of four proved to be tricky but not impossible, and once Larinna had strained to raise the anchor and partially unfurl a single sail so she could see where she was steering, she found herself able to lean against the helm and let the ship's compass guide her way. As long as she didn't have to fight, she'd make it home. Her leg was feeling better and her spirits were lifting slightly, though her mind still drifted back to Adelheid and the others from time to time.

She would have to sell the ship when she made it back to an outpost, she decided. Then, well, perhaps she'd buy a little sloop she could manage on her own. She wasn't certain she was ready to find another crew, not so soon after her first disastrous voyage. *If I had only let Faizel and Ned walk past me when I first landed at Sanctuary Outpost*, she thought bitterly, *they would never have been able to reach the map and Adelheid might still be alive*. She shook her head, refusing to let herself wallow in might-have-beens, and focused on the horizon that was in front of her.

A horizon, she realized, that had sails on it. Another galleon was sliding into view ahead of her, previously hidden from sight by the rocks of the nearest island. She was already altering her course to try to avoid a confrontation when she spotted the figurehead—a fearsome woman holding two crossed pistols.

Letting out an unintended, joyful laugh at the sight, Larinna dashed all around her stolen ship, weighing anchor and getting as close to the island as she could for a better look. It was definitely the *Unforgiven*; she could even make out Ned and Faizel roving around on the shoreline, gathering food and supplies for the return journey. It felt better than she expected to see them again, and barely had they spotted her approach before Larinna had abandoned ship, diving overboard to meet her crewmates.

They reunited in the surf and Larinna was startled, but not displeased, to find herself picked up bodily by Little Ned for a bear hug. Together, they made their way back aboard and clustered around the map table to tell their stories. Faizel seemed no worse for wear, so Larinna demanded to know why he hadn't been crushed under the tumbling masonry deep within the ruins. "I have a very thick skull, yes!" he said, by way of explanation. "And my good friend Ned was kind enough to break my fall with his head."

"We'd have come back for you, but we thought you was dead," Ned added apologetically.

"And I for one do not believe that the Gold Hoarder was about to let us form a search party," Faizel declared. "To see a Skeleton Lord such as he up close is not a sight I shall soon forget. I expected him to chase us all the way back to the ship."

"Well I don't think he'll be bothering anyone, at least not for a while," Larinna said, a trace of pride creeping into her voice. As they listened attentively, she told them all about the collapse, the fight, the escape, and the battle at the bridge when she finally put an end to the monster's pursuit.

"Such a pity," Faizel said sympathetically. "To think of the largest fortune any of us have ever seen. Lost down there, possibly forever. We were unable to grab more than a handful of coins. Enough to repair and refit the ship, perhaps, but hardly Athena's Fortune." He pointed across at a distant fog bank. "From the crow's nest I could see the Devil's Shroud appears to be advancing, perhaps even moving in to claim this place. I think perhaps we will be the last ones to come here for some time."

His expression grew serious then, and he leaned forward across the map table. "We have a long journey home," he declared, "and we are once more a crew of three. Would you, Larinna, consent to being the acting captain of the *Unforgiven*?"

Shocked, Larinna looked back and forth between them, unable to tell if they were joking. "Me? You want *me* to be the captain?"

"We need a steady hand upon the helm, and I see no reason why it should not be the mighty pirate who single-handedly fought off the Gold Hoarder!" Faizel said, encouragingly. "At least until Adelheid returns."

Larinna stared at him, uncertain if he was cracked or simply making a joke in very poor taste. "Adelheid's dead, Faizel," she said, as gently as she could manage.

Now it was Faizel's turn to look at her as if she was playing some cruel joke, and the two of them stared at each other in mutual incomprehension for a moment. Ultimately, it was Ned who broke the deadlock.

"Faizel," he said, a low rumble of mirth making his shoulders quake. "I don't think anyone's ever told Larinna about the Sea of the Damned."

Emotions appeared to be fighting for control of Faizel's expression, and Larinna felt like she was going to launch herself across the table at whoever said the next thing she didn't understand. "What," she growled dangerously, "is the Sea of the Damned? And so help me, if either of you laugh at me, I'll—"

"Forgive us, forgive us," Faizel interrupted, holding his hands up in supplication. "Sometimes I forget that you are still new to the Sea of Thieves, though you have had quite the maiden voyage. Let us try to explain." Larinna marshaled what little patience she had left while Faizel settled back with his arms behind his head, deep in thought.

"You must understand that what I am about to say is the result of much conjecture and half-remembered experiences," he said slowly. "No one truly understands the Sea of the Damned, not really, and I hope you will come to understand why no one really enjoys talking about it. We do not even know if the place has a real name. If it, itself, is completely real."

He caught Larinna's glare and continued his story. "Whatever it may be, the Sea of the Damned takes the form of a vast, dark ocean whose waters are icy to the touch. There are no stars to chart by and no sun with which to tell the time. You cannot see the horizon as there is only ever an endless fog through which vague shapes can be seen but never reached. Down in the waters, if you look closely, you can see writhing shapes that seem to be neither mer nor human. Are they the spirits of the dead? Could they be the same lost souls who find their way back to our world and plague us as skeletons? Some would say so, but who knows for sure?

"When you wake up in this strange place, you have a body and you have your belongings, but you are not quite alive either. Caught between two worlds, perhaps, on the deck of a ship that is not your own, a galleon that sails this endless ocean. She is an ancient ship with a strange creature for a figurehead, and her walls and railings are marked with the names of some who have sailed in her before you."

This was sounding more and more like a ghost story to Larinna, but she found herself captivated by the idea nonetheless. "A ship? Does she have a crew?"

"Indeed! They are gaunt and bloodless, shambling and obedient, for their captain is a tall and fearsome man with wild hair and an outfit that seems as ancient and ragged as his ship. The first time you encounter him, you wonder if you are perhaps his prisoner, or if you have been plucked from oblivion to serve as a deckhand on his endless voyage through limbo. In truth, you are more like a passenger, rescued from an unknown fate."

"That's why we calls it the Ferry of the Damned," Ned cut in. "The cap'n hardly ever speaks, though. S'pose he's not got much to talk about except how he's sick of the job."

"And where the door to the captain's cabin should be," Faizel persisted, "there is a great portal, sealed tight, with no lock or handle. And so you remain aboard until the ship's captain, your Ferryman, decides the time is right. That is when the door will open in a burst of light—true light—from the living world. And when you step through—"

"You wake up." Ned shuddered. "And it feels like you had the worst dream of your life."

"He just lets you go?" Larinna's eyebrows were raised in surprise. "I'd expected you to tell me he takes your soul as payment, or something. What does he do it for?"

Faizel shrugged. "Everyone has their own ideas, of course. Some say that he is paying off a great debt, or that he is cursed somehow. Others that he is searching for his lost love and will cast those of us he finds back to the land of the living, like a fisherman of souls. I think that perhaps it is wiser not to ask him too many questions. Do not bite the hand that feeds you, yes?"

"An' we know dead used to just mean dead," Ned added, ominously, "which is why the taverns ain't stuffed with pirates from the olden days. No one wants to take the Ferryman for granted and muck about, in case next time he ain't there to save you."

Larinna imagined desperately treading water in an endless, ethereal ocean, calling and pleading as the Ferryman stared implacably down at her ... and then turned the ship's wheel, vanishing into the fog and leaving her soul to sink beneath the waves. Despite the heat of the day, she shivered. "You mean to tell me that Adelheid is on this Ferry of the Damned right now? Waiting for the door to open? What if she's not allowed through?"

"Then that will be the start of another adventure, perhaps," Faizel said guardedly. "One we may all have to face one day, when we are very old or very sick and the Ferryman decides he would prefer not to take us aboard. Until then, we must forge ahead in her name and hope that she finds her way back to us. At least there is still hope that we will see her again, yes?"

Larinna was trying to take all of this in. She still had a thousand questions that she suspected there were no answers for, at least for now. A world of lost souls and skeletons, ghoulish ferrymen and the dead coming back to life?

She stood up.

"As acting captain," she said firmly, "I say we go and wait for Adelheid at the nearest tavern. I need a very, very large drink."

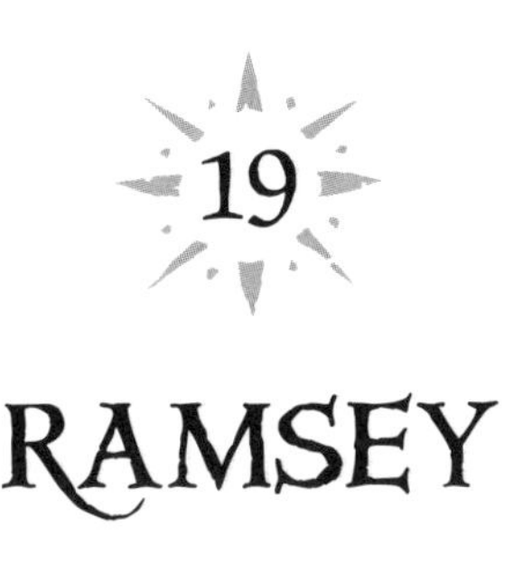

RAMSEY

The vessel that approached Tribute Peak was dazzling, considered by many to be the most magnificent on the Sea of Thieves. Her sails were a bright scarlet, trimmed with silver and bearing a crest known by everyone that saw it, for this was the ship of the Pirate Lord. She far outmatched any other galleon, and many smaller vessels sailed in her wake like chicks following their mother.

Her size meant that she needed to remain far from the shore and out in the deeper waters, but this was no concern for those aboard her, for she had been designed to hold a number of rowboats at her stern that could be lowered to ferry her crew when needed. It was in one of these boats that Ramsey sat, stroking his graying beard pensively as he stared at the distant statues. Word had reached him of an old acquaintance who lurked in the ruins below, and there was much that had to be said.

Three of his crew rode with him, burdened with the provisions Ramsey had instructed them to assemble, but as ever he insisted on being the one to row them ashore. His great arms grasped the oars as readily as they ever had, propelling them toward land with an ease that belied the man's advancing years, and before long they were marching up the shore in a long crocodile formation.

Twenty men and women trailed behind Ramsey. Together they carried lengths of rope and chain, stout axes and sturdy planks—everything that they would need to reach their destination. Each of them was a pirate of renown and normally sailed on voyages of their own, but today was a momentous one, and each of them wanted to say that they'd been there to witness it.

A fine drizzle swept them as they made their way across the island to where the fallen statue lay. They moved without haste, Ramsey limping slightly on his wooden leg, which had been carved to resemble the fore claw of a griffin. One man struck up a shanty as they traveled, and one by-one they took up with it, until the island rang with their voices:

Cloaked in folds of midnight waters
Side by side, we sons and daughters
We set forth on no king's orders
But we sail together.

Ours is a life of wild ambition
Take all we please, need no permission
Woe unto those in opposition
For we sail together.

Hold fast! Tides are turning
Flames roar, fires are burning
We'll all be returning
If we sail together.

All on the waves shall know our story
Sing of the battles fought ashore, we

All shall thrive on fame and glory
When we sail together.

Hold to our course and no surrender
See how she gleams in all her splendor
Fight to the last, we must defend her
As we sail together.

Words of warning have been spoken
Ancient creatures have awoken
Still, until our bond is broken
We shall sail together!

Their song carried them across the glassy shore to the base of the fallen statue, where Ramsey had long ago determined the entrance to the ruins would be. They hefted their lanterns as they descended and now there was no more singing, only the clatter of booted feet as they followed their captain down the many steps and through the silent passages.

Finally, they reached the great chasm, and it was here that Ramsey's crew began their work. First, guide ropes were cast across the divide using powerful harpoon guns, then the bravest of the pirates began to climb across them, hand over hand with tools at their belts. Anchors were driven deep into the dark rock either side of the abyss and wood was cut to length. They toiled through the night, working to create a sturdy rope bridge that would span the abyss.

Through it all Ramsey stood, patient and impassive. He ate nothing, said nothing, drank nothing, and might well have been taken for a statue himself—if not for his eyes, which were very much alive and focused on the tunnel that lay across the ravine. Only when the bridge was finally completed did he turn to inspect it, plucking at the ropes that served as handrails and nodding in appreciation. "Should be good for a century or two," he commented. "That'll do, all of you. You can go back to the ship."

There were several protestations, concerns for Ramsey's safety among them, but he waved them all away. "There are many things pirates should do together," he informed them, "and some they must do alone. I'll see you all back aboard in time for the feast."

His crew left him only reluctantly, abandoning the tools and supplies they'd used during the labor, and retreated one by one until Ramsey's lantern was the only light remaining. He crossed the newly formed bridge without much fanfare, his griffin claw clomping heavily on each wooden plank, and made his way deeper into the ruins. Finally, he reached the large stone door, shook his head with wry amusement at the glittering key that adorned it, and surrendered a golden coin from his purse so that he could enter.

Two skeletons were emptying the contents of a freshly plundered chest under the silent supervision of their leader, who sat reclined on his golden throne. Upon seeing Ramsey's frame outlined in the doorway, the two abandoned their task and promptly dived into the pile of treasure they'd been attending to, attempting to make themselves as inconspicuous as possible. Ramsey grunted in satisfaction, for his reputation now seemingly made even the undead think twice before facing him. He ignored the cadaverous cowards, instead striding purposefully across the great treasure chamber. He stood before the glittering chair and stared into two sightless, emerald eyes.

"Hello, Rathbone," he said calmly. "Too greedy to die, I see."

Insofar as a skeleton could display emotion, the Gold Hoarder seemed to be both furious and fearful at the reunion, but Ramsey's hand did not stray to his weapon. "I came to talk," he said, simply. "Nothing more. You always did think I did too much talking, but you'll listen to me today. You'll have to forgive me for coming into your little lair by the front door, but I'm too old and too worn out to be traipsing through a secret passage at my time of life. Besides, I'm sure you've filled it with all manner of traps and devious little schemes."

He turned, slowly, taking in the piles of treasure that filled every corner of the room. "You're doing very well for yourself, I see. Barely a day goes by that I don't hear stories of the fearsome Gold Hoarder, the mysterious Skeleton Lord who strikes in the darkness and steals every last coin and copper from the pirates he encounters. If only it could make you happy.

"That's the trouble with greed, Rathbone. The more you feed it, the more it grows, and the bigger its next meal has to be. When I lured you here all those years ago with rumors of treasure, it was your greed I counted on. I knew you wouldn't be able to resist this place, but I never imagined it'd lead to—" He paused and gestured at the skeletal form that sat motionless before him. "—all of this. How long did it take you to pick up all of those coins and jewels from the bottom of the sea, I wonder? Months, I'd wager. Years, perhaps. Long enough for the flesh to fall from your bones, at any rate."

He sighed. "I should have faced you myself with a sword in my hand and given you the death you deserved, not left you to this lingering torment you've created for yourself. But no, I was off chasing my own ambitions. Living out all those grand adventures I'd dreamed of since I was a boy. And now, Rathbone," Ramsey leaned in closer, grinning down at the glittering figure, who seemed either unwilling or unable to react. "You're going to hear all about them."

For many weeks after the fateful kraken attack, all Ramsey saw of the Sea of Thieves was the view from his tiny window, for he had been ordered to bed. He lacked the strength or will to argue, for as Mercia pointed out, he had been lucky to survive at all. Had the merfolk not carried his unconscious form back across the waves to Golden Sands, he would surely have perished along with his plans for a brighter future.

Ramsey remained listless and inconsolable even once he was up and about, staggering against the walls of his room as he struggled to get used to his new leg and finally electing to walk with a stout cane.

He was a captain without a ship, and he had no means to procure another, for his fortune was now locked away with keys that only Rathbone possessed.

Eventually, boredom overwhelmed him and he took his first steps outside for many months, wandering down to the dock to stare wistfully at the sea, until somebody clapped a hand on his shoulder. To his surprise, he found Briggsy at his side, her cheerful demeanor undiminished by the passage of time. She had been sent to fetch him, she explained, for they greatly needed his counsel.

To Ramsey's utter astonishment, "they" turned out to be a gathering of pirates, Shan and Captain Slate among them, who had taken his fateful speech to heart. His dream of an alliance, far from being crushed by Rathbone's treachery, seemed to have been bolstered by it. The people of Golden Sands had seen what it meant when pirates bickered among themselves rather than paying heed to what might still be waiting out upon the Sea of Thieves.

"If there's krakens out there, there could be *anything*," Briggsy explained. "The more we know about the world, the better." The kraken they'd defeated was spotted from time to time, she informed him, though it always stained the sea an inky black and kept its body safely out of sight. Evidently it had learned a valuable lesson about preying on pirates, though such creatures were rumored to live for centuries, and Ramsey doubted he'd seen the last of it.

They sailed under a single flag from that day forward, sometimes journeying as a convoy and sometimes spending weeks apart before coming together to tell their tales and share the spoils. Ramsey was immensely gratified when Slate yielded captaincy to him for their maiden voyage, and before long their adventures had provided enough coin for Slate to afford a new ship of his own. Before long, they were being approached by others who wished to join their cause, to master the Sea of Thieves in its entirety.

The alliance was never without its conflicts, for some who were welcomed aboard turned out to be false in their intentions, taking more than their share or hiding the largest hoards for themselves. One thing Ramsey refused to tolerate was stealing among members of the union, and those who were caught doing so were summarily dismissed, often with a volley of cannon fire to speed them on their way.

There were also those who thought, as Graymarrow had, that to truly live the pirate life meant anything and anyone was fair game. Those pirates soon learned not to attack any ship that sailed under Ramsey's flag, however, for a slight against one was a slight against all, and his support was growing by the day.

The more they traveled, the more experienced they became, soon learning to spot the telltale signs of a storm on the horizon and how to tell when skeletons might be lurking nearby. Even so, the Sea of Thieves always had something new to surprise them. Curses, and cursed objects, in particular, continued to add an element of danger and uncertainty to every crumbling shrine or ancient talisman they came across.

Many famous pirates, both within the alliance and without, succumbed to these malign forces and became dark legends in their own right. One by one, they were consumed by ambition, aggression, or other driving forces that left them twisted or transformed just like Rathbone, even beyond death.

They were known as Skeleton Lords, for they seemed to hold some sway over the undead pirates who'd served with them in life, and they continued to sail across the Sea of Thieves and wreak havoc. People soon learned to tread cautiously if a Skeleton Lord's ship had been reported in the area.

Not every magical artifact led to calamity, however, and Ramsey and followers also discovered plenty of trinkets and talismans that granted great boons—positive effects that could calm the waters, raise shipwrecks from the bottom of the sea, and even heal wounds more readily.

Many of these were studied at great length by Mercia, who spent more and more time on land as the years passed, writing down her findings in great tomes—though she insisted these should be locked away until they were needed.

Ramsey had found her slumped over one such an artifact, a skull necklace that bore the Reaper's Mark. She was smiling peacefully in her stillness, cold hands still holding the quill with which she had penned her final advice to him: *This will suit you.* He had no idea what magic resided in the necklace, but he wore it, always.

Shan, too, had long since given up constant life on the waves, though he continued to tinker and improve on all manner of contraptions and devices—anything that took his fancy. Shan could be found crouched over a lathe refining a telescope's lens small enough to be mounted on a rifle one morning; the next, he might be whittling a graceful dancer out of driftwood to spin atop an ornate music box for his grandchildren back home.

Their deeds were mighty and their reputations had spread from one corner of the oceans to another. There was nowhere they hadn't been, nothing they hadn't tasted, fought, stolen, or sold. And yet, as the days, the months, the years of brawling and battling and laughing and looting blurred together, something still seemed to be missing.

Ramsey was standing at the helm of his mighty galleon when it came to him. He turned to crack a joke, looking first to Mercia and then to Shan. Neither was there, of course, and it was then that he realized he no longer sailed with his friends at his side. Oh, he had a crew who were loyal and brave, but they called him Captain and not Ramsey. They thought of him as the fearsome Pirate Lord, a living legend to be admired and respected. Someone to be aspired to. But they'd never dare to share a drink with him.

And that, Ramsey realized, was what he'd been searching for all along. The missing piece of the puzzle. That was when he decided to retire.

The words bounced back and forth, echoing in the vaulted chamber that the Gold Hoarder had chosen for his lair. The Pirate Lord stood waiting, tapping his cane impatiently, but if the skeleton was even able to respond, he gave no sign of doing so. "Retiring!" he repeated, impatiently. "I've sailed the length and breadth of the Sea of Thieves. I've left footprints on every island and fought off pirates, sharks, and krakens. I've cracked riddles and dodged traps and plundered everything from teacups to tiaras!" His voice rose as he spoke until he was practically bellowing. "There is no pirate more famous, more feared, and more ferocious than I!"

Just like that, he sagged, and was Ramsey once more. "But if you can't share the memories with your friends in a tavern afterward, none of it matters. If you can't boast or brag about it, can't share your stories and pass on what you've learned, then what's the point in having a reputation? Well, I'm going to do something about that. Make sure that anyone who's really made a name for themselves always has a place to tell their stories. Maybe even ask for advice, if they're not too proud.

"I've got a fine ship, but this will be my final voyage on the Sea of Thieves. It's time for someone else to stake a claim to her, I reckon. Trading Companies, merchants, gangs, soothsayers . . . The world is always changing, and maybe that's not such a bad thing after all. Oh, those Gold Hoarders of yours are welcome to any of my fortune they can find, and so is anyone else. I won't need it anymore. It's always a give and take, see."

He paused, then said slowly, "I'm sorry, Rathbone, that I couldn't be a better captain to you. Sorry I couldn't make you see that there's so much more to the world than just its precious stones. Sorry that we couldn't be friends."

His expression hardened as he continued. "But even so, you were *wrong*. Wrong to think the Sea of Thieves exists so people like you can make a profit. Wrong to betray your crew. Wrong to believe all that matters on a voyage is the reward at the end of it. And yet you came damn close to turning our home into everything I despised. I hated you for that."

Ramsey's face was so close now that he could see his own anger reflected in the Gold Hoarder's emerald eyes. "And now look at you. The man will be forgotten, and all people will see is the monster.

You can plunder every last coin from the Sea of Thieves, Rathbone, but you'll always be the poorest pirate I know."

Having said his piece, Ramsey straightened. He took one last look around the chamber, drinking in the piles of treasure and wondering how much of eternity the cursed figure before him would spend trying, in vain, to lay claim to every last piece of gold. His eyes alighted on the black diamond ring that the Gold Hoarder still wore upon his curse-stiffened finger, and for a moment it seemed as though a great sadness overtook Ramsey—as though he had yet more to say. Then the moment passed, and he lumbered toward the exit without another word, ready to set sail for the last time. Gradually, the light of his lantern faded and his echoing footsteps fell silent.

Hunched upon his usurped throne, lingering among his stolen treasures deep within the ruins of a forgotten sanctuary, lost far beyond the edge of civilization ... the Gold Hoarder began to scream.

LARINNA

Under Larinna's steady hand, the *Unforgiven* made its way carefully out of the Wilds and back toward the familiar sights and smells of Sanctuary Outpost. Faizel had suggested that they sail to a more distant destination, one where they were less likely to be recognized by members of the Order of Souls, but Larinna stood firm. "Adelheid will be expecting us back there," she insisted. "Besides, I should think our little run-in with Captain Quince will make any other pirates think twice before accepting bounties on the likes of us."

Grinning, Faizel conceded the point, and they made landfall just as the sun was bidding the day its last goodbye. The lights of the now-familiar tavern were calling to them like a beacon, but there were arrangements to make before they could really relax.

They called first at the shipwright, who scratched her long locks in bemusement at the impoverished condition of the captain's cabin but gamely began taking measurements to replace all of the furnishings that had been thrown overboard. Most of what they'd been able to loot from the Gold Hoarder's lair vanished into the folds of her apron, but she assured them that she'd have the *Unforgiven* repaired and restocked by morning.

Faizel clutched their last few coins tightly in his hand as they made their way up to the tavern, where some smooth talking and the promise of a good story transformed his gold into several large tankards of frothing grog. Faizel did the lion's share of the telling, as ever, but Larinna was surprised to find herself rather more talkative than usual and frequently cut in with corrections, contradictions, and when the time came, her own part of the anecdote. As they talked, they noticed more and more listening figures emerging from the shadows to hear their tale.

There was a quiet cheer as they talked about their escape from the Order of Souls, and a rather louder one when Larinna gleefully described how they'd finally scuppered the *Black Gauntlet* using a Chest of Sorrow. She suspected a few ships with unpopular captains might find themselves unexpectedly soggy in the days to come. By the time Faizel reached the part of the story where they arrived at Tribute Peak, the tavern was overflowing with an attentive audience, and the tankards before them seemed, mysteriously, to have been refilled.

Just as she'd expected, the story of their descent into the ruins and the eventual discovery of the Gold Hoarder drew the most interest from the crowd, although many scoffed at the very notion of Skeleton Lords, let alone an immense underground treasure pile.

Larinna coyly invited the naysayers to head out to Tribute Peak to see the ruins with their own eyes. "Although," she informed them, "you'll need a sharp sword, a lamp to see by, and an eighty-foot rope bridge. I'm sure Salty the Shopkeeper has one lying around somewhere!"

This got the biggest laugh so far, but also seemed to signal the end of the evening's entertainment. The assembled pirates began to disperse, making their way back to their bunks for the night.

Larinna had expected to be toppling over of sheer exhaustion by now, but the thrill of recounting her first voyage across the Sea of Thieves had made all of the excitement and terror feel new again.

She felt sure that more grog would cure her wakefulness in time and poured another glass for Ned, Faizel, and herself.

Together, they toasted both Adelheid and the *Unforgiven*, as well as the original inhabitants of Thieves' Haven, whoever they may have been. It was at this point that Ned fell over backward, toppling off his stool with his eyes closed, smiling happily and dreaming of whatever it was Ned dreamed about.

Larinna and Faizel shared another laugh and clinked their glasses, and Faizel pulled a battered deck of cards from his pocket. He taught Larinna how to play Karnath, a game she had never heard of but which was apparently a popular way of passing time across the Sea of Thieves. In return, she taught him a few sleight of hand tricks that she'd picked up from a deckhand in her younger days. "She had very nimble fingers," she said with a slight smile, and produced the ace of hearts from behind Ned's pink-tinged ear with a flourish. She expected Faizel to ask her how it was done, but by the time she turned back to the table she found that he too was asleep, snoring contentedly with his head on his arms.

Chuckling to herself, Larinna gave a long, luxurious stretch and slipped the cards into her pocket for safekeeping. It was then that her fingers brushed against the ring she'd found during her battle with the Gold Hoarder. She'd completely forgotten she'd taken it, but now she pulled it free and turned it over and over in her fingers, hoping to find some clue as to whom it might belong. The black diamond shone oddly in the firelight, reflecting the flames in a way that seemed to draw her gaze deeper and deeper.

It was as she contemplated the heart of the dark stone that she heard the scraping sound. If the tavern hadn't been deserted, save for those few pirates now dotted around in a drunken stupor, the noise might have gone completely unnoticed. It sounded for all the world like stone sliding against stone, like when she'd uncovered the secret passage that led from the Gold Hoarder's lair.

Larinna stood up, a little unsteadily, and began a slow examination of the room, for the noise had filled her with a strange curiosity. There was a mystery, and she simply had to have the answer. She checked behind the bar and beneath the tables, poked at the dying hearth with a poker, and examined the brickwork of the fireplace closely, in case there was some sort of mechanism or entrance being disguised by the flickering flames.

Finally she spotted what was different. The far corner of the room, dingy and unoccupied as it was farthest from the fire, seemed to have shifted. Four of the flagstones that made up the tavern's floor were recessed, forming a series of steps that led down and out of sight. Larinna couldn't remember ever seeing them before, but surely they'd been there all along, hadn't they?

The drink's made you daft, she told herself, standing again. *It's just a stock room, or something*. As she turned to leave, a light breeze raised the hairs on her arm, though the tavern's door remained tightly closed, and a burst of distant music tickled the edges of her senses.

She was convinced it had come from the stairway. Scowling at her own irrationality, Larinna found herself moving down the steps. She was extremely glad that Faizel and Ned were sleeping soundly, for she knew the Voyage of the Wine Cellar would be a joke she'd never live down if the steps turned out to lead nowhere more exciting than a musty old basement.

The stairs didn't seem to be guiding her anywhere so mundane, however, and the floor was already getting more uneven beneath her feet. The stone slabs of the tavern floor gradually gave way to a fine white sand, and the walls had the rough coolness of natural rock to them. She could smell salt, and suspected that the passageway in which she'd found herself eventually led out to the ocean. *An old smuggler's passage?* That didn't seem to fit either, for this was the Sea of Thieves. Smugglers didn't need to sneak into the building, not when they owned the place.

She soon realized that whoever had built this passageway was no mere bandit, for the corridor came to its end and Larinna was presented with an imposing threshold: an open doorway through which a blinding light was shining. The searing brightness made her headache even worse, but the distant music seemed even louder than before. It seemed that all she had to do to solve the mystery was keep walking, and so Larinna stepped tentatively through the portal, shielding her eyes with her hand.

The salty aroma was stronger here, and as Larinna's eyes adjusted to the light, she finally understood why. The cavern she'd stumbled into was monstrous, larger by far even than the treasure chamber of the Gold Hoarder, though much of it was filled with seawater. Huge stalagmites rose up around her, many taller than the mast of most ships—including the vessel that dominated the scene ahead of her.

Long ago, though how long was impossible to say, she had clearly been a fearsome galleon, perhaps the most impressive on the Sea of Thieves. And yet, at some point in her past, someone had sailed her into this cavern, likely right through the roaring waterfall that cascaded endlessly in the far distance. They'd threaded her between vast pillars of stone and brought her to rest atop the rocks, beaching her once and for all. Then, they'd cracked apart her hull, exposing the inner decks.

There had been a toymaker on the island where Larinna grew up, and she remembered passing by his shop one day while he was displaying his latest creation—a dollhouse whose entire front could be peeled away to reveal all the little rooms and tiny people within. This unusual ship felt the same to her, as if some great giant had seized the vessel and opened her up to stare at all the little pirates inside.

The pathway Larinna was following led her to a maze of boardwalks and planks that snaked out across the water. She was much closer to the music now, the distant trill of a violin and the wheeze of a concertina in something approaching harmony.

She wove her way across the walkways, noting as she did that there was another ship shored up nearby. It was an impressive galleon in its own right, a ship fit for a pirate of renown, but it seemed to be unoccupied. *Who else knows all of this is down here?*

Following the sound of singing, Larinna made her way to the ship itself, taking the time to examine the various details and seeking out some clue to its history or purpose. Finally, she found what she was looking for—a large, wrought iron metal sheet, held in place with massive bolts that had long rusted into position. The ship's nameplate.

A layer of deep green moss had built up across the engraving, and she impatiently pulled at it until the whole fuzzy mass came away and she could make out what was written underneath.

It said: *Athena's Fortune.*

Larinna stared at it for a long while, thinking back to the note that had greeted her when she'd first woken up in the tavern. She suspected she was being toyed with, and that alone was enough to make her want to turn on her heel and storm away—but her curiosity, as ever, proved more influential than her anger. She climbed the final few stairs, reaching the level of what she supposed would once have been the ship's lower deck.

She wasn't sure what she'd expected to find at the heart of the huge vessel, but she certainly hadn't expected a tavern. That was where she found herself, however; the spacious interior of the ship had been converted into a pub far more luxurious than the one where she'd left Faizel and Ned asleep. There were plush hangings adorning the walls, paintings and portraits here and there, and fine crystal goblets to drink from.

There were also ghosts, and Larinna was surprised to find that detail didn't bother her in the slightest. They sat around the tables, talking and joking in groups of three or four, apparently unwilling to let a mere trifle like their own mortality get in the way of a good time. They seemed solid enough, other than the eerie green glow that surrounded them, and as she watched, one of them picked up a tankard of grog and downed its contents seemingly without difficulty. Upon spotting Larinna, they raised their glasses in a toast and gave her a raucous cheer, as if she were a welcome regular. Despite the unusual circumstances, it felt very much like stepping into any other drinking den.

An otherworldly pirate band was playing in the corner, the source of the tunes she'd been hearing, and one of them nodded cheerfully as she moved through the tavern to its far end. There was another ghostly figure here, larger than the others, seated at a table by himself—no, not a table, she realized, a captain's desk. He glanced up as she approached, and his eyes crinkled with the lightest trace of a smile.

"Nice to see you at last, Larinna," he said. "Welcome to the Tavern of Legends." He remained seated, gesturing toward a stool on the opposite side of the desk to his own high-backed chair. Although Larinna usually preferred to remain standing in situations like this, she sat herself down and leaned forward with her elbows upon the wooden surface, so that they were face to ghostly face.

"You," she said, "must be the Pirate Lord."

"I must," Ramsey replied agreeably, "although people in here usually just call me Ramsey."

"You're a lot more—" Larinna hesitated. "—*dead* than I imagined."

Ramsey laughed at this, a big belly laugh that shook his spectral fame. "Noticed that, did you? Well, it was bound to happen sooner or later. We didn't have a Ferry of the Damned in my day, after all. But when you live as long as I did, you tend to pick up a few little tricks and trinkets for sticking around even after your body's worn out its welcome." He fingered the Reaper's Mark that hung around his neck absentmindedly as he said this. "Although I suppose you could also say that a pirate never really dies out here on the Sea of Thieves, not as long as their legend lives on."

Larinna nodded. "I'm starting to believe that. I mean, I came to the Sea of Thieves because I wanted to see things that no one else had seen. Leave my footprints on the sand of uncharted beaches. To see what lies in the creases of the map. I still do, but I'm starting to realize that that's only part of it. When you're with your crew sharing a grog and your stories, that's when it becomes real. Not just living it, but *reveling* in it."

Ramsey made a sweeping gesture that took in the entire tavern, nearly spilling his drink in the process. "That's what this place is all about. A pirate needs a fine ship under their feet while they're out on their adventures, and they need a good tavern in which to tell their tales afterward. Well, I thought, why not combine the two? I sailed mine into this cave, laid her onto the rocks, and built a tavern where real pirate legends could live on. What do you think?"

Larinna considered the question, looking around slowly. "All I see are ghosts," she said finally, glancing over her shoulder at the distant pirate band. "If you have to die to become a regular customer, I don't think you're going to do a lot of business down here."

Ramsey snorted. "Well, anyone who's still living, breathing, and fit to sail a ship is out doing so, or so I should hope. I spent a good many years out on the open sea, and I've still got a good head on my shoulders, green though it may be. I know about all sorts of dangerous creatures, hidden treasures, ancient curses, and I offer them up as voyages to my guests here. They're better than anything those damnable Trading Companies have to offer, believe me."

He leaned backward, gesturing toward the curios and items that littered his desks. "Weapons, provisions, and all of the spoils I gathered over the years, too. I have everything a crew needs to sail out together and do what pirates do best. Then they can head back here together and tell everyone all about it."

"So it *was* you," Larinna said softly. "You were the one who put the map in the bottle. And back at the beach, too—"

"I arranged for that to happen, yes."

She shot him a look. "Why me?"

"Why not you? Why not anyone?" Ramsey took a deep draft of his grog. "I like to keep myself informed as to who follows my maps, even now. Sometimes a new arrival will catch my interest and I'll help point them in the right direction. Not everyone heeds the note, of course, and some people are more stubborn than others. There will always be pirates for whom fighting and feuding is enough. But if I think they've got potential, I do my best to steer them here."

"My potential?" Larinna blinked. "What are you talking about?"

"You plucked a ring from the hands of the Gold Hoarder and lived to tell about it," said Ramsey, mildly. "Not bad for your first voyage."

Larinna realized she was still clutching the ring in her hand, and slowly uncurled her fingers. "This? I suppose I did." She placed it on the table between them. "What's so special about it?"

"Everything you see here is special," Ramsey reminded her. "That ring in particular once belonged to a young man who made a very foolish mistake, as young men often do. He fell in love. If you'd like to buy a drink, you could sit and hear the whole story."

Larinna hesitated. There was no denying that the warmth of the room, the cheerful music, and the smell of good drink were all extremely comforting. *More than that*, she thought, *this is the Pirate Lord! Possibly the greatest captain who ever lived, and he wants to have a drink with you! Imagine everything he could tell you. The voyages he could send you on. The voyages he* will *send you on . . . one day.*

As much to her own surprise as to Ramsey's, Larinna got back to her feet. "You said it yourself: This is a tavern of legends," she said firmly. "And I'm not a legend. Not yet. I don't even know what my legend will be, but I think I'm going to have a lot of fun finding out.

"I know that the Sea of Thieves was very different in your day. No Gold Hoarders to trade with. No Ferryman to help you back to the land of the living. No maps and charts for sale to guide your way. But everything out there, right now, that's where my stories will come from, and I need to go and find out what they are." She paused. "They say you sailed in a Golden Age of Piracy. Well, I say that a new Golden Age is just beginning out there, and this one's for us to enjoy."

She could tell from the pleased look on Ramsey's face that she'd made the right decision, and now Larinna leaned forward and tapped the stool with her finger. "You save this seat for me, understand? One day I'm coming back to swap stories and learn all about you. I'll be bringing my crew, too, so you'd better find some more chairs, and don't you even think about charging us for the grog."

Now Ramsey stood as well, and for the first time Larinna spotted the remnants of several injuries. She couldn't help but wonder what final fate had befallen the Pirate Lord of the Sea of Thieves, but that was yet another story she'd have to wait to hear. She shook his paw-like hand as it was offered, pleased to find that his grip was as strong as if he'd been made of flesh and blood, and made her way back along down the tavern. The ghostly pirates watched her once more as she departed, smiling.

At the stairs, Larinna found that she couldn't resist one last look around, to drink the room in and hold it in her mind like a painting. It would have to do until the next time she crossed its threshold. Her eyes lingered on the tavern's ethereal proprietor as he turned the glittering ring over and over in his ghostly fingers.

"Ramsey!" she called out across the room. "What was her name?"

The Pirate Lord smiled, wistfully. "Athena."

Only when the tavern was out of sight did Larinna let out a long, slow breath. It was a magnificent hideout, she had to admit, and she allowed herself the luxury of a moment's daydream; she saw herself standing at the prow of a glittering galleon, flanked by Adelheid and the others as their ship burst through the silvery curtain of the waterfall and off on a new journey. *All in good time*, she thought.

She stood aside for a group of pirates as they staggered past her on their way to the tavern, struggling with a cursed chest that seemed to be writhing and moving as if it was alive. Even as she watched, they lost their grip on the box, and it bounded merrily along the docks as if it were an overexcited puppy, forcing the red-faced crew to tear after it before it could get away. *Always something new*, she reminded herself with a smile.

She ambled back along the passageway until the sandy floor gave way to flagstones, and was not terribly surprised when the stairway began to grind closed behind her, sealing itself away. Squatting down and running her fingers along the floor, she could feel no trace of the secret steps. No matter. They'd appear for her again when she was ready.

Faizel and Little Ned had slept long enough, she decided, and nudged the latter repeatedly in his ribs until his snoring gave way to a choking cough and he lurched upright, looking confused and disgruntled. Faizel proved somewhat harder to rouse, and eventually they settled for Ned carrying him outside to the rain barrel and dunking him briefly inside by his ankles, much to the amusement of those stallholders who were setting up for another day. Faizel, for once, was not amused, though his good humor was restored when Larinna promised to buy the pair breakfast. "I know a man who does excellent bacon and eggs," she promised.

"Feasting without your captain!" came an accusing voice. "Honestly, I drop dead for five minutes . . ."

There was Adelheid, alive as ever and looking no worse for wear other than a large tear where the Gold Hoarder's shovel had ripped through her outfit. Her crew surrounded her, all clamoring to tell the tale of everything that had happened during her stay on the Ferry of the Damned. "It's a story you can tell me over breakfast," Adelheid insisted.

Together, the crew of the *Unforgiven* coaxed the tavern keeper into providing them with a fine meal, and then they made their way to the docks where their ship was waiting. The shipwright had been as good as her word, and everything was once again in its rightful place. Adelheid vanished into the captain's cabin for a few moments and returned wearing a shirt of vivid crimson in place of her torn tunic.

"Well," she declared, "I'm pleased to say that we don't have to worry about more bounty hunters getting in our way. Furthermore, thanks to me, we're no longer blacklisted by the Order of Souls, so we can pick a voyage with them whenever it takes our fancy."

"We aren't?" Larinna stared. "How did you . . . ?"

"You must've hit someone *really* hard," Ned said admiringly.

Adelheid smirked. "Imagine my surprise when I woke up on the Ferry, and who should I find lurking there but our old friend Captain Quince? It seemed as though he'd offended the Ferryman by virtue of being his usual charming self and was destined to spend all eternity sailing the Sea of the Damned because he was too stubborn to apologize. Being a magnanimous and forgiving sort, I offered to have a quiet word with the Ferryman, and in exchange Quince agreed to have the Order of Souls forget our little misunderstanding over Simeon's riddle. Anyone fancy a skellie hunt?"

"An intriguing suggestion," mused Faizel, "but I feel like I would like to put a few more meals between myself and another encounter with the living dead. Perhaps we could introduce Larinna to the opportunities offered by the Merchant Alliance?"

"Not pigs again," groaned Ned. "What about the Gold Hoarders?"

"I've seen enough gold to last me a life time, thank you, Ned."

"No such thing, Larinna." Adelheid put her hands on her hips. "All right, then, the next voyage we make ourselves. Time to get back out onto the waves where we belong." She hesitated, then added graciously: "Take the helm, Larinna. You can pick a heading for us."

Larinna was both surprised and pleased, and took the sun-bleached wheel of the *Unforgiven* in both hands. "Aye, Captain. What are we looking for?"

Adelheid grinned. "Someplace . . . fun. We'll know it when we see it. We always do."

The *Unforgiven* shone in the sunlight as she flew across the waves, carving a path across an untamed sea beneath an azure sky. Aboard her, her crew joked and laughed together, raising their tankards in a toast to the adventures they'd had, and all that were yet to come.

Beyond the horizon, Larinna knew, there would be places that not even the Pirate Lord and his crew had ever discovered. Places filled with strange and troublesome treasures that were begging to be claimed by any pirate brave enough to seek them out. Somewhere out there, her legend was waiting for her.

This, she thought with satisfaction, *is what being a pirate is all about*.

ABOUT THE AUTHOR

Chris Allcock is a game designer and writer whose career began at Rare Ltd. in 2003. He has helped create a wide variety of acclaimed titles, including *Kameo: Elements of Power*, *Kinect Sports*, *Rare Replay*, and most recently *Sea of Thieves*. He currently lives in the English Midlands and is probably drinking tea.